USA TODAY BESTSELLING AUTHOR

Dale Mayer

TERK'S GUARDIANS
ROYCE 11

ROYCE: TERK'S GUARDIANS, BOOK 11
Beverly Dale Mayer
Valley Publishing Ltd.

ISBN-13: 978-1-778866-16-6
Print Edition

Books in This Series:

Radar, Book 1

Legend, Book 2

Bojan, Book 3

Langdon, Book 4

Walker, Book 5

Reid, Book 6

Sanders, Book 7

Nate, Book 8

Royal, Book 9

Alex, Book 10

Royce, Book 11

Trevor, Book 12

About This Book

In a world where diplomatic immunity can shield the darkest of sins, a sinister pattern emerges where wives mysteriously vanish without a trace. When MI6 finally connects the dots, even their hardened agents are disturbed by the implications. Terkel's team faces their most challenging mission yet—navigating international politics, while racing against time to prevent another tragic disappearance. The clock ticks by even faster when they discover the diplomat's latest target: the missing sister of dead wife number four.

Trapped in an opulent prison, Heather's heart aches, not just for her lost sister but for the freedom slipping through her fingers. Each passing day brings her closer to an unwanted fate—becoming wife number five to a man she suspects of unspeakable crimes. Her desperate plea for help echoes through secret channels, but the response brings only tighter security and darker shadows. The golden walls of her cage begin to close in, threatening to suffocate her last hopes of escape.

Enter Royce—dangerous, determined, and devastatingly attractive. His calculated rescue plan seems perfect on paper, but the crackling tension between them threatens to complicate everything. As they navigate a deadly game of cat and mouse, their growing attraction becomes impossible to ignore. With both their lives hanging by a thread, Heather and Royce must trust not only each other's skills but also their hearts ...

Sign up to be notified of all Dale's releases here!
https://geni.us/DaleNews

PROLOGUE

TERKEL WALKED THROUGH the big patio doors out onto the deck of his own apartment, just seeking a few minutes of peace and quiet, something that was hard to come by in his household. He sat down in a comfy deck chair with a scotch and tilted his glass to the sky above.

"Not sure what you had in mind when you set this all in motion," he muttered to the world at random, "but good job." At a soft laugh behind him, he turned to see Celia. She wore a long soft gown and appeared to be floating, as she walked toward Terk. Her body was slim now, after only six weeks since the twins were born, mostly back to normal but riper. The births of their twins, when it finally happened, had been an experience Terk would never forget. Celia had come through it like a trouper.

"What are you doing out here all alone?" she asked him.

"It's the all-alone part I was looking forward to." When she stopped next to him to grab his outstretched hand, he added, "Except for you."

She chuckled. "Of course, but, hey, if you need alone time, that's totally okay, you know?"

"Nope. *Alone* is one thing, but *alone without you?* That's not what I meant at all."

"And yet it would still be okay."

"That's fine. ... It can be okay but some other day."

She just smiled, and he opened his arms. Instead of sitting down beside him, she sat in his lap and curled up against him. "It's been a hell of a ride," she murmured.

"Are you kidding?" he asked, then burst into laughter. "That doesn't do it justice. A hell of a ride can entail all kinds of things," he clarified, "including the way you got pregnant."

"It sure as hell doesn't even begin to equate to the happy chaos that our world is now." She raised her head to see his face and smiled. "Any regrets?"

"None," he stated instantly, "no regrets, just a few little concerns. You know, some money issues, a little worry about the bills, all that stuff," he shared, "but definitely no regrets."

"Don't worry about the money issues either," she countered, with a chuckle. "We're making do."

"Yeah, *making do* won't cut it," he noted. "I am responsible for an awful lot of people now."

She traced his lips with her finger and whispered, "It's not just your responsibility. You're not alone in this," she said. "It's all of us together, and that makes a whole lot of difference."

He smiled, held her close, and whispered, "It sure as shit has been a ride. We've expanded way more than I even thought we could."

"And yet I don't think we're done, are we?"

"Oh, I don't know," he said, with a heartfelt sigh. "The world's such a mess. Sometimes it seems as if we might never be done."

"We may not," she acknowledged, "but you have created a special place, and … I hate to say, *a rescue*, but—"

"Oh, yeah, *rescue* fits," Terk agreed. "Jesus, we're creating a rescue for psychics." Then he burst into laughter again.

"Who knew?"

"Who knew what?" she asked.

"Who knew that so many psychics were in need, that so many psychics were out there? Who knew there were so many jobs out there that everybody desperately needed us psychics to do them?"

She smiled at him and added, "I think everybody but you." He rolled his eyes at that, and she giggled. "You're very special."

"*Right*," he muttered, but it was hard to argue with her. If ever somebody could turn his ugly day into something beautiful, it was Celia. "I presume the babies are fed and asleep?"

"They are," she replied, with a happy sigh. "Something else I never expected to happen, and, *boom*, there it is. *Motherhood*."

"Right. None of us expected that."

"And yet," she added, staring at him, "I can't help but feel that we're blessed."

He held her close and nodded. "Absolutely."

"What are we doing about Riff?" she asked.

"Yeah, I'm not sure what we're doing about Riff," he shared in a somber tone. "We still haven't had any news, and yet I feel as if we've been blocked time and time again. Then there is Angela, who just keeps coming back."

"Like a homing pigeon," Celia added.

"I don't know if either one of them are prepared to realize that the homing pigeon keeps returning because of Riff."

"I don't know that even she's ready to accept that yet," Celia agreed, "and the kids make her excuses all too real. Good excuses for her to keep showing up, you know?"

"Exactly," Terk noted, "though I was hoping maybe

some of that would slow down."

"It will soon," Celia pointed out. "Several more births will come, and then we shouldn't have any more pregnancies." She wiggled in his lap. "Unless you want one."

"God, no." He stared at her in shock, and now she burst out laughing. "You were joking, right?" he asked in horror. "Please say it."

"I was joking—or maybe I was just testing the waters."

"You mean, two isn't enough?"

She gave him a brilliant smile and shook her head. "*Hmm*, no. I don't think two is enough," she whispered, "but we don't need any more right away."

"Thank God for that," he declared, facing her. "We have lots more headaches to deal with before I want to go down that road."

"I don't disagree. I would like you to be a little bit more set up, a little bit less stressed, and a little bit more capable of taking some downtime with the babies."

"Babies?" he asked slowly.

"Yeah, babies," she repeated. "Another set of twins awaits us."

He sucked in his breath and winced, but almost instantly two tiny red-haired cherubs popped into his mind. "Good God, red-haired twins?"

Celia chuckled. "Red-haired *girls,*" she clarified, almost too excited. "Yep, and I can't wait."

"Maybe," he said cautiously, "but we do have jobs to do."

"I thought you were out here, thinking about Jonas's latest MI6 op."

He sighed. "I came here to try *not* to think."

"What is it about and where?"

"Somebody in Iceland," he began. "I'm just not sure who to send yet."

"If it's somebody Jonas already knows, that would be an even bigger draw for him."

"Possibly, but I'm pressured on this because I'm pretty sure Jonas will be calling anytime now, looking for an answer."

"If somebody's hurt and injured, there isn't much time to decide anyway."

"True, and he had somebody on the job, but apparently that fell through."

"When you say, *fell through* …"

"Yeah, they were killed," Terk stated, his tone grim, "which is why I've been holding off."

"And yet?"

"And yet nothing," he replied. "I'm not sure that we want to get into something like that. I don't want anybody here risking their lives anymore. Everybody's got families now, and somehow it just seems different."

"Sure, but that also needs to be their decision," she noted. "Everybody here has been affected by a case, one way or another."

"That's true," he conceded, "but at least it doesn't involve trafficking kids this time."

"What is this one about though?"

"I think someone is marrying and then killing their spouse and then marrying and killing again," he said.

"So, why is MI6 concerned?"

"Because they think it's one of their diplomats, and nobody can touch him."

"Ah, so diplomatic immunity means he can travel the world, can keep committing all kinds of crimes, and nobody gives a crap?"

"We give a crap, but it's hard to do anything about it when someone has diplomatic immunity all around the globe."

"So, Iceland really?"

"It's not as if he's an Icelandic minister, if that's what you mean. He's from Iran, but he's currently in Iceland, and his fourth wife just died."

"But is Iran where the husband owes the wife a dowry after marriage, yet there is no rule about when to pay it? Oh, don't tell me that this was about not paying the dowry?"

"She did have a dowry due to her, and the problem is, he's now taken his wife's younger sister captive. The sister wasn't even raised anywhere close to his world, and, from what I am told, she's English. She reached out and asked for help to get away. That call went out two days ago, and nobody's heard from her since."

"Oh shit," Celia murmured, twisting in his arms to face him.

He nodded grimly, then picked up his drink and tossed it back. "So, we need somebody who can handle all kinds of BS. There is also a chance that the sister might have abilities. Apparently she kept her married sister entertained over her last months by reading tarot cards, thinking she could hide her gifts that way."

At that, Celia sucked in her breath. "That's dangerous," she muttered.

"Very dangerous, and nobody wants to acknowledge that she's gone missing. The diplomat has absolutely no ideas, of course, and says he's completely innocent. It's got nothing to do with him, *blah, blah, blah,* and he's heading home."

"So, we have two separate issues here. We have the sister

missing, and we have a diplomat who's killing off his wives." Then she frowned at Terk and asked, "Do you know that for sure?"

"No, not for sure I don't," he admitted. "However, with every marriage, he didn't have to pay a massive dowry debt, plus he gained an inheritance. So, my take would be an absolute flat-out yes on killing his wives. On an energy level, I can't read him," Terk added. "And whenever I can't read someone's aura or energy, I get very suspicious."

"Well, crap," Celia muttered. "I thought maybe things would calm down a little bit now."

"No, that won't happen. The real questions become, who do I send, and what abilities can we utilize in a situation like this to stack the deck in our favor?"

"I don't think there are any," she muttered. "Almost all of us know enough to hide our gifts from the world, so it's interesting that the sister was openly using tarot cards. That just makes her an easy victim for con men who want to use her gifts for their own selfish advantage."

Terk shook his head. "They had a Ouija board first, but it was removed from their possession."

"I'm not against removing that as well," Celia agreed. "That can be dangerous too."

"Absolutely. We must actively protect ourselves."

She then asked, "What about Elena? She and her brother were involved in something similar," she reminded Terk. "They were part of one of the groups that I started up since we moved over here."

"Yeah, but I'm not sure that she's exactly what I would call *operative material*."

"I wasn't so much thinking of her as of her brother. He's ex-navy."

"His name?"

"Royce, I think."

"Royce," Terk repeated. "Seems as if I might know that name. Have you mentioned it to me before?"

"I think I did, but honestly, we've not had two seconds to even talk to each other," she muttered. "So who knows?"

"I feel as if I know that name."

"And you might. He had done a mission in Iceland and was stationed over there for quite a while, so he would know the area to some degree, and he might even know the players."

"I'm not sure that's a good thing though, is it?" he asked her.

"In this case it's hard to say, but it feels as if a connection is there."

Terk groaned.

"So, what's this sister's name? The one who's gone missing?" Celia asked suddenly.

He frowned at her and sighed. "Heather."

"Okay, Heather," she repeated slowly. "And we're helping because she's calling, or we're helping because Jonas is calling?"

"Jonas brought up the issue of the diplomat and the wives he keeps murdering. I guess this diplomat has been on the MI6 watch list for quite a while, but they haven't done anything about him yet. However, now after the contact from the sister herself, it's more of a humanitarian mission. So at least we could dive in and see what we can do to help both cases."

"Right," Celia muttered. "So you need to contact Royce and Heather in whatever way you can. It definitely feels as if some connection is there."

Terk pondered that for a moment and then agreed. "I'm not exactly sure what that connection is at the moment, but yeah. It's there." He smiled, then reached for his phone and added, "Boy, did I ever luck out when I got you."

"You sure did," she declared, with a fat smile. "You need to remember that. You make your phone calls, and I'll go check on the kids." After giving him a big smacking kiss, she walked out, leaving him feeling as if he were the luckiest man alive.

CHAPTER 1

R OYCE HARRINGTON STEPPED out of the airport in
Helsinki, his duffel bag slung over his shoulder. He
looked around, wondering at the circumstances that had
brought him here. When a shout came from his left, he
watched as Rick, an old friend, separated himself from the
crowd, and lifted a hand in greeting. Royce responded in
kind and then quickly walked toward Rick.

"Hey," Rick greeted him, giving him a big bro-hug. "My
God, it's good to see you, man."

Royce stepped back, eyed Rick, and shook his head.
"You look way better than you deserve to be, considering
you got attacked, almost died, but still survived."

"I'm not only looking way better than I deserve to," Rick
noted, with a smile, "but I am doing way better than I
deserve to, and I plan to keep that advantage."

"Of course you do." Royce studied his old friend. "And
this is one hell of a request you've brought me in for."

"It is, indeed," he murmured. "Actually Terk's wife, Celia, had the intel on your sister's work and so knew about
you. Therefore, as soon as your name came up, I recognized
who they were talking about. Naturally I volunteered to
come along," he explained, followed by a big laugh.

"Sure you would." Royce gave him a headshake. "So,
what is this about? We're supposed to go rescue a kidnapped

woman?"

"Yep, we sure are. Yet, in this case, there's a little more to it."

He groaned. "Sure, there is. If there weren't, you wouldn't need me."

"Now that is self-confidence, and I like that," Rick replied, flashing his friend a big grin.

"What's this I hear about your being a father now?"

"Yep, married and a father," he stated proudly. "My wife is an incredible healer, and we have twins. And her twin sister also had twins," he added, with a laugh. "I don't know if you heard this, but Terk and Celia have twins as well."

At that, Royce frowned at him. "I did not know all that. Honestly it sounds as if the government blowup was the best thing to ever happen to you guys on Terk's team," he suggested, staring at him.

"If you'd said that not so long ago, I probably would have beaten your brains into the pavement," Rick shared, "but now I can honestly say that I'm doing great, but I have to give credit where credit is due. If our own government hadn't tried to dismantle our team on a permanent basis," he detailed, with an eyeroll, "I wouldn't have found Cara, and I wouldn't have this new life." Rick shrugged and gave a big sigh. "Having gone private with Terk, I see everything is completely different."

"You really think this is a long-term solution?"

"It is for us," he declared. "Are you still trying to keep your *intuition* hidden?"

Royce glared at him. "You know what it's like out there. If people find out"—he raised both hands in the air—"you of all people can understand that *anything* can happen."

"I do know that," Rick agreed. "Believe me that I do. I

guess that's why I'm just checking to see if you're still utilizing your abilities."

"Yeah? So, you tell me. Is there any way *not* to?"

Rick chuckled. "We never found a way. As soon as we lost them in the attack, even temporarily," he clarified, sobering instantly, "I felt deaf, dumb, and blind. It is not a state I recommend."

"It's not happened to me, but I suspect that—at some point in time in this lovely world that we live in—it's quite possible."

"It might be. Sorry if it does." Rick shook his head vehemently. "In my case, I was blessed that Terk knew healers who could help us. In fact the whole team is healed and greatly because of Cara and Clary and Terk," he shared. "Plus everybody that we brought into the fold has gotten married and has added to the big family our team represents." Rick laughed. "Everyone is or was pregnant. So watch out, if that's *not* the future you want for yourself."

"Now that just blows me away."

"None of us thought that pregnancies would be the end result of the craziness that our world had become, but we're not arguing against it."

"Everybody? Really? All the guys on your team?"

"Yes, all of us. Calum got back together with his wife. You remember Mariana and Calum Jr. That kid has some pretty impressive powers of his own already. Damon and Tasha finally got their crap together," he shared, with a laugh. "Even Brody was smitten, and he is with Clary."

At that, Royce stared and asked, "Brody, that cantankerous bastard Brody? Are you kidding me? Somebody fell in love with him?"

Rick snorted. "Yeah, he's my brother-in-law now," he

shared in between the laughter. "How's that for a twist?"

"Actually I can see that on many levels," he noted. "You two were always close."

"We've *all* been close," he clarified. "That hasn't changed, and I'm really glad that it's turned out this way. As a matter of fact, the team has grown tighter. Then, with Terk pulling us all out of the fire and setting up the company—although he's overwhelmed with the process—he's done one hell of a job bringing in people to give him a hand. We've got an incredibly different life than we had just a couple years ago."

"You're happy?" Royce asked his friend.

"Very happy," he replied, nodding. Then he motioned Royce to move along. "Now let's go. I've got a vehicle over there, waiting for you."

"Waiting for me or waiting for us?"

"Us," Rick confirmed.

As they hopped into the truck, Royce looked around inquisitively. "This missing woman, is she here?"

"Our latest intel says she was brought in here last night," Rick noted. "However, that can change minute by minute. Plus a few more things about this case might make life a little difficult for us."

When he explained about the diplomatic immunity, Royce groaned. "That just pisses me off. There was a case not very long ago of a diplomat's wife running over a teen in the street, just a regular old village street. Her husband got her out of the country right away, and she never did face any repercussions for killing that innocent seventeen-year-old kid."

"That sucks," Rick grumbled, looking over at him. "I think I heard about that."

"Yeah. There's been all kinds of efforts to bring her to justice, but every time it's been blocked by bureaucratic BS of one kind or another. Thus she doesn't have to face the reality of her actions."

"Nobody else would get away scot-free."

"Exactly. Anybody else would have been crucified. Even if it was an accident, she still needs to take some responsibility. There's still a penalty involved. Anyway, tell me more about the woman in our case."

"Here's a couple files." And, with that, Rick reached beside his seat and pulled two folders from there and held them up. "One is what we have on her, and the other file has what we have on him." He handed Royce the two folders.

"You have a much thicker file on him," he noted, opening the fat folder. "Why does that not surprise me?"

"Let me give you a few of the salient details while we drive," Rick began, pulling out of the parking spot. "Bottom line is that his fourth wife has just passed away, and he's supposedly holding hostage this young woman, the sister of his last wife. I'm not sure that *hostage* is quite the right word for it, but he's keeping her prisoner."

"And you know this how?"

"She somehow got word to MI6. No one knows how yet. She hasn't been able to get free, as the diplomat watches her all the time. She wants to get away from him before she ends up like her sister."

"As in dead?" Royce asked, turning to Rick.

"Or as wife number five first, then potentially dead."

"Yet the deceased sister had money?"

"The family business," Rick confirmed, carefully watching the road ahead. "This diplomat travels with an entourage, so he's not easy to get at, and he leaves anytime he wants to. He might run out of luck and run out of countries that will allow him to stay hidden, but that's not the case right now."

"Do we think that the missing sister is still here? Is there any current evidence of that?"

"He has a private plane, which supposedly came in last night. According to the intel, he came in alone, meaning with his usual entourage but not her."

At that, Royce frowned at him, and Rick nodded. "I know. Which means in theory, she's not here."

"You don't believe that though, do you?"

"According to what MI6 was told in a hurried phone call, the diplomat never leaves her alone. She hasn't been away from him or his brother or some guard since his latest wife died."

"How did she die?"

"Supposedly a heart attack." He made an air quote, before grabbing the wheel again.

"Of course. And I'm guessing there was no autopsy."

"No, of course not."

"Does heart failure run in the family?"

Nodding, Rick replied, "Yeah, and that made it harder to get anybody to give a crap."

"Lovely. What about the wife's family? Which is also Heather's family, right?"

"Heather is the only one left, which is why the two of them have so much money. Now Heather's net worth is significant to many and potentially why she is quite likely to end up being wife number five, whether she wants to be or not. Faheed is that kind of person."

"Well, crap," Royce murmured. "That's not a good way to go through life, is it?"

"No, it sure isn't, and yet we know it happens a lot. Hannah's and Heather's family started a big whiskey brand, many decades ago. When the parents passed six years ago, the business went to the sisters."

"So, did this diplomat get a controlling interest?"

"That I don't have any details on, at least not yet," Rick noted. "In theory, the missing sister should have the company now, on paper at least, and the deceased wife, … she also had a large life insurance policy."

"Of course she did," Royce replied, with irony.

Rick smiled over at him. "I feel as if I'm hearing that same old tired note of *This again, really?*"

"It's an opportunistic grab, isn't it? Somebody wants something, and they don't care what they have to do to get it. They just reach out and take it."

Rick nodded. "It does seem to be that way," he said in a resigned tone. "Even though we do help dozens and dozens of people on an annual basis, the world just never seems to run out of assholes."

Royce laughed. "I hear you there," he muttered, feeling more in control. "Let's hope that we can take this particular asshole out of the game." His words were followed by an odd silence. Royce frowned. "So, what is it you aren't telling me?"

Rick sighed. "It depends on how much you hate governments, but this is a job that we're doing for MI6."

"Hang on a minute. Are you getting paid by two parties for this job?"

"No, MI6 brought it to our attention first. We would have helped Heather directly, if we'd heard from her first, but we didn't. MI6 brought it to our attention, after the death of the diplomat's fourth wife."

"So, we're information hunting for MI6 at the same time as rescuing Heather."

"Yeah, but MI6 is focused on us getting a nice clean case against our murdering diplomat."

"Which will never go to court," he interrupted, "because you know Iran will bury it, or else Faheed will just disappear quietly into the night because he caused too much trouble."

"You and I both know that. My main concern, and MI6's too, I suspect, is Heather's safety. But, if she has any information to give on this Faheed, … then MI6 also wants her alive and testifying."

"Is that a condition of her release?" he asked, looking over at him.

"No, I don't believe that it is, and it certainly isn't a mandatory part of our rescue," Rick stated. "We want to take this Faheed guy off the streets, for sure. Yet we want to save her at the same time."

"Got it."

"You'll see a picture of her in the other file."

Royce opened the file that he had yet to study, and there was a picture of a young woman. Intelligent looking, but more than that was there. She had a sparkling grin on her face, as if the world was something she was more than ready to take on, while living her life to the fullest. "Interesting," he murmured.

"What's interesting?" Rick asked, as he quickly changed lanes and took a turn at a corner.

Royce looked up at the area they were traveling through, then returned his gaze to the file. "Something's almost familiar about her."

"I don't know about familiar, but we've all, from the time we've seen that photo, sensed something."

"Sensed?" he repeated. "Oh boy, here we go again."

"Yep. It could just be that she might have a highly developed ability. Have you ever seen her before?"

"I don't think so, but I definitely sense something about her energy."

"And that's *your* thing," Rick declared. "You can see energy off photographs, can't you?"

"We can see energy off anything, as you can see the energy off this truck," Royce clarified, turning to face his friend. "So, that's not unusual. But seeing something that's worthwhile off a photo, ... something we can use to our advantage? Now that's a whole different story."

"Oh, I agree with you there," Rick replied, chuckling.

Royce smiled at his buddy. "It's really good to see you, Rick. You do know you could have called at any point in time, like when you and your team needed help."

"I could have, but, between getting our asses kicked, trying to recover and to protect ourselves, finding the woman of my dreams, getting married, getting her pregnant," he explained, with an eyeroll and a flashing grin, "it's been kind of crazy. Then having twins? ... Well, my life has been a little bit complicated."

"Jesus," Royce muttered under his breath. "So, you guys managed to accomplish all that in a fraction of the time anybody else ever does."

"When it came down to it," he said, with a smirk, "we really didn't have time to do anything but move—and move fast."

Royce nodded. "I'm glad it turned out okay for you. So few of us are out there, very few like us. You have got to be one lucky bastard."

"Exactly. Unfortunately that is part of the problem.

Since very few of us are out there, and, when you consider that this Heather might very well be another person with abilities, you can bet that Terk will be very protective and very proactive about trying to save her."

"That's fine. He can be as proactive as he wants. We're still up against a diplomat who can jump countries in a heartbeat and apparently even get into a country like Finland without trouble."

"Yes, and that just makes it a bigger challenge."

"I thought the initial request mentioned something about Iceland?"

"It did because that's where they were at the time, but they've already changed locations. So now here we are in Finland."

"How long is that likely to be for?"

"I can't tell you," Rick admitted, trying for a neutral tone, but he clearly had something on his mind. "If Faheed thinks we're onto him, he'll be gone in a second."

"The better question is, will he take her back to Iran? If he did decide on that, it would make our process even more complicated. … Finland for us would be a walk in the park comparatively."

"I'm not sure why he chose Finland. Iceland either for that matter. It seems to be random, but we need to figure out whether he's here on a diplomatic mission or has something else on his mind. So far we don't think he's into human trafficking, but my current theory is the usual criminal activities, involving guns, drugs, killers-for-hire."

"His schedule doesn't help much," Royce pointed out. "Just the basics are listed. It says that he's meeting with people to *strengthen ties, fostering good relationships through conferences and peace visits.*"

"Of course," Rick quipped. "Meanwhile, Iran has absolutely no idea that they have this murdering wild card running around, or, if they do know, they're protecting him."

"If they do know, they'll do their best to take him out because he'll cause them no end of headaches." Royce stared out at the countryside, disappearing rapidly beside him. "You can't have somebody like Faheed running around the globe, giving your country a bad name, particularly if you're doing it under the guise of the home country allowing it."

"And that was definitely our take on it, but, so far, nobody has stepped up and done anything about pulling him back. So basically Jonas is looking for some evidence, anything that he can use against this Faheed guy."

"Remind me again why Jonas and MI6 are involved?"

"Because wife number four was English, as is Heather. Plus the wife, Hannah, died in England."

"*Great*," he muttered. "So, Faheed slipped through their fingers at that point, right?"

"They disappeared through diplomatic immunity channels within twenty-four hours of Hannah's death. Nobody even realized he was there or that there was an issue. Faheed tried to say he was separated from his wife at the time, had no idea what happened, was locked up in meetings, *blah-blah-blah*. He also made it look as if he was devastated because he was hoping to reconcile with his wife, but then added something to the effect of *Hey, it just wasn't to be, and somebody decided otherwise*. Yet he arranged for a cremation, and the remains were taken back to his country."

"Right. Not that they would do us any good at this point. And whether he still has them is questionable, but who knows? He may have just tossed her ashes into the ocean."

"You do seem to understand how this works," Rick noted, acknowledging Royce's long career of dealing with similar assholes.

"When you get a bad seed with money and a free pass to travel the world without any restrictions, doing whatever he damn well pleases, that makes it easy to do what he wants to do and to feel as if the world owes him. Yet, if he already has money, why the hell is he killing his wives for more?"

"Do these assholes ever have enough money?" Rick asked him snidely.

"*Right*," he agreed, "Greed is alive and well. I have yet to meet any rich person who had enough."

HEATHER ROTHCHILD PACED the small suite, her tarot cards clutched in her hands. Just like the last one, this was a high-class, elegant space. She wouldn't even be surprised if silk sheets were on the bed, but she couldn't have cared less. All she wanted was to escape this gilded cage to the freedom of the world she used to know, a world that she hadn't had the chance to enjoy in a very long time, not since coming to visit her sister months ago. Not for the first time in this hellhole had she wished she had taken her sister's advice and run while she had the chance. However, Heather wouldn't leave Hannah alone, but Heather had been completely misguided in thinking that she could help her sister escape too.

Instead her sister was dead, and Heather was the one captive. Her hand instinctively rested against her heart. The tarot cards vibrated in her hand. The loss was … crippling.

The fear was … almost as crippling.

Her sister had been happily married—although how that was possible, Heather didn't know. When asked, her sister would just smile and say it had seemed to be a good idea at the time. Precisely when marrying that monster could possibly have seemed to be a good idea, Heather surely didn't know. And yet her sister had never spoken a word against her husband. Maybe because they were constantly being watched, constantly monitored, and anybody saying anything untoward would get their punishment. And, of course, all explanations were twisted to make it sound as if it was all about keeping the women safe.

The ugly reality had kept them both in line.

Heather wasn't into revenge, but she sure had a burning anger to see Faheed pay for her sister's death—if he had been involved. He swore passionately to her that he had absolutely nothing to do with it, but Heather didn't believe him. He had seemed grief-stricken at Hannah's death, but Heather just assumed he was a very good actor. After all, he had treated her sister like a china doll and had kept her a prisoner for five years, the entire time that they were married. Her sister had told her that she was totally okay with that. Very much the fragile type, Hannah had never been the kind of person capable of handling life in the real world.

Whether that was an image Hannah had deliberately cultivated or not, Heather didn't know, but having grown up with her sister, she knew that it hadn't been that way forever. Only as her sister became an adult did Hannah seem much less capable of living in the world around her. Certainly Faheed had understood and had protected her from every-thing. The trouble was, Heather was too damn suspicious and pretty damn certain that he had been involved in her sister's death.

Not to mention the fact that he refused to let Heather leave, telling her that, when the time was right, he would, how he couldn't afford the bad publicity after her sister's death. That didn't make any sense to her, but he would not give her another explanation. So, until he changed his mind, Heather had no choice. He also mentioned how it was too dangerous, but, as far as she was concerned, the danger was sitting right there, with her. Wherever Faheed was, trouble seemed to follow.

Heather knew better than to seek help from Faheed's adult children, three sons and one daughter from his first wife. Those offspring were not terribly impressed with their father marrying Hannah, many years younger than their father. So they stayed out of Faheed's personal life, probably as long as the adult children's own fortunes weren't affected—or maybe they'd learned to not cross that line. Hannah had been depressed over her lack of children, but, after much questioning by Heather, Hannah had finally confessed that Faheed wouldn't tolerate a pregnancy.

When a knock came at her door, she quickly slipped her boxed tarot cards into her pocket. She deliberately had a small set, tucked away in its original packaging, so she could keep them on her person at all times. "Come in." She'd already learned that arguing and going against Faheed's wishes didn't turn out well for her. And that went for any attempts to avoid answering. Not that he would ever hit her, but she could easily be locked in her room for days.

When the door opened, Saheed—brother to Faheed—walked in, his usual smug smile on his face.

"There you are," he greeted her in a bright, cheerful voice.

She glared at him. "Where else would I be?" she snapped. "You escorted me here, doing your brother's bidding, as always."

He just gave her that same genial smile that he always did when she got snappy. "A little tired and stressed from traveling, I see," he replied, with that same smarmy tone that made her skin crawl.

"No," she corrected him. "Tired and stressed because I want to leave. I want to go home. I don't want to be here." She chewed on the last part and rolled her eyes. "Then you already know that."

"Yes, yes, yes, I know," he said, with a wave of his hand, completely ignoring her demands. "Dinner is more or less ready, and we thought maybe you would wish to eat with us."

"And if I say no?" she asked, with a wry smile.

"Then, of course, we'll have a meal sent in for you," he replied, his fake smile brightening in anticipation. "I'm sure you're feeling peaked after all the traveling and could use a few days to rest."

She stared at him, wondering how he could live with himself. He didn't sound fake, and it bugged the hell out of her that people out there so enjoyed others' suffering. "No, I'll come. I want to get out."

He nodded. "I figured you would." His smile turned into a triumphant grin, as if he knew which direction she would choose to go. "You'll make Faheed very happy."

She glared at him. "How come you keep traveling with Faheed, instead of going off and doing your own work? Or rather living your own life, instead of being attached to his?"

"It is my honor to be his *assistant*," Saheed stated, his shoulders stiffening at the criticism. "That's what you call me, isn't it? Of course I do have an official title and all that, but I understand that you're not feeling very kind toward us at the moment. Until you recognize that we haven't had anything to do with your sister's death, that probably won't change. So, I'll be here for a while I guess."

She didn't say anything, but he stepped back from the doorway and motioned for her to walk out. She did so immediately, grateful for the chance to at least get out and see a little something about where they were. "You didn't even tell me what country we are in this time."

"We're in Finland," he said, with a bright smile. "Probably for a couple days but I'm not too sure yet."

She nodded and didn't say anything to that. She had never been to Finland and wouldn't it be nice to think she could spend some time here, but, in this situation, not likely. She dreamed of being free whenever she got to go on a trip. This captivity she would definitely not have chosen. Yet it would be forced on her, no matter what she did. Chafing at the prison, she followed her ever-present *helper* down to a hotel lobby, then into a private dining room on the other end.

Faheed hopped up with a delighted smile. "I'm so glad you decided to join us. I was afraid that you weren't feeling well enough."

"I'm fine," she declared, using the strong tone she always tried to adopt when speaking with him. "I'm not my sister. I keep telling you that."

"No, no, of course, forgive me," he muttered, with that same fake genial smile.

She sighed, then took the seat being held out for her and sat down. It was just the three of them, and that was not right. Normally his secretary was here as well. "Where's

Ana?" Heather asked curiously.

"She's resting," he shared, with a casual wave. "She might need to go back home a little earlier than I do. We have a fair bit of work to be done, and I need to make that decision tonight."

Heather didn't say anything and just nodded slowly. Ana at least understood the situation Heather was in, though didn't understand why Heather was fighting it. But then her sister Hannah never really did. Her sister seemed to have been much happier in the gilded cage than Heather was.

Dinner was served without her being offered a choice, something else that Faheed did on a regular basis. She had some chilled soup, followed by salmon and vegetables. She ate well, knowing that, depending on the whims of both Faheed and Saheed, she could be sequestered in her room with only sandwiches at any point, should she not please Faheed. Tonight she ate without complaint, not wanting to take a chance of pissing him off, not while they were in a country where she might get away from him.

If there was any chance of that happening, she wanted to ensure she had her strength up.

"Good," Faheed said, as he noted her appetite. "The change of location seems to have been good for you."

She nodded. "I'm feeling decent now," she muttered, as she looked around with interest. "I've never been to Finland before." Huge windows overlooked the city, but seeing it from the inside wasn't the same as walking the streets and inhaling the very essence of the city. "Any chance of going out for sightseeing or maybe a quick tour?"

"Oh, I don't think so," Faheed replied, with a sad look in her direction. "I have many appointments to attend while here. I doubt there will be time for sightseeing."

She sighed and nodded. "Of course not. Why would you want to do anything that would make me happy?" she muttered, and her tone rang like flint on stone. She quickly finished off her meal and sat back, then looked over at Saheed and announced, "I would like to return to my room."

He glanced at Faheed for confirmation.

"Of course," Faheed agreed. "After eating all that, I'm sure you need a digestive nap."

There was the usual jab at the amount she had eaten, which was very typical of him too. Faheed had controlled her sister's food fanatically to ensure she didn't get fat. In Heather's case, she was almost too thin. Therefore, eating was something she often took advantage of when there was a chance because, as soon as she got stressed, she dropped weight very, very quickly. Then it was hard for her to put it back on again. As usual, Saheed was there to pull out her chair the minute she made any attempt to stand up, a move she found most disingenuous.

And, with that, she rose and followed Saheed from the dining area and back to her hotel room. He opened the door for her, ushering her in with that same smarmy smile. "Have a good night." Then he quickly locked the door behind her.

She stared at the door in frustration. You would think that there would be a way for her to lock her own door and keep them out, but sadly there wasn't. Not that she'd ever had a problem with either of them coming in during the night, but that wasn't something she even wanted to start thinking about. That would be enough to make her cringe and stop sleeping.

Once again, she thought about Hannah, who had blossomed in this cloistered atmosphere. She'd often laughed at Heather and told her that there was a lot to be said for it and didn't seem to mind her restrictive lifestyle. Besides, she genuinely loved Faheed. Heather often wondered about that too, but then love blossomed in the darndest places. Heather's reaction to Faheed had been totally different.

Faheed had gotten it into his mind that he was now responsible for Heather. The problem with that was that she didn't want him to be responsible for anything of hers. She was a legal adult in the eyes of the rest of the world, but, he and those in his home country felt women weren't smart enough to do much. So, as long as Faheed was around, Heather worried that he would be working hard to overtake control of her company.

"Sorry, sis," she whispered into her room. "I didn't think everything would change so quickly."

And yet, from Faheed's point of view, he was just doing his duty, as brother-in-law to Heather. She snorted at that because the *brotherly duty* had everything to do with greed and controlling Heather's company. She felt he was still trying to figure out how to get it away from her. She understood that her father's will was unbreakable and that her position as majority owner of the company was secure. Upon her sister's death, Hannah's shares went to Heather, and there was nothing Faheed could do about it, or at least Heather hoped he could do nothing about it, except maybe try to make it look as if she were incompetent.

That was a very real possibility, an angle for Faheed to tweak, and something she often worried about. While she had been staying with her sister, Heather ran the business via emails and calls and online meetings. That was hampered once Hannah died. Still, Heather had managed to get out one message to her manager, telling him to notify the proper authorities how she was being held against her will. At least she hoped it got to him. If so, hopefully he had passed it onward. Yet here she was, wondering if anybody had even gotten the message. Not for the first time she wondered if Faheed had gotten a hold of her manager and had made some deal with him.

Faheed was all about making deals, and she could totally see him doing just that. He was all about feathering his own nest and making his world turn the way he wanted it to, so Heather wasn't surprised. However, the thought of losing her family's company was enough to make her vomit right now. It just wasn't fair. She'd put in so much time, effort, and work to make it what it was today that it didn't seem possible that somebody else could just step in and take it from her.

However, this world functioned on strength, and those who had power took what they wanted, and it didn't matter who or what stood in the way. In her current kidnapped status, she didn't know how to stop Faheed from stealing her company from her. Alone, in the privacy of her room, she pulled out her tarot cards and sat down to read them.

She'd been reading tarot cards all her life. It had been a way to separate herself from her parents, who both had been very domineering as she grew up. They'd been absolutely horrified to find her with tarot cards, to the point that they were frightened of her. While it bothered Heather, it had also given her a certain sense of power that she could do something or was doing something that upset them to that extent.

At the time, it was typical teenage crap to her, but, as soon as she'd started working with the deck, she found that she had an affinity for it. An affinity, almost a calling, really, and she was too accurate in her predictions. Her sister used to ask her all kinds of questions, and Heather had answered them through the tarot, and they always ended up being right. When her sister had asked her about marrying Faheed, Heather didn't need the tarot cards to tell her to run as far and as fast as she could, but her words had fallen on deaf ears.

As far as her sister was concerned, Hannah had absolutely no need to worry, and Heather hadn't been able to convince Hannah otherwise. To Heather's dismay, the tarot hadn't lied. She had argued with Hannah about the results because her sister was willfully ignoring the messages from the beyond, or whatever it was. Blinded by love, Hannah had discounted all the evidence suggesting that marrying Faheed would be a terrible mistake. Instead, she had adjusted her filters, tuning out anything she didn't want to hear.

The word of the tarot made sense to Heather, but it didn't make sense to her sister, at least not when it came to Faheed.

Whether listening to her psyche, other people, the universe, or God, Heather had any number of answers for the way the results came out, but she liked to think of it all as just being *intuition*.

Pulling from the tarot deck, she chose one card for her future, asking if she was to stay where she was, and, when she flipped it over, her heart froze.

It was *that* card, the one that she always hated, not because what the card implied always came to pass but because it could potentially sometimes be true. As she stared at it, this was the same card she had pulled over her sister's future. Heather looked around, almost in panic, wondering how the hell she was supposed to get out of this nightmare.

That card, that card staring her in the face, was the Death card.

CHAPTER 2

T HE NEXT MORNING Heather woke up, determined to find a way out of this mess. When the housekeeper came to clean the room, Heather asked her, "Any chance you could send a message for me?"

The woman frowned at her, then glanced back at the doorway uneasily. "Can't you leave?" Her English was decent but the accent hard to decipher.

"No, I'm being held prisoner."

The woman gave her a half shrug and a commiserating look.

Heather muttered, "*Great*, nobody'll help." Yet the presence of a guard at her door probably was threat enough for this housekeeper.

Heather wasn't even sure what it would take to get somebody to help, but she knew good people had to be out there. She certainly couldn't blame the cleaner for being terrified of the guard outside her door, plus the high-profile diplomatic presence of Faheed. He was a pretty imposing figure to begin with, and, since he got to hand off all responsibility, using all that lovely diplomatic immunity BS, it made him even more terrifying because he could do whatever he wanted, with no repercussions. Heather didn't know how he'd gotten away with so much for so long but suspected that his brother, Saheed, had facilitated his efforts.

When the woman was almost done cleaning, Heather smiled at her. The woman hesitated but then quickly laughed nervously. That was a good sign, or at least it was something. Yet, if Heather had a chance to give her a message to send, who would she call? She didn't know who to call. That was the problem. Who did you call when you found yourself in this situation? It's not as if she had any experience with criminals. She was in the whiskey business, for God's sake.

Yet here she was, desperately looking for somebody, anybody who could give her a hand. She had access to the internet, but she also knew that Faheed and Saheed checked out what she did on a regular basis. So it's not as if she could search for avenues of escape or who to contact at this time. She knew better than to even type in *how to hire a hitman*, which would bring instantaneous repercussions on her.

She didn't want to kill Faheed. She just wanted to get away from him. As emotions momentarily overwhelmed her, the cards vibrated in her pocket. She placed her hand over the pocket to calm them. She knew when she calmed that they would too. They were direct conduits to her own emotions.

The next day followed the same pattern, and it drove her crazy. As the days continued to blend one into another, she was getting more and more frustrated. Letting her go was a choice on Faheed's part, not hers.

She would end up leaving Finland without anybody the wiser. At that, she pondered leaving a note behind. Would Faheed notice? How could they notice, if Faheed and Saheed left with her? With a groan, Heather felt sure Saheed would inspect her room the moment she packed up to leave. If not himself, via a surrogate.

Heather worried that Faheed or Saheed had a greater chance of finding any note she left behind. Even if somebody nice found her note, Heather had no guarantee they would take her note to someone who could help. There were too many ifs and buts—and possible retaliatory threats.

She pulled out her cards from her pocket and mentally asked if she would safely escape this nightmare and received a strong yes. Frowning but delighted, she looked around nonplussed, wondering where a rescue could come from.

Yet the cards hadn't lied to her yet, so she would go on trust.

She had two worries prominent in her mind, getting free and protecting her company. They were her constant companions.

While she had a good relationship with her managers and her directors, the company ran more or less without her. Thus, if people out in the world at large were willing to take bribes, she wouldn't be surprised if someone in her company would do so as well. She didn't want to think of that, but she wasn't a fool. There had been multiple attempts at espionage in the past. Even now, Heather felt in her gut that Faheed's lawyers were trying to break her father's will, trying to break the family trust her father had set up for just such an event.

Yet her sister had already made further provisions to leave everything to Heather that had to do with the family business. Those legal documents existed with both sisters' signatures on them. That had been mandatory per Father's will, which was not terribly unusual with a family business, except that Hannah may not have told Faheed about this— the tiny little fact that the family business wasn't Hannah's to hand off.

As far as Heather was concerned, if Hannah had held

back even that much from Faheed, Heather considered that to be a good thing. But then again, it would explain the argument that Faheed and Hannah had not long ago. She refused to talk to Heather about it, yet it upset Hannah greatly. Maybe it had even brought about her sister's death.

Hannah hadn't been in the same situation that Heather was in right now, being locked in. Her sister had always had a certain amount of freedom to come and go, mostly because she was thoroughly in love with Faheed and would never have done anything to change that. Little did she know that it was probably her beloved Faheed who was responsible for her death.

Heather shook her head at that. "Why does the world not care?" she muttered out loud. Not that anyone knew to care about it.

She had her laptop with her and her cell phone, but she couldn't even use them. Everything went through Faheed. She knew that, right now especially, she was being closely monitored. He'd warned her not to even attempt to contact anybody, and, since he had a lot on his mind that she wasn't privy to right now, she needed to do her best not to piss him off.

It hadn't been a light warning. She knew exactly what he meant and had done her best to maintain a certain aplomb around him. As long as he thought she was being coopera-tive, there was a chance that she could get out of this alive. She was afraid that she was about to become Faheed's next wife, whether she wanted to or not, and, in Faheed's world, that was certain death. She had never wanted to be in his company for even a minute, so marriage was an absolute *no* as far as she was concerned, but, for him, it would just make economic sense.

It would be one more notch on his trophy stand, giving him a valid reason to retain control of Heather's whiskey company, whether she wanted that or not. And that was half the problem. He seemed to always do whatever he wanted, and nothing seemed to stop him.

"But not me," she vowed. "He won't get what he wants this time. Not from me."

And, with that, another knock came on the door, as Saheed came to escort her to Faheed's suite for brunch, whether she wanted to or not. With that little gesture, she became even more determined to get word out to someone, somewhere, that she was being held against her will.

Surely someone would care.

"IF SHE'S HERE," Royce noted, "surely she would be in the same hotel as the diplomat."

"And yet," Rick replied, as they walked up to the front entrance of the hotel in question, "nobody has reported seeing her."

"How is that even possible?" he muttered.

"Because Faheed is touting Heather as his actual wife."

"But his wife, Hannah, is dead."

"Yes, except, and this is potentially very pertinent, the two of them looked a lot alike, almost to the point of being mistaken for twins."

"Ah, crap," he muttered in understanding. "So there is a chance that he is trying to pass off Heather as his wife in order to keep any questions at bay."

"Maybe, it's hard to say. He won't tolerate personal questions, which is fairly standard for diplomats."

"If Heather is free to walk around …"

"We don't know that. If she were free, as in free to come and go as she pleased, that would be a different story," Rick replied, frowning at him. "You and I both know that women can walk around with their kidnappers or guardians, yet not be free, not say anything to anybody, and still look perfectly natural, as if they are happy to be there."

He nodded. "I guess that's quite true, isn't it? Damn." Royce was frustrated as they walked into the hotel. He looked around and asked Rick, "Are we staying here?"

"We are. Mostly because Faheed is here."

"Interesting. What are the chances that we'll even see him?"

"Not likely. He keeps to himself, using a private dining room. Nobody's allowed in or out. Meals are served by one server and passed off to his team. Then he's served from there. Or he eats in his suite with security in the hallway."

"Great, so security's heavy, and Heather may or may not even be here."

"First of all we must confirm that she's even here. If she is, then we have to verify if she is the woman who reached out to MI6 because we don't know that for sure. We also have no confirmation that Heather is really a prisoner. Once we figure all that out, the real work begins—getting her out of here."

"*Great*," Royce muttered. "Rescuing damsels in distress appears to be the call of the day."

"We've done a lot of it lately," Rick agreed, "for one reason or another."

"And that won't stop, since women are often kidnap victims," Royce noted, "but the circumstance in this one seems just a little bit off."

"More than a little bit, if you ask me," Rick replied, "but some cases are just that way."

"Yeah, they sure are," Royce muttered, as they quickly checked in. They were given their rooms as requested, and, as they walked up slowly, Royce checked out the security in the area. "I wonder if we'll even catch sight of them."

"Not likely. Our intel says they have an entire floor to themselves."

"All that for one diplomat?" Royce asked.

"A very wealthy one, remember that. He doesn't travel in standard style and always has his entourage."

After they checked out their rooms and dumped their bags, Royce and Rick set out on a fact-finding mission. Picking up a coffee in the hotel coffee shop, they quickly did a full-on hotel sweep, checking out each floor, including the floor where she was potentially being held.

By the time they had the layout, Royce frowned. "Where are the guards? That absence alone is curious, plus normally we don't have a location this fast."

Rick whispered, "Maybe the guards are in each room."

Royce groaned. "Which means we can't single out which room houses the diplomat and which one has Heather?"

Rick nodded. "Faheed may just be that cloaked in his immunity that he has no need to post guards and simply doesn't worry about people like us," Rick pointed out. "Faheed's obviously of the opinion that he can do what he wants and that it doesn't matter."

"I think you're right there." By the time they had checked out everything, Royce summarized, "Okay, so we have four main exits, six other exits, plus the fire exits, all leading to the ground floor and on to the garage for parking. We need a source of information to find out when they leave the building, so we can enter her room."

"Yeah, good luck with that, finding a source and knowing which room is hers." Rick laughed.

Royce cocked one eyebrow at him. "I was thinking of coming from the roof into her room, straight to the source."

"Except we don't know what room is hers though," Rick pointed out. "I'm okay with the roof as a starting point, though we still have to confirm she's here."

"Yeah, that'll be a slightly different challenge," Royce conceded. "I wonder what window washers they use at the hotel."

Rick smiled at him in approval. "Now that's a good point. We'll have to get that information from Jonas." He quickly sent off a series of texts.

Royce laughed. "Can't say I've had too many occasions where I got to put MI6 to work for me."

"That is also partly their deal, and they want her, so she can testify against the diplomat."

"Sure, but getting her has to be paramount, with the testimony secondary, if you ask me."

"Agreed. We just want to ensure that nothing happens to make our lovely diplomat pull out of the country on the run with Heather."

"He does that on a regular basis, I gather?"

"Yeah, he has uncanny instincts when it comes to smelling trouble, and he very quickly books it."

"You think it's more than uncanny instincts?"

"It's something to keep in mind," Rick nodded, "but the sense of self-preservation is strong. So, if he's been listening to it all these years, he won't question it. He'll just jump ship."

"And take his entourage with him."

"Exactly. Wouldn't you? He's gone to a lot of effort to do this repeatedly."

"We also need to check with her company and see if she's had any communications with them and if they've had any with Faheed."

"We have to go about that indirectly, so I have Terk on that right now," Rick shared. "We have some pretty good hackers on board."

"You've got Sophia working for you, don't you?"

He looked over at him and smiled. "Yep, we sure do. She's Wade's partner now."

"Cranky Wade?" Royce couldn't believe it.

Rick burst out laughing. "Man, it seems as if you have a bad impression of us all."

"Antisocial, living on the edge of society, not terribly friendly with the outside world. Then there is the talk of energy-working miracles and all that shit. So, you tell me. How does that look to the average citizen?"

"Hey, we're not that bad," Rick protested. Then he shot him a look and grinned. "Okay, so maybe we were. And we were probably worse as we each made our way back after the attack, way worse," he admitted in a flinty tone. "Nothing like an apocalyptic betrayal to make you paranoid and to cause you to pull back again."

"Understood," Royce muttered. "But obviously Wade must have something going for him, particularly if Sophia is with him."

"Apparently they had a bit of a thing before, and then he was sent off on a job that was quite dangerous, so he ended it, didn't want to get her involved."

"I'm sure she didn't appreciate that," Royce noted, staring at Rick. "The little bit I remember about her is that she was a hell of a spitfire."

He laughed. "Yep, she still is. She moved in to help him when he was down, so he couldn't escape her this time. Plus, since he was still recovering, as we all were, he was vulnerable and needed any support he could get. You should see the two of them together."

"I guess that's probably about the only way she could have made it happen. Besides, you have to love a woman who goes after what she wants."

"As long as they're happy, I'm good with it," Rick added. "God knows, mine didn't happen any easier."

"No, I can't imagine that it would have, particularly if you two were dealing with that whole betrayal scene."

"We all were," he muttered. "No way we couldn't be, and, trust me, we all had our struggles."

Royce nodded.

Just as they headed back to the coffee shop again to grab some food, Rick's phone rang. He looked down at it and smiled. "That's Jonas." Rick stepped into the hallway several feet away from everybody and answered it.

Royce quickly placed their order, then rejoined Rick. He couldn't hear all of Jonas's side of the conversation, as too many people were around for it to be on Speakerphone, but Royce got the gist of it. When his order was ready, he picked it up and returned to Rick. Together they walked out of the hotel.

When Rick disconnected the phone, he nodded to Royce. "One woman is here with the group, right now. There were two, but one just left."

"Interesting, I wonder which one left. With our luck it'll be the one we wanted," he stated, with a half laugh.

"Maybe, but neither has been seen very much anyway.

The one woman did show up for a meal last night, left early and was escorted back to her room. She was seen going to Faheed's suite for a late breakfast. That could mean she's the one we are looking for, considering she was escorted both ways and isn't staying in his suite with him, yet still showed up for a meal. Thereafter, she went to her room."

"We need that room number," Royce muttered.

"The problem is that he's rented an entire set of suites. So, the reality is that she could be in any number of the rooms."

"Right, so back to the window-washing idea. That's got to be the best we've got, but we'll need to make it happen fast."

"Jonas is on it now," Rick assured him.

With that, Royce nodded. "Any news on her family business?"

"I haven't heard back from Terk on that yet."

"Okay, so moving on to the next problem we need to address," Royce paused, looking around to ensure they were alone. "We'll need an exit plan."

"Yeah, and that could be a little bit more of a challenge," Rick muttered.

"Do we have any contacts here?" Royce asked, carrying the to-go bag of food.

"I thought we would do a reconnaissance around this part of the city and see what we can come up with."

"Any safe houses around? Does Jonas have anything? Because, as soon as we nab her, we'll have to book it."

"It won't be quite that simple."

"Nope, it won't, but that doesn't mean that we won't pull it off," he muttered.

Rick grinned. "You see? That's why I knew you needed

to come." He smiled openly. "That confidence is hard to beat."

"Sure, but I always think, if we don't believe we can succeed, what are we doing here?"

They sat outside in the warm sun on a nearby bench and quickly ate their sandwiches, while they took a look at the area. "I'm not seeing any guards," Rick murmured.

"No, neither am I, which means Faheed either has them traveling with him, which he likely does, or doesn't think he'll need more than what he currently has upstairs. Which is also interesting because that shows a certain level of confidence on his part."

"Too much. Maybe it's gone beyond confidence and into arrogance," Rick pointed out.

"That's possible too," Royce muttered. "But then when it comes to any of these diplomats, particularly from some of these other countries, there is almost a requirement of arrogance," he noted, with a snort.

"Maybe, but, when they cross the lines, they still need to pay the piper."

"And yet diplomats don't."

By the time their sandwiches were gone, they had a good idea of the ebb and flow of traffic in the immediate area. The vehicle traffic coming and going was huge, and where Faheed and his entourage were staying was among the highest tier of hotels in the city. The hotel had what appeared to be a top-notch logistics system. Their clientele were extremely well protected from the masses, and there didn't appear to be very much in the way of public traffic in that hotel. Not many people came in and out of the front entrance, and those who did were escorted into vehicles already waiting for them.

When he got a nudge and a whisper to check his three

o'clock, Royce casually looked around to see the diplomat stepping out of the hotel, talking to somebody on the phone. At least that was the face that Royce recognized from the file. "He's not alone, of course."

"No, he has two men with him. Left one is obviously a guard, and the second one is the brother," Rick shared, "at least according to the photo we have in our files. He travels with him all the time."

"Interesting, and yet to be expected, I guess."

"Sure, but then we'll have to consider that he's keeping an eye on Heather too, which won't be an easy job, considering she wants out."

Just then Rick's phone rang. He looked down and muttered under his breath, "Terk."

Again because they were outside with people passing by, Royce kept an eye on the vehicle as the diplomat got into it and quickly disappeared, taking his brother with him.

Rick disconnected the phone and nodded to Royce. "The window-washing idea is a go. Jonas came through, so we know now that it's done on a biweekly basis, but they do different windows each visit, so all the windows get hit on a monthly or bimonthly basis," he explained, looking up at the huge hotel. "A lot of windows are here."

"Right," Royce confirmed, "so what is the news?"

"Apparently they are currently working on the far side, near the penthouse floor."

"Do we have any response from her company?"

Rick nodded. "Terk read through the energies of the employees. From Terk's initial pass, he found that Heather is well-loved. Sophia made a test call, passing herself off as a journalist, asking for an in-person interview with Heather. Sophia got a runaround response. Nobody would confirm

Heather was out of the office. Nobody would book a time and a day for the supposed interview."

"Of course. We still must talk to them eventually, even by phone, to ensure that everything is above board and no one there is involved," Royce noted. "Also, did Hannah have anything to do with the business? Why just Heather?"

"Waiting for more company info to come through," Rick replied, "so we can get started on that soon."

"I want to check out the window washers," Royce said, "but better if I get a room number. With Faheed and Saheed both gone, that means we have a window of opportunity that I don't want to lose."

And, with that, they quickly retraced their steps to their rooms, where they sat down with the hotel schematics, sorted out the rooms, the placement of rooms on the entire floor where she most likely was. "She's got to be somewhere along this side," Royce suggested. "This area right here is secluded. This is the perfect vantage point for Faheed too." He frowned. "Do you really think he paid for the entire floor below, or has he just got this entire penthouse level?"

"I don't know. I've seen them do both in the past, and our intel could be wrong or no longer current. Maybe he has a standing invitation to stay at this hotel. We won't know until we get a little more information."

"I hate bad intel," Royce declared, staring at him.

"You and me both," his partner replied cheerfully.

"In that case, I think I'll go see if I can get my own intel." And, with that, Royce hopped to his feet.

"Whoa, whoa, whoa," Rick cried out. "Where are you going?"

"To find out what room she's in, and, if I have a chance to see her because nobody else is around, I will talk to her."

And he quickly walked out of their hotel suite. Royce knew Rick thought this was a bad idea, but Royce wasn't listening. He needed to move and now …

CHAPTER 3

HEATHER CURLED UP on the couch, reading her book, with a pot of tea she'd had delivered sitting cold beside her. One of the things she was allowed was a digital reader and eBooks, as long as they were fiction. She wasn't allowed to read nonfiction books or anything else that might in any way improve her mind.

She snorted at that. She'd been reading business books since she was twelve. She'd taken an interest in the family business right from the beginning, and yet here Faheed was doing whatever he could to ensure she didn't have any input into her own damn company. But the reality was, no matter where her eyes were focused, her mind was scurrying through the options to escape.

She figured she always had a guard on her door, so, on a whim, she stood and opened the door. Yes, a guard was standing there, looking at her inquiringly. She asked if she could wander around the hotel and get a breath of fresh air, and he stated that he could take her up to the rooftop deck, if she liked, but that was the only place he was allowed to escort her to. That pissed her off. "I guess I can't go without an escort, can I?"

When he looked at her askance, she smiled. "Just kidding."

She walked back inside and closed the door. At least if

she went up on the rooftop deck, it would give her a chance to get out and maybe see the lay of the hotel, yet likely the same as every other hotel she'd seen in the last few months. It just seemed pointless.

While her sister was alive, it hadn't seemed to be such a prison. Heather had had every avenue available to talk to Hannah, plus the freedom to fly back and forth. Heather had been a free spirit back then. Only after her sister's passing did things go bad. Heather didn't know how long Faheed would keep this up, but, so far, he wasn't doing a bad job of keeping her under lock and key.

It just drove her crazy that she didn't have the skills to know how to get out of this scenario. She'd always trusted herself to get out of messes on her own and to learn from experience. Should she go up on the rooftop deck now? She found it frustrating and unbearable to sit here and do nothing. She got up and wandered over to the window and stared out at the streets below.

The windows were open, but they weren't open in such a way that she could stick her head out. These windows opened at the top, and Heather would have to be ten feet tall to get that breath of fresh air. She understood it was probably more of a security thing here, but, for her, it just made her situation even more frustrating. She could see off to one of the other wings, where the window washers were.

She wondered if that could be an avenue of escape. If they were coming her way, perhaps she could talk to them. At least, it would be somebody to talk to that the guard couldn't scare off. Still, her lovely guard, knowing that window washers were nearby, might come inside her room soon to ensure she didn't talk to anyone. She groaned at that thought.

She wasn't good prisoner material, whereas her sister had taken to it just fine. Hannah didn't want to make any decisions in the world, didn't want to do anything but look pretty and set up nail appointments. Heather loved Hannah, but, even at that thought, she winced because it wasn't fair to her sister. They were just very different people. And now with her sister gone, any disparaging comment about Hannah made Heather feel even worse, even if it was just a thought in her head.

Her sister had been a very lovely, gentle soul, something that had attracted Faheed. Hannah had been very much the epitome of a good, obedient wife, whereas Heather herself, well, that was a whole different story. She didn't do obedience well. As her family had found out, she'd gotten herself involved in the business very early on, even if they didn't want her to.

Her father had laughed and just noted that she was a chip off the old block. The deaths of her parents had been crippling for her. Although Heather was sure Hannah was affected by their parents' deaths too, that loss wasn't the same thing for her sister. Hannah seemed to be more into her social circles, while Heather had been at work, alongside her father. And that was what? Six years ago. … *Six years, yes.* It echoed in her mind, and Heather could remember it as if it were yesterday.

She'd immediately stepped into the CEO slot, took over the business, and ran it for both herself and her sister, who had signed over all voting rights because, well, … Hannah didn't want anything to do with it. She'd done that transfer before she had married, without Faheed's knowledge.

Heather didn't think Faheed had any idea that Hannah even had those kinds of voting rights to sign over. Heather, on the other hand, had been relentless in not giving up any votes she controlled or influenced, and she'd kept the company flourishing. She knew that her father would be smiling with joy and pride if he knew just how successful she had been, as she optimized several of the factories, kept up with some traditional methods, yet had modernized what could be modernized.

She'd also opened up brand-new marketing programs to get their product out into the whole world, and two years ago they'd won the first set of awards, winning two more the following two years as well. Last year was by far the most productive year they had ever had. Heather knew she was doing a hell of a good job, and the thought that anybody would apply pressure to take that away from her just made her want to scream with fury. Her ending up captive to a man like Faheed drove her even more crazy.

Yet here she was. Imprisoned. Her freedoms stripped from her.

That little-woman syndrome stuck in her craw, as she again stared out at the window washers, wondering if she could post something on the window. If she got caught, Faheed's response would likely be traumatic, and she would probably not see the light of day for a long time.

As she turned to frown at the couch and her e-reader, an odd noise caught her attention. She pivoted to see a man dropped in front of her. He flashed past, and she wondered if he was part of the window washers or something complete-ly different because of his panther-like movements.

She was afraid of alerting her guard if she called out to the mystery man, so she just waved frantically, trying get his attention. Meanwhile she wondered what he was doing. Then suddenly he reappeared, slowly climbing back to face her. She stared at him in shock, as he climbed higher to where the window was opened. "What are you doing?" she whispered.

He poked his head into the room, flashing a grin at her. "Don't suppose you're Heather, are you?"

Shocked, she nodded. "Yes, yes, that's me. Please tell me that you're here to help me."

"I am here to help you," he confirmed, "but I can't get you out this window. Yet, no matter what, I will get to you. Understand?"

She looked up and nodded. Yet she also knew she was on the twenty-first floor. The windows were ten feet high, and they opened from the ceiling, and she had no way to get up there. She glanced around frantically.

He spoke to her in a soothing tone. "Just stay calm. Now that I know you're here, I'll find another way to get to you." He smiled and added, "By the way, my name is Royce."

"Heather," she whispered. "Please, please help me. There's a guard at my door."

At the word *guard*, he frowned and nodded. "Good to know. I'm heading to the roof now and will find a way to get to you inside."

"I can get to the roof," she cried out in a hoarse whisper.

He looked at her in surprise. Then nodded. "Do so now if you can." And, with that, he was gone.

With determination, she walked quickly to the front door and gave the guard a sweet smile. "If you wouldn't mind, I would love to get out and see the deck, the rooftop deck as you mentioned before, please."

He nodded. "Of course, ma'am."

She cast one last glance back at the door as he closed and locked it to ensure it was secure, and then he said, "Follow me."

"Thank you very much." With a smile, she walked up to the rooftop deck with him. For the first time, hope and excitement filled her. Now to keep it all dampened so as to not alert the guard.

ROYCE MADE IT back up to the roof and phoned Rick. "I found her, and I spoke to her through the window."

"What?" he asked in astonishment. "Already?"

"Yes, she's being held on the twenty-first floor." Then he gave him the room number, describing what he'd seen about her location. "She told me a guard is at her entrance."

"Of course there is," Rick muttered. "Faheed has to keep his … valuables protected."

"Right. She did ask for help, and I gave her my name and told her that we were on it and to just calm down, as I would find a way to get to her."

"You've located her, so that's something."

"Yeah, she's fine and looks to be in good health but obviously scared and wants out."

"Of course she does. Anybody would," he muttered. "Where are you now?"

"I'm up on the service roof," he replied. "There is a rooftop deck below, with a running track and some seating areas. She told me that she could get to the roof, so I'm staying put to see if she manages that."

"And, if not, can you retrieve her the same way you found her?"

"No. I wasn't prepared for those windows. If I could have accessed her that way, I would have snagged her right then and taken her out of the room."

"That would have been good too," he admitted, "if your cables were rated for that level of added weight, that is."

"I would have taken the chance anyway. Even if we fell at a slow rate," he explained, "it would have been fine. As it is, the windows are completely inaccessible because of the way they're built."

"Okay, so that's a no-go."

"Yes, but now at least she knows that somebody is here. Hopefully that will help her to calm down somewhat," he shared. "So now it's just a matter of making a plan."

"Good, I'm glad to hear you got that far." Rick asked, "Did you see anything?"

Knowing what he was asking about, Royce replied, "Nothing unusual. Her energy is excited and worried, but she's healthy. Apart from some bits and pieces of other people's energy attached to her, she looked normal."

"Well, that's something. What about her energy?"

"You mean her abilities?" he asked drily. "Nothing out of the ordinary. However, there is a hot spot on her hip. Intuitively I would say those were her tarot cards. They are closely affiliated to her, matched to her energy. I doubt they would work for anyone else. Her abilities drive the answers she receives." Hearing noises, he whispered, "I have to go. Somebody's coming up here."

"Hey, wait. Somebody's coming up to your level?"

"Up to the roof, or they could be down a level."

"It could be her."

"Only if the guard is bringing her."

"And yet, if she had that kind of access, maybe that was her own doing."

"I'll find out in a minute," he whispered. "She didn't

exactly look or sound like somebody who would wait for life to happen."

"No, according to her file, she's quite the go-getter."

"Complete antithesis to her sister, I gather."

"Yes, that's what we're hearing. Be careful," Rick reminded him. "Those guards are paid well, and failure is not an option for the one assigned to her."

"No, it won't be," Royce agreed. "Sounds as if somebody's on the deck where the chairs are."

"Which would make sense, but go carefully."

"Yep, will do. I'm out." And, with that, he disconnected. He was on the very top of the service roof, which was a different level of roof than the other decks where guests were allowed, fairly common in these big hotels. As he walked up and around the top tier, he had a chance to peek over the edges. Sure enough, it was her. She had a guard with her, and she walked to the edge and stared out into the city streets below.

The guard cautioned her, "Not too close."

She smiled at him. "I'm not interested in committing suicide."

Even from where he sat, Royce could see the guard flush. Rick was correct. The guard himself, if he were to lose Heather in any fashion, that would make his life almost impossible. Failure was not an option, particularly if it was a woman who you were guarding for Faheed. Royce felt sorry for him, yet this world the guard had gotten himself into was harsh. So Royce had only so much sympathy for the guard. Royce was a little short on that right now.

As he watched, Heather walked around, as if checking out the area. Royce was grateful he was close enough to hear the conversation between her and her guard. The guard was clearly uncomfortable and kept very close to her. Finally she sat down on one of the chairs and just took several deep breaths. "It's beautiful up here," she murmured.

The guard hesitated. "I would feel better if you were back in your room."

She looked at him in surprise. "Why? Nothing can happen to me up here, can it?"

He just looked around uneasily, and that was his instincts at work, the instincts of a man who could sense Royce's presence. Royce smiled because it still wouldn't be enough to stop him from getting her.

She just smiled at the guard. "You worry too much. You made the offer, so I took you up on it. I can't tell you how much I'm enjoying the fresh air. Do you have any idea what it's like when you don't have five minutes to yourself outside of that room?" she murmured. "It's tough. I understand that it's a gilded cage and all that, but it's not a cage that I chose." He looked at her in surprise. She nodded. "Or did you not know that I'm a prisoner."

The guard frowned at that, not liking to hear anything obviously.

Royce could only hear so much from where he was, but, if she was attempting to convince the guard to let her go, it wouldn't go well by the looks of it. The guard couldn't afford to make a mistake, not on this.

She sat there happily, staring up at the sky, and Royce wondered whether she was just trying to show him where she was or to give him an opportunity to get down there. He looked around, then realized it was possible. He quickly shifted roofs, jumped across to another one, silently coming up behind them. As Royce moved closer, she stared up at the sky and smiled.

"Tell me something about yourself. I'm dying for a normal conversation."

He shrugged. "Nothing to say."

She nodded. "Right. Of course you're just being friendly because it's part of the job." He looked at her and frowned again, as she shrugged now. "I get it. Kidnapping women is part of the job. God, what kind of a life do you guys all live?" she murmured. "I feel almost sorry—"

"It's time to go back," he interrupted briskly.

He didn't like hearing her words. That was obvious. She sighed. "Why? It's beautiful up here, and it's not as if I'm going anywhere, and nobody else could possibly get up here," she muttered.

"I don't care," he replied. "I don't like anything about this."

She stared at him in surprise, and Royce knew he had to act. He made a wide jump, coming down behind the guard. As he turned around, Royce clocked him one and dropped him. He looked over at her and smiled. "Hi, this time we get to meet in person," he stated, with a grin. "As I said, I'm Royce."

"Heather," she replied. "Please get me out of here, and we better make it fast."

He nodded. "The question is how, and how long before this guy is found?"

She shrugged. "I don't know."

"Is there any place to hide him?" He looked around, took off the man's belt, and quickly used it to secure him. "We'll have to move fast." His phone buzzed just then. He glanced down at it and shared, "It looks as if your entourage is on its way back. They're just coming in through the front of the hotel."

She stared at him in shock and started to shake.

He quickly picked up the guard, dumped him behind the ventilation shafts, and whispered, "Come on." He held out a hand, and she placed hers in his without a question. "Now we have to run."

And rather than go back inside the hotel, he took her down a fire escape to an empty window-washing scaffolding and down onto the rooftop garage parking. By that time, he pulled out his phone and called Rick. "Hey, I've got her. We're in the garage on the rooftop. I'll grab some wheels, and we'll need a safe house."

Rick replied, "I'll clean out our rooms and be on my way."

"Find us a safe house," he repeated.

"Yeah, working on it," he muttered. "Keep her safe, keep her out of sight. They're here, and, once they figure out she's not in her room, all hell will break loose. I'm texting you an address and will meet you there."

And, with that, an address came through very quickly. Royce looked over at her and said, "I'll hijack a vehicle. Once they find out you're missing …"

She nodded. "Hurry, hurry, hurry."

He smiled. "Your wish is my command."

He walked over to the nearest vehicle, managed to unlock it, and quickly fired it up. She got in beside him, and he looked back at her. "You need to duck down and stay down, until I tell you otherwise. I wish you had a blanket or something."

"Me too," she muttered, "but we don't."

And, with that, he drove down to the ground floor, noting he would likely have a toll to pay. He at least hoped it was an automated exit, not a manned one. As he approached, the fencing opened automatically, and he smiled. "Look at that," he muttered. "This must be an employee's vehicle, and their bills are probably sent to them automatically."

"I'm sorry for them then," she said, "because I don't think anybody who works here is paid anywhere nearly enough."

"Particularly not your guard," he pointed out. "He'll have a hell of a headache."

"But that's all?" she asked anxiously.

"That's all," he said, and, within seconds, they were back out on the street and driving away from the hotel.

CHAPTER 4

S AFE FOR THE moment, Heather slowly slid upward into her seat, looking around carefully before buckling up. The tarot cards vibrated happily in her pocket. They were tuned into her emotions in the most incredible way.

The incessant buzz of the seat belt alarm stopped. Royce smiled. "Thanks for doing that. That thing is pretty annoying."

"I would take that over the sound of Faheed's voice any day." He glanced at her sharply, and she shrugged. "I only became a prisoner after my sister's death."

"Do you know why?"

"No, but I have a good idea," she shared. "I don't think Faheed realized that the controlling interest of our family's company was never in my sister's name. So, with her death, all her shares reverted to me. I just know that he's got lawyers on it right now, trying to break my father's will, but I'm really hoping it doesn't happen."

"Well, considering he kidnapped you and held you prisoner," Royce stated, "I'm sure there's something your lawyers can do to stop it."

"Maybe," she muttered. "Yet I'm not in England, and they haven't been able to reach me."

"Once we get to a safe house and off the streets, we'll see about having you call them." With that said, he immediately pulled into an alley, behind a dumpster, and grabbed her phone, opening it. Then he nodded and returned it to her. "Checking to make sure your phone wasn't bugged."

"Oh wow," she muttered.

"Yep, we don't want to waste this opportunity. Let's make your freedom useful and permanent."

She grinned. "Now that is an attitude I can get behind. Who the hell brought you into this?" she asked curiously.

"The British government is looking for your assistance in putting away Faheed."

She shuddered. "Will they send me back if I don't help?"

"I would never let them do that. Your safety should come first, even though we know that governments tend to be a little fanatical when it comes to making things happen their way."

"You're not kidding," she muttered.

"Does Faheed have any enemies?"

She nodded. "I would imagine he has lots. My sister used to laugh about it because he was so powerful. I guess he's powerful either way."

"Was she happily married?"

She winced at that. "Unfortunately I'll say yes. I say *unfortunately* because I don't think she ever really realized what he was truly like, but the *yes* is also because I do know that she was happy. Therefore, I can't really be that angry with him."

"What if he had something to do with her death?"

"I always thought he did, but I have no proof," She stared at him, her heart breaking. "Do you?"

"I don't, but it is something that we're all looking into."

She sank back against the seat, tears forming in her eyes. "My sister had a history of health problems. She was delicate, but I … Look. I don't mean to speak ill of the dead. I just don't know how much were health problems versus convenient excuses for attention."

"Oh, that's interesting," he noted, staring at her.

"And I feel like an absolute shit for saying that." She groaned. "So don't mind me."

"No, I think it's important that we understand what's going on here because this? … Well, it's confusing."

"Yeah, it is," she muttered. "I don't really know what I'm saying right now. I'm just confused and upset at the thought that Faheed had something to do with my sister's death."

He nodded. "As you should be. What I can say is that this is a government-sanctioned rescue, and that's why I'm here."

"Thank you," she whispered.

He grinned at her. "No problem. Also, your phone call came through a group called The Guardians."

She stared at him. "My phone call? Guardians?"

"Yeah, Guardians," he confirmed, with a grin. "Terk is the leader of that group."

"Terk, Terk, Terk," she repeated. "Why do I know that name?"

"I don't know," he replied. "Do you know that name?"

She shrugged. "I feel as if that is a name I should know."

"I don't know how you should know it," he began. "They used to work for the CIA, and now have gone private and are living out of England, where they do jobs like this for MI6."

"He has my thanks," she stated in a formal tone. "I'm sure a price tag is involved, and I would be happy to pay for my freedom. I told Faheed that I would pay for my freedom too, but he just laughed and told me not to worry, as I would, indeed, pay."

"Ouch."

"I know, right? How is that for finding out that you'll pay in ways that you can't even imagine," she muttered. "If it was anyone other than Hannah, … I wouldn't have stayed."

"I'm curious why you did stay," he replied.

"Because she was … She was this lost bird," Heather shared. "You had to meet her to understand. She was very unique to the rest of the world around her, and Faheed was fascinated by it, but he didn't understand her. Although she was happy to be taken care of and happy to be part of his world, I don't know how long that happiness would have lasted. I thought her fascination of it all would end fairly quickly and knew that she would need my support. Instead, well, … it ended in a way I wasn't expecting."

She stared out the window, her fingers clenched tightly together. "I was hoping he would continue to treat her well because she was spoiled in every way. So, for a guy like Faheed, spending money was easy, and so spoiling someone like her with money was also easy because no emotions were required."

"Of course," Royce agreed.

She looked over at him, seeing his firm jawline and his capable handling of the vehicle as he drove swiftly and surely. She questioned whether she should be quite so open and honest with him. Yet, unless he had some ID on him, she had no way to verify his identity. "I guess I should ask you for an ID."

He laughed. "Yeah, you probably should have," he confirmed, "but I don't have time to take it out of my pocket right now. As soon as we get to the safe house, then I'm all for exchanging details."

She smiled. "Honestly, the biggest thing about all this is the fact that I'm out of there," she exclaimed. "So, even if you're not who you say you are, … I still thank you."

"I am who I am," he declared, with that same note of laughter in his tone again, "and you're perfectly safe with me."

She sank back into the seat. "That would be very satisfying to know," she whispered. "It's been very hard to know who to trust here lately."

"What about Faheed's brother?" he asked, looking over at her.

She shrugged. "He makes my skin crawl."

"That's an interesting observation. Do you have anything a little more tangible? Any way to elaborate on why that is?"

She snorted. "You mean, a reason to hate him? I guess there isn't, outside of the fact that he does his brother's bidding all the time and that he made my sister uncomfortable." She cringed at the expression on Royce's face. "No, not really in *that* way. He was just one more of Faheed's minions."

"And yet a loyal one, I presume."

"Very," she declared. "Uncomfortably so. It's almost as if he relished his role."

"Any reason why he wouldn't?"

"I don't know. I have no idea what Saheed's role really is," she admitted, "but he got all the perks without the responsibility that his brother supposedly has."

"That alone is a very interesting observation," he noted. "When you think about it, with a brother who is a diplomat, Saheed would get to travel the world like the truly rich do, plus get the same immunity as his brother because Saheed is part of Faheed's entourage, and still Saheed can do whatever he wants."

"And he does," she stated.

"What about women?"

"They both have women whenever they want them," she shared, staring out the window, hating to even get into that discussion.

"And your sister?"

"She hated it. She hated that Faheed had other women over all the damn time, but he did. She knew it, and there wasn't anything she could do about it, just accept it or not, and, in her case, … she found acceptance was the easier path of life."

"You're saying she really loved him, or was it the lifestyle?"

She frowned at that. "You didn't know her, so I can forgive you for questioning that, but I'll tell you right now that she loved him."

"Good enough," Royce replied. "The bottom line is that she lost her life because of him, and now we're trying to prove that Faheed had something to do with it. Not just her death but all the wives who went before her. Every one of his four wives died, and, in each case, Faheed inherited a very substantial fortune." He paused for a short beat.

"Four wives?" Heather repeated.

Royce nodded. "Did your sister know?"

"She knew that he had been married before. Faheed told her that his wife died in a car accident a long time ago."

"She did," Royce confirmed. "That was wife number one. Your sister was Faheed's fourth wife," he pointed out, "but the diplomatic immunity makes it damn near impossible to nail his ass to the wall, even if he did kill all of his wives. Yet I don't want to just nail him to the wall. I want to ensure he's off the streets, out of commission, and pays for every one of those lost lives."

"What if he didn't do anything to cause any of his wives to die?" she challenged.

He smiled at her. "If he didn't, then he's innocent, and he can go free. Maybe, just maybe, it's possible, but somebody will have to prove it to me first," he stated, giving her a hard look. "Because those four women dying, all while married to him, is not a coincidence that I'm willing to ignore."

"I'm not sure I ever believed in coincidences," she whispered. "You're right. That's a bit of a stretch. If it was just two …"

"Two?" he asked. "I suppose that two could be bad luck on his part but not four," he declared, as he took a left-hand turn onto a small road and then into a driveway, where a garage door opened right in front of her. He pulled in, shut off the engine, then turned to face her. The garage door shut behind them. "Come on out now. We're at a safe house."

She stared around, realizing the chance she had taken, coming with him, a stranger to her.

He smiled again. "It's okay. I'm really not the bad guy here."

She took a deep breath. "Glad to hear that because I've had enough of those to last me a lifetime." And, with that, she got out of the vehicle, slammed the door hard, and walked toward whatever awaited her on the other side of that connecting door.

WATCHING HER INSIDE the safe house, Royce noted how she checked all the windows and doors and spaces to confirm she was truly safe here. He watched with his arms crossed and leaned against the wall in the hallway. "You're not a prisoner here, you know?"

She shot him a glance, nodded, and then added in a curt tone, "But essentially I am until I'm free."

He pondered that. "I guess if you mean that you're a prisoner here in the sense that you must hide from him, as he'll be coming after you, then yes." He noted her hand instinctively going to her pocket, recognizing the security the tarot cards gave her, as in confirmation or reassurance of the psychic message she was receiving. "On the other hand, you're free to walk out that door anytime, which you weren't at the hotel."

She snorted. "I might be free to walk out that door, but I'll also get my ass kicked if Faheed or Saheed find me."

His smile fell away. "Was Faheed abusive?"

She shook her head. "No, he doesn't need to be. He controlled my sister quite easily by keeping her delicate and completely useless." She groaned and raised both hands. "That sounds awful, though I don't mean it that way. However, my sister was totally okay to be this pampered orchid. She didn't want to do anything with her life, and that suited Faheed because that's how he wanted her, as an arm piece, as a showcase for his *whatever*." She gave Royce an eyeroll. "That's not me. I'm very active in my company, and I don't want him having any part of it, and I certainly don't want to be a prisoner and kept as a replacement."

"Has he made any attempts to talk to you about being a replacement?"

She shook her head. "Not directly but he made veiled

comments. However, I definitely got the impression that I wasn't quite up to snuff." She gave a half laugh. "He likes his women beautiful and stupid—but Hannah was definitely not stupid. *Quiet* is probably a better word for her. I know that I certainly wouldn't fit the bill. I also can't stand the man, and I would never marry him," she declared. "So, in the future, should it ever look as if I've changed my mind on that, rest assured I am being forced by him. So please get me the hell away, if you can."

"It won't happen," Royce replied. "I'll ensure that."

"I would love to believe you," she noted. "Yet you don't understand what he's like. He gets his own way at everything. So, the minute Hannah died, I couldn't wait to get away. I wanted to get away earlier, and I wanted her to come with me, but she refused to have anything to do with that idea."

"She didn't think her life was in danger?"

"Not seriously enough, it seems." Heather frowned at that. "I saw no dissension between Faheed and Hannah, and there didn't appear to be any sign that he was unhappy with her. So I just don't know. And Hannah seemed happy enough with him, except for the other women he had and …" Heather looked over at Royce sadly. "It would be horrific to think that she had outlived her usefulness."

Royce stared at her intently. "Particularly if Faheed thought he was getting your company."

She studied Royce and nodded. "I imagine he was quite angry when he found out that Hannah didn't have the controlling interest in the company and that it's essentially mine and not something he can take over. They had a fight shortly before her death that Hannah refused to talk about. It could have been about my business."

"Yet he might control your company if he has control of you."

"And that was the next unpleasant thought I had," she admitted. "Yet I'm no fool, and I am very aware of the machinations that had been going on," she stated. "If Faheed had anything to do with my sister's death, then he can rot in hell," she declared passionately. "Not that it will be easy to prove, as she was cremated instantly."

"His own religion would be against that."

"Yes, but she wasn't part of his religion, so that apparently wasn't an obstacle."

"Right. Of course." Then suddenly he looked around, as if he remembered something. "How about food? Do you need food?"

She grimaced. "If I could calm down enough to eat, then yes. However, at the moment, I'm still too wired," she admitted. "I fear he'll burst through that door at any moment."

Royce walked to the garage door and threw the bolt at the top of the door. "Now, they'll have to get through the lock and the bolt at least."

"No," she argued, "they just have to slam the door open. I've seen his cronies do that more than once." She hesitated. "Do you think my guard is okay?"

"Do you want me to phone the hotel and ensure they check for him?"

She nodded. "Yes, please. I don't want anybody hurt because of me."

"It could already be too late for that," he shared. "You know that, right?"

She winced, wrapping her arms around her shoulders as she collapsed in the nearest chair. "What was I supposed to do? Stay a prisoner in order to not have my guard get hurt? Faheed doesn't tolerate dissension. Faheed doesn't tolerate arguments. Also he doesn't tolerate any resistance or failure. His plan is his plan, and that's just all there is to it."

"Would Faheed hurt the guard?"

"No. He wouldn't get his hands dirty."

"And his brother?"

"His brother is one creepy SOB," she snapped. "Nothing about him is normal or nice."

"He does Faheed's bidding, without question?"

"All of it, usually with a big smile on his face—as if he can't wait. He's never touched me though, and he never touched my sister."

"We can be thankful for that."

"Sure, but it still doesn't make him a nice man. If Saheed found me now, believe me that he would be quite happy to teach me a lesson."

"I presume that lesson would be physical."

"Yeah, it sure would, probably involving rape." She grimaced. "He's very much that domineering male where women are chattel and not a whole lot else," she reminded him. "So, just the fact that my sister didn't run the company in Faheed's mind meant that I couldn't run the company either because we women didn't have the brains for it. He would never accept that I lived for that company all these years. Hannah didn't even want her shares in it, but our father insisted, and I was okay with it because she didn't want anything to do with managing the company. I just cut her checks all the time," Heather shared, with a laugh. "And, when she married, I was really worried that's what Faheed was after, but he already had so much money that it didn't make sense."

"He may have a lot," Royce agreed, "but I think he also spends it at a pretty good rate. All his other wives also left substantial inheritances behind, so he may have money, but that's the thing. It's never enough for those types."

"My same conclusion."

"I have to ask, outside of Faheed, would anybody else have had the temerity to hurt his wives?"

"Meaning did somebody else close to Faheed kill them? I don't know why that would be the case," she replied, thinking about it. "Yet I guess it's always possible. I hate his brother, but that doesn't mean that Saheed's a killer. He's just … an abusive psychopath who likes to inflict pain."

"And that's quite a bit right there. What if he was out to create pain for his brother?"

"Which also doesn't make sense because, if you think about it, his brother was the source of everything given to Saheed."

"Maybe it was a way to get back at him."

"Maybe." She raised both hands. "That's a mental twist that I don't have any experience with," she murmured. "Would it be possible? Absolutely. I just don't think Saheed would do anything to go against his brother."

"Do you think Faheed would have killed Hannah himself or would have arranged to have your sister and his other wives killed?"

"If it's what he wanted, yes," she said instantly. "Something is very cold about Faheed."

"Yet your sister loved him."

"She did. I know she did."

"So obviously he had some redeeming qualities."

She glared at him. "If he did, I never saw them."

"That's not true," he countered. "You told me yourself

that he treated your sister exactly as she wanted to be treated."

"I guess, but that doesn't excuse him if he had something to do with her death."

"Which we don't know yet," he muttered, as he looked down at his phone. "My partner will be here in a few minutes, so don't freak out about it."

"I won't freak," she replied, staring at him. "I am getting tired, but I'm not tired enough to unwind and sleep, but too tired to make a run for it, if we need to," she noted in resignation. "Adrenaline only goes so far. We got lucky today, but now I feel as if we were *too* lucky."

"We got lucky. Yes, that's exactly what we did," he said. "And it worked, and you're free, and now we need to figure out how to get you out of the country and back home again."

"That would be lovely," she murmured. "I arrived on a private plane but without any paperwork. Faheed kept it all."

"Paperwork we can manage, but, more than that, we need a way to get you safely home."

CHAPTER 5

HEATHER WOKE FROM a nap on the couch and stared around her in a half-bleary, half-panicked state.

A hand landed softly on her shoulder, pressing her back down again. "Relax. You're safe." The man's voice was calm, strong, but firm.

She blinked up at him and slowly recognized Royce. She groaned and collapsed back down again. Her mind raced to check that all was well in her world. The warmth of her tarot cards was a welcome reassurance. "You know that first moment when you wake up, and you're not sure if you're still awake or asleep?"

"I know," he murmured, smiling at her. "It's all good."

"Maybe," she conceded, "but, even in sleep, I can't seem to escape him."

"That's likely to continue for quite a while."

"Yeah." She shifted upright, scrubbed at her face, and looked around. "It might be time for a meal and some coffee though."

"Good. I asked Rick to take a detour to pick up food before he arrives."

"Good. He was due in, wasn't he?" she asked, frowning at him. "How long was I asleep? What happened to him?"

"Not long. He had a couple errands to run first."

She didn't say anything to that but wondered if they

were errands she needed to know about. Should she mention her tarot cards to these men? No, not yet—if ever. She'd seen Faheed's horrific response and didn't want to do anything to jeopardize her position here. "I don't suppose you have any intel on what's going on at the hotel, do you? We need to know the situation and soon, in order to see what's happening and what our next move will be."

"That's right, and I do have some intel. The hotel manager has absolutely no word of anything amiss so far."

She stared at him blankly. "Meaning that Faheed didn't raise an alarm?"

Royce nodded. "Nobody came to the front desk and asked if you were there. Nobody asked anything. So, it seems as if they are keeping your absence quiet for now."

She frowned and stared down at her stockinged feet. "If he were to acknowledge that I was missing, it would be an acknowledgment of a loss or failure, and that would cause them to lose face. So, it makes sense that he would choose to keep it quiet," she explained, with sudden understanding. "On the other hand, do I dare ask about the security guard?"

"He's in the hospital and under guard by the Finnish police. They've been briefed on his role, and they're trying to keep his presence at the hospital a secret because they don't want him talking to anybody."

"That would be good because otherwise it would let others know that I escaped, wouldn't it?"

"The hospital just knows that the guard disappeared."

She winced at that. "So the local police might very well think that the guard took a bribe from me and then helped me to get out of there. That'll leave him in terrible danger."

Royce shrugged. "I get that, but let's not forget that he was taking money to keep you a prisoner."

She couldn't argue with that because it was true, and he'd shown absolutely no interest in helping her get away from her imprisonment. "It's sad to think about really," she murmured. "People could do so many things in life to become successful. Instead they turn into being assholes."

When an odd knock came on the door, she bolted off the couch and ran into the far corner.

"That's my partner." Royce held up a hand reassuringly to her.

She just nodded, crossed her arms over her chest, and remained there, watching as Royce walked to the front door, tossed back the bolt, and unlocked it. When he pulled it open, she studied the newcomer curiously.

He stopped when he saw her, and a big grin crossed his face. "Hey," Rick greeted her. "Are we happy to see you."

Her shoulders sagged, and she nodded and smiled. "Not as happy as I've been to see you two," she murmured. "Although it'll take a while to believe that I'm safe."

"Oh, you definitely need to keep your awareness up for a bit," Rick stated. "While your position has improved, you're not out of danger yet. And, if you have any tools or abilities to help us keep you safe, let us know, okay?"

She froze. Her heart slammed against her chest. "Abilities? Tools? Do you think if I had a way to escape before that I wouldn't have?"

"Of course. Just keep in mind that we're not safe yet."

"*Great*," she muttered, giving him a droll look, trying to hide the uneasiness inside her. Surely he didn't know about her cards? No one did. Well, Hannah had, but even she didn't realize how connected and useful they were for Heather. "Aren't you supposed to tell me that we are safe and that it's all fine now?"

"No. That would be a complete disservice to you," Rick replied, his tone now serious. "This is a very dangerous step in the process. In this situation, if you relax and assume everything is fine, you could take one wrong step, and he's got you again." When her face paled, he nodded. "So don't relax. Don't think this is all over with," he warned. "We'll do our best to get you home and well away from this nightmare, but you are far from out of the woods yet. So, we've got a lot to get through before you're back in England."

She looked over at Royce. "Your friend's not very reassuring."

"No, he isn't. Rick is all about making sure the job gets done and gets done properly," Royce explained. "So don't take it as a scare tactic. Instead just understand he's trying to ensure that we don't let down our guard and lose the ground we've gained."

She nodded and didn't say a whole lot more. Yet it made her think more about the process. "So, is this a good time to possibly check in with my company to let them know that I'm here and that I'm safe?"

Royce shared a look with his partner.

Rick pondered that and asked, "Is there any chance anybody in your company would have double-crossed you?"

"I would love to say there's absolutely no chance," she responded, "but I'm not an idiot. They are employees, and every employee has a price tag. So, in this case, I don't know exactly how to answer that."

Rick grimaced. "And that's the concern. It is quite possible that, once the word spreads, somebody there will let these guys here know that you're alive and somewhere here in town, and we'll be up against a much harder battle to get you home."

She let out her breath in a slow release, as she thought about it. "I really don't want to think that somebody in my own company would betray me," she murmured. "Yet is it possible? Absolutely, though honestly, it's really one of those unthinkable things."

Royce nodded. "That's understandable, and Rick could tell you one hell of a story about betrayal at work. We're not trying to make you suspicious of everybody you've hired. We just want to ensure that we don't have any setbacks."

"Got it." She turned to Rick. "Did you bring food, by any chance?"

"I did bring food." Rick held up multiple bags. "Food, plus I also brought you a change of clothes."

She bolted toward him. "Seriously?"

He nodded and laughed. "We've been in this position a time or two," he shared. "So, it's nothing fancy, and I didn't know about sizes. I had to depend on Royce for that."

She flushed. "At this moment, I couldn't care less if you brought potato sacks. If it is clothing that Faheed didn't buy and wouldn't recognize me in, I'm all for it."

"Unless you're some fashion icon who makes an entrance, it's all good. He won't likely recognize you in these."

She laughed when she opened the one bag that he'd identified as clothing. "No, this is perfect."

"Just leggings and a T-shirt. Not the quality you're probably used to, and there are no underclothes. Sorry."

"That's fine," she replied, with a wave of her hand. "I can wash them and hang them up. Besides, one change of clothes will go a long way, but it certainly won't take care of things forever."

"No, but hopefully we'll get you back home again before it becomes too big of an issue."

"That sounds good to me," she said, with a bright smile. Wrinkling up her nose, she sniffed the air and asked, "So, what did you bring for food?"

"Hungry?" Rick asked in a teasing voice.

"Absolutely." She looked over at Royce to see him smiling at her. "I know. I know. I said I wasn't hungry earlier, but then I had a nap and a chance to reassess. Things are looking brighter now than they did a few minutes ago."

"You mean, an hour ago when you fell asleep."

"Yes," she conceded. "All kinds of things can change in an hour."

"Absolutely they can, especially if sleep is involved," he murmured. "So, let's eat."

She sat down at the table and listened as the men discussed their options. She didn't interrupt. She just worked her way through the food. While in captivity, she hadn't eaten that much, as the reality of being held prisoner became more and more concerning the longer it went on. Now, with a taste of freedom, a chance to get away from that controlling nightmare, with some backup at her side, her outlook had changed considerably.

Royce looked over at her. "How much do you think he wants you?" She stopped, chopsticks in the air, and stared at him. He shrugged. "I guess the real question is, do you think he'll come after you down the road for any reason?"

She frowned at that. "If he's after me, I expect he wants the company. If it is established that he can't get it no matter what and that my father's will can't be broken, then I suspect he won't want anything to do with me. I don't know that for sure though. Of course I'm not of the opinion that he's holding some torch for me," she pointed out. "So, beyond his interest in the company and the assault to his ego, I doubt very much that he'll care. I don't even know if he cares now."

She shrugged. "I've never really understood what was truly on his mind. I don't know whether he'll pose a danger when I get back home or not. I hope not. Yet I could never have imagined he would confine me either. However, if you put him away for murdering his wives, then it's not an issue." Neither of the men made any comment, just kept eating. "So, is there any update or new information about getting me out of here?" she asked, searching their faces.

"Some," Rick said in a noncommittal tone. "We've told the British government you are free, but, of course, they want something in return."

She winced. "Royce mentioned that before, but what could I possibly give them?"

"Their goal is to put away Faheed, so evidence, proof of some sort, is what they'll be after, likely with some enthusiasm. It's not that they want to hold it over your head in exchange for getting you out of here, yet—"

"Got it. They do want to hold it over my head. But how do I give them what they want? I certainly can't go back in there."

"No, but do you have any information that could help them?"

"I don't know how," she said, bewildered. "I was a prisoner. They do know what that means, right?"

"Of course, but you weren't always a prisoner, and I suspect that's probably what they're pinning their hopes on."

"No, I wasn't," she agreed, then considered that for a moment. "I could come and go during those five years of their marriage, although that seems like such a long time ago now with …"

Royce nodded. "That freedom changed once your sister passed away."

Even the reminder that her sister was gone caught her by surprise, and the tears flooded her eyes. Her cards warmed in her pocket in sympathy. She brushed away the tears impatiently and nodded.

"Could her death have been accidental, or did somebody else in Faheed's life do it?"

"I don't need to think about that," she stated, shaking her head. "That's your deal."

He smiled at her. "It is and it isn't," he began in a calm tone. "We came to get you, yet MI6 hopes to stop Faheed, and we want to ensure that no other young women end up like you or worse, like his first four wives."

She winced at that. "God, I can't believe he's had four wives who died on him. Hannah told me that his first wife died, but she never mentioned any subsequent wife who had died. I didn't question it either. I guess we both thought Faheed divorced thereafter."

"Four dead wives makes it very suspicious, don't you think?" Rick asked, looking over at her.

"But Hannah believed she was his second wife. I'd heard there were more, but Hannah didn't want to hear those rumors, so I didn't delve any further into it."

At that, the two men looked at each other. "I wonder if that's what set it off."

"Set what off?" she asked, frustrated that they seemed to understand so much more than she did.

"His behavior. Maybe the first one was an accident, and maybe he loved her, and she died in a tragic but legitimate accident. Yet he ended up in a significantly improved financial position at the end of the day. So, that may have been enough to compel him to marry a second time, but with more of an eye toward potential fiscal benefits. When taking that one out down the road worked out so well, it became a hard pattern to stop."

"That's a disgusting way to look at life though," she muttered, aghast. "All those young women deserved to have beautiful, fulfilling lives and not have Faheed take them out because he was greedy and wanted what they would leave behind."

"Yet it happens time and time again," Rick noted.

She frowned and went back to her Chinese food. When she hit the end of it, she pushed the carton out of the way. "Whew, I'm done. That was excellent, thank you."

"*Done*-done or done for now?"

She stared at him, then back at the food and shrugged. "Good point. I don't know. I haven't been eating that much recently. Honestly, I haven't had much of an appetite since my sister's death, and it's gotten progressively less as I began to realize my situation. However, I've tried to keep eating to maintain my energy. Even now, if we have to run, I want to be ready."

"That's a good way to look at food anyway," Rick agreed. "Hopefully you won't have to run, but there's always the possibility that we may have to and quickly," he pointed out in a cautious tone. "I'll leave this food here for a bit. So, if you want to tank up a little bit more, you can. We'll stick it in the fridge when it cools, the kitchen does have a microwave."

She yawned just then, and Royce nodded. "That's a good sign too."

She stared at him. "How can it be a good sign?"

"Sleep is something you need every bit as much as food.

The adrenaline from earlier is wearing down now that we've got you here, but you're still in a state of shock. It may not have registered yet, but it will hit you. Plus, you're frustrated, and sleep would help take off some of the edge to that as well."

"Or else I'll wake up from nightmares," she muttered, as she slowly stood up, walked over to the kitchen, and poured herself a glass of water. She drank the water, leaned against the counter, and stared out the window. "I keep thinking about what I could share with the British government, but I don't know what I could possibly offer them." Then she turned to looked at the men. "Tell me honestly. Will I not get out of here if I can't give them that kind of help?"

Surprised, Royce stood up and joined her. "No, that's not the way it works."

"Are you sure?" she asked. "Because it feels that way all of a sudden."

"We certainly won't let that happen. That's not the way we function. The British government may want to do something different, but that's their problem," he said, with a smile. "If you had some information, anything, some history, documents, something that pertains to Faheed, MI6 would be very interested. So think back. Did you overhear how Faheed got the best out of all these deals? Maybe he named somebody, like an associate of his? Keep in mind that every one of these wives died by a different method of death," he pointed out, deep in thought. "So any detail you can share could be helpful, from the time before you were a prisoner."

She sat back down again, relief washing through her. "I have some photos, and I have some stuff from the years when I could visit with my sister. A couple times I saw things that were a little irregular. At one point I was highly suspicious of him, but Faheed always treated my sister so well that I didn't ever want to rock the boat."

"Highly suspicious in what way?" Royce asked.

"His business dealings. It seemed as if he was constantly getting paid, but I don't know who paid him or what it was for. I know he paid his brother in a big way, with fat envelopes of what seemed to be cash."

"Do you know what it was for, or for sure that it was intended for him to keep?"

"I heard parts of conversations, with comments of a job well done. So, I always assumed that it was a bonus for something Saheed had done and that Faheed used cash so it was nontaxable."

"And that's possible too, depending on what the jobs were."

She frowned, considering that. "I didn't hear all the details. … I don't have my laptop, but, if I did, that would help."

"Did you keep information on your laptop?"

Then she started to laugh. "No, I keep everything on the cloud, so any laptop would help. I've always been fairly safety conscious because of my own company as much as anything, but, of course, my version of safety consciousness versus yours is likely to be very, very different."

"Not necessarily," Rick countered, as he got up, then walked over to one of the bags he'd brought in. When he brought out a laptop and handed it to her, she was surprised but recovered quickly and opened it up and brought up her emails. "One of the things that I always used to do was email everything to myself. Everything was backed up daily to a secret email address."

"But Faheed would have that now, right?" Rick asked.

She shook her head. "Once I was his captive, he threatened me to not use my phone or my laptop. So no. Unless he checked my backup settings …"

"Just as a backup?" Royce asked.

"You never know when you can't get back into your email again because that can certainly happen nowadays with hackers freezing you out of your accounts and demanding a ransom. Plus, I don't always have internet service out in the warehouses. So I would do a lot of stuff on my phone, which was backed up as well, just to ensure I had copies of everything."

She signed into her secret email address and went back several months, frowning as she tried to remember what had piqued her attention earlier.

"Do you think you have something?" Royce asked.

She shrugged. "I didn't quite understand a couple things, but give me a minute." She quickly went through her emails with photographs. "I think this is the one that concerned me at the time." She brought it up and twisted the laptop around so they could take a look at the picture.

Royce frowned.

Seeing the odd look on his face, she asked him, "Do you know who that is?"

"Yeah, he's a known contract killer," he stated, frowning at her. "Do you have a date on that?"

"These pictures were taken from my phone, so the backup date should be the same day. I do have my phone with me, but I haven't had a chance to sort all the photos. So that'll take a little more time." She grabbed her phone and pulled up her special folder for that.

"Stop," Rick called out. "If Faheed was monitoring your

phone usage, don't do anything on your phone. Wait until Sophia has a look at your settings."

"Sophia?"

"She works with us at Terk's place. Send me that photo that you brought up, and I'll contact the British government." Rick walked a few steps into the living room and started talking on his phone.

She looked over at Royce. "Is that helpful?"

"It's hard to say whether MI6 can do anything with it, but it certainly cements the idea that Faheed had a contract killer in his employ."

"So did he shoot to kill any of his wives?"

Royce nodded. "If not for killing his wives, would Faheed have killed any business associates or competition?"

Heather snorted. "I don't know what his business dealings were even about. I just know he's some diplomat, but I have no idea what that means."

Royce chuckled. "All too often nobody knows what it means. It's a job title with no actual duties. They get to go around the world and try to make people happy," he said, with a smile. "Keep international relationships open and flowing properly, but that doesn't necessarily mean the same thing in this case."

She nodded, then forwarded the requested photo to Royce. "I have a couple other photos similar to that one. Again the backup date would have been within a day or two of the actual photo being taken."

"Good enough. I'm surprised you saw him."

"He came to the house one day, and I was outside, walking around. Faheed met him outside and was angry, then went back into the house and came back out with an envelope and gave it to him. I was sitting in one of those arbors with vines growing all over it that he had created for my sister, and I saw the whole transaction. … I got it on video and just lifted out the photos." When he stared at her, she just shrugged. "I'm always looking for shifty business practices to protect my own business from. So, if it was shifty, I wanted to know about it." She gave half a laugh. "Not that it ever did me any good. I didn't do anything with it because I didn't know what to do and still don't."

"But we do," Royce stated, with a smile.

She nodded and quickly forwarded the video and the other material that she had to both Rick and Royce. "I think that's all of it. Now check your phones." She looked up at him and asked, "You got coffee?"

"I'll put on coffee. Now put away your phone. Work off either Rick's laptop or mine, if you need to."

"Yeah, I probably should," she muttered. "Thankfully I had my laptop backed up because I left it back at the hotel. Faheed has it now. Regardless I had my phone and my laptop backed up but also buried in files that Faheed wouldn't ever look at. Since I've been captive, he monitored my phone and my laptop all the time, so I didn't dare try to do anything after Hannah's death. Sorting those photos I secreted away would be a worthy project for me to do today."

"Then eventually, after you get Sophia's all clear, you can transfer them all to your computer."

"I'll start deleting the ones that I don't need right away," she muttered, getting comfy on the couch.

Hearing Rick's voice in the background, she flicked through the photos, keeping a few beautiful ones of her sister. A couple brought tears to her eyes as she realized that such a gentle soul was no more. Giving her head a shake, she sorted and deleted the ones that she didn't want to keep. Anything to do with Faheed, she emailed to the men. By the time Royce sat down beside her, with a cup of coffee, she had gone through about one hundred photos already.

She looked up at him and sighed. "I didn't realize how many photos I'd collected. I'm surprised my phone even works with such a backlog on it."

"Another good reason to remove them, *after* Sophia ..." he said, with a smile.

"I know. I know," she muttered and kept at it. Later she lifted her head and announced to the room in general, "I think that's it. You should have all of my Faheed-related photos."

"Good," Rick replied. "You've sent me some fascinating images."

In a croaky voice, she replied, "Just something about Faheed always struck me as wrong, and I never liked him. Still, he treated my sister so well and acted as if he accepted and liked me, which always made me feel guilty. It drove me nuts for the longest time, and slowly I finally accepted him. Then, after her death, I became his prisoner and wondered if it had been just a slow, silent grooming on his part."

"It could have been, but your instincts were sound at the beginning, so you took photos. You did what you could, and you held it together," Royce stated, admiration in his eyes. "That's more than a lot of people would do."

"Yet, if he had anything to do with my sister's death ..." she began, now staring at him.

"We don't know that yet," he reminded her. "So, let's not jump the gun."

She closed her eyes and nodded. "Easily said, not quite so easily done."

"None of this is easy, but you're doing great."

She laughed. "I don't suppose you were a cheerleader in school, were you?"

Royce burst out laughing. "Nope, I sure wasn't. I was too busy playing football and baseball and all the other sports that let me get out there and be competitive."

She assessed him for a moment and finally nodded. "Yeah, you seem to have a competitive edge to you."

He snorted at that. "Most people in my industry have a certain level of competitive tendencies. It keeps us fit and healthy. Plus, it keeps us alive."

"I hadn't thought of that," she muttered, staring at him. Then she nodded. "You're quite right. That would definitely have something to do with it, would it not?"

"It would certainly be harder without that edge," he added, with a smile. "You've got to really want to stay alive in these industries, which is beginning to change a bit as a lot of the guys have partners nowadays. It used to be unheard of, but now the ones who do really well have partners at home and tend to focus on good planning and recon, working smarter, then fighting like hell because they have so much to come home to.

"The ones who are more impulsive, taking more chances at the last second, tend to be single and do things that you think about afterward and say, *Oh God, that was just nuts.* They don't have those same instincts to step back and to think about this because they don't have kids or even a wife at home, which keeps them grounded. So, when opportunities arise, they jump out there and are absolutely kamikaze about it," he noted, with a hard flint in his tone.

"Sometimes they go too far, but, in the process, you see absolutely incredible feats of physical endurance and heroism. Yet sometimes it puts everyone at risk, which is the trade-off," Royce explained. "So, generally speaking, if you want people protective of your country, who will work at being safe and yet diligent, keeping themselves and those around them alive, married men have the edge, hands down."

"I didn't even consider that," she noted, staring at him. "Of course it's not exactly anything that I would normally consider anyway, since it's not my reality."

"Yet," Rick said, with a half laugh, "the two of you are getting along very well."

"Sure we are. He saved me, even if I just met him today."

"That was yesterday," Royce corrected, with a bright smile.

She stared at him. "What do you mean?"

"It's midnight, in case you hadn't noticed."

She blinked and looked around. "No wonder I'm tired," she muttered. She got up unsteadily, and Royce was there to hold her arm and to keep her on her feet. She smiled. "You've been keeping track of me all day. Maybe it's time for you to go to bed."

"I will," he said. "We were just waiting for you to crash."

She frowned at that. "You could have told me so, and I could have gone to bed a while ago."

"We also needed those pictures. So, with your photos sorted and deleted, maybe you should check your emails? On one of our laptops, of course." He studied her inquisitively.

She frowned at that. "I'm too tired right now." Even with Royce's assistance, she staggered toward the nearest bedroom.

He stopped at the bedroom door and asked her, "Will

you be okay?"

She looked up at him and nodded. "I'm just exhausted."

"Shower tonight or in the morning?" he asked.

She yawned. "As much as I want one tonight, it'll be tomorrow. I've got to get some sleep before I drop," she murmured. Then she crashed on the bed and waved him off. "Go, get some rest. It all will just hit me like a ton of bricks. … I'm done."

As soon as he shut the door, she sighed, got up to strip off her clothing and to pull back the blankets. With the last of her energy, she headed to the bathroom. Smiling when she saw a new toothbrush and toothpaste still in the original packaging, she quickly filled a sink with soapy water, washed her underclothes and hung them up to dry, then brushed her teeth, washed her face, and, nude as the day was long, slipped in between the sheets. Closing her eyes, she was sound asleep in minutes.

ROYCE WALKED OUT to the living room to rejoin Rick. "She'll be out like a light in a matter of minutes. She's exhausted."

"She's held up surprisingly well, considering," Rick noted, with something akin to admiration in his tone. "I'm still going through these photos. I don't recognize everybody, but Jonas has gotten back to me on a couple of them that they are fascinated by. They had been trying to make connections between Faheed and a few of the Russian oligarchs as well. And plenty of good photos of them are here, so they're quite happy with this information. Of course, now that they have all that, they're dying to know if she has any other information."

"Of course they are." Royce sighed. "That doesn't mean she does though. Although it's interesting how her hand hovers over her pocket. It's instinctive and constant. It's almost a weather vane, telling her about the circumstances surrounding her."

"It seems to work for her. The fact that she even had all these photos is amazing and very helpful."

"We need her to sleep and sleep well. Then we can brace her on it tomorrow," Royce said in a considering tone.

At that, Rick got up and asked, "How are you doing for sleep?"

"Not too bad," Royce replied. "You want me to take the first watch?"

He nodded. "Sure, if you can. I'll see you in four." And, with that, he quickly disappeared into the second bedroom, leaving Royce alone.

He sat down at his laptop and started going through the photos she had sent. He noted an interesting pattern to them. Almost always, Faheed was in a deep conversation with somebody, almost always on the front steps of the house, or houses, as if he didn't allow any of that business into his private world. Which would make a lot of sense.

Also several photographs of the brother, Saheed, showed a similar habit. Royce briefly contemplated whether it would be worth a trip to Iran, the diplomat and his brother's home base, to see if Royce and Rick could gather more personal intel. That wouldn't be an easy job, and it wouldn't be sanctioned by the UK government, which meant, if they ran into trouble, they would be on their own.

As he flicked through all the pictures she had sent, one of them struck him as being even odder than the rest. It was the brother, Saheed, and the contract killer, standing out on the front steps, as if mimicking Faheed's actions. Royce had to wonder how the two brothers' wills were set out and if Saheed would inherit anything from Faheed on the off chance that he passed away first. Or would it all go to Faheed's adult children?

Despite four marriages to young child-bearing women, the only children came from the first marriage, none thereafter. Based on what Hannah had shared with Heather, Faheed had been so angry with Hannah for even thinking of getting pregnant, another aspect to contemplate. And more questions to ask Heather in the morning. To that end, Royce sat down and started a list of things to go over with Heather when she woke up.

The hours passed very quickly, and, before he realized it, Rick staggered into the kitchen and put on coffee.

"You ready to get your four?" Rick asked him.

"Yeah, I've started a list of questions for her," he shared, leaving the list on the countertop. "I suggest we go over some of the salient points when she wakes up."

"Got it," Rick said. "Go get some sleep, and I'll check in across the world."

"Sounds good."

With that, Royce quickly headed to the same bedroom that Rick had come out of, stretched out on the bed, and crashed.

CHAPTER 6

HEATHER WOKE A couple times in the night, reassuring herself that she was still safe. Suddenly self-conscious to be naked, she checked her underwear in the bathroom, happy to find them dry and put them on. She went back to bed and seemed able to fall asleep each time. Then suddenly she bolted to her feet and raced out to the living room. She stopped partway, realizing she only had on her underwear, and bolted back into her bedroom again.

Royce laughed and called back, "As much as I really want to see that show again, I do hope you have clothes in there to put on."

"I do," she muttered, mortified at her actions. "Sorry about that."

"Don't be sorry. Hey, I'll never pass on the opportunity to watch a beautiful woman come out in almost nothing."

"*Right*," she quipped, as a way to get over her embarrassment. She certainly wasn't a prude. What bothered her more was her panic and instantly bolting, "At least I realized it before I got too far." She quickly dressed, brushed her teeth, and, as she walked out once more, she smiled at them. "I wasn't expecting to bolt out of bed already running," she admitted. "So, that's my lesson from now on."

"Once you get used to being free again, those reactions will calm down," Royce noted. He motioned to the kitchen counter. "There's a fresh pot of coffee on."

"Yes," she said, as she headed toward it. "Do we have any plans?"

"We do, indeed. Rick is taking some time to sleep again. He only got four hours, so I gave him a few more, and then we'll be hitting the road."

She stopped in the act of pouring coffee, then turned around and looked at him. "Are we going home to England?"

"We're getting to that point," he clarified, with a small smile. "I'm not too sure that we'll make it all in one trip though." She frowned at him. "We're heading to Holland first."

"Why don't we just go to France and take the Channel across?" she asked.

"It's not me doing this planning. That's all up to MI6," he explained. "Plus, Terk and his team are trying to keep our exit quiet and low-key."

"Sure, so no flights I gather is what you're saying."

"There'll be flights, but they'll mostly be private."

"I never flew in a private jet until my sister married Faheed, and that's all he travels in," she murmured. "I found it incredibly luxurious, yet almost criminal, knowing so much of the world was suffering, and here they just traveled like that all the time."

"And a certain luxury is always afforded to the rich." He smiled, as she sat down across from him.

As he studied her face, she felt the color flushing up her cheeks. "I know. I know. I got some sleep, but I still don't look all that great."

He laughed. "If you're hedging for compliments, don't bother. You are beautiful as you are. Even yesterday, when you were struggling to come to terms with the shift in your reality, you were beautiful then too."

She shook her head. "If that is how you see it, then you're blind," she announced. "But thank you for the compliments. It does a gal good to know that she's not a walking disaster."

"Oh, I didn't say that," he teased, with a cheeky grin.

She gave him an eyeroll and smiled. "You get me back to England, and I will be a very happy camper and will definitely be looking better in no time."

"That's the plan," he confirmed cheerfully. "I've got some intel here, and we also have a bunch of questions we need to ask you."

She groaned. "Of course you do." He pulled out a pad of paper, and she could see a long list. "All of those?" she cried out.

He nodded. "Yes, unfortunately all of them."

She sighed. "There's not nearly enough coffee for that to happen."

"We can always put on another pot," he stated.

"Fine, fine," she muttered. "Let's just start in and get it over with."

He began with questions about Faheed's brother, about some of the photos, about conversations she may have overheard or not overheard, other people who came visiting, women who came visiting.

By the time Heather was done, she felt completely exhausted again. "I need to go back to bed now."

"If that's what you need to do," he said, looking at her sharply, "go ahead and do it. Once we head out to England, it'll be stressful again."

"It's already stressful," she said, pointing at his pad of

paper and all the questions. "I couldn't even answer most of those."

"No, but you did answer some," he noted. "I find it interesting that you never saw any female visitors. Didn't your sister have any friends?"

"No, she wasn't allowed friends, female or otherwise. She wasn't the kind to have very many girlfriends to begin with, so I think it just suited her. However, I did find it odd in the sense that she had no friends. Then she was pretty isolated even before marrying Faheed."

"Which also suited the both of them apparently."

"Yes, but I didn't think it was all that healthy, and anytime I tried to convince her to change, to go outside, to do something, she wouldn't hear of it."

"Okay, I've got another question for you. Do you think that she was being drugged in any way to keep her that docile?"

Heather stared at him, shocked. Dear God, she hoped not. Swallowing hard, she whispered, "I didn't even consider that."

"It's just a question that comes to mind because that's not a common behavior."

She stared off in the distance, nodding. "It isn't all that common, but I'm not sure it's all that uncommon either. ... My sister was always a loner and just—" She frowned. "This will sound terrible, but she always wanted to be taken care of. She didn't want to work, to have responsibilities or to earn accomplishments. All that stuff was just too much effort for her."

"What did she do with her time?"

"She painted a lot," she shared. "In fact, she was quite gifted at it. She also played music and was good at that too, but she never wanted to do anything more with those gifts. Though she enjoyed them, she was never interested in putting in the effort to reach her full potential."

"Him too presumably."

"Actually yes. He loved it when she played, and she would spend hours playing for him, particularly in the evenings."

"Maybe that was partly what the draw was."

"I don't know," she murmured. "It did seem as if, whenever they were together, they were happy. If I hadn't seen it myself, I wouldn't have thought it because he's very controlling in so many other aspects. Maybe after years of marriage to my sister, he decided it was time to get rid of her. I don't know."

"Maybe it wasn't Faheed. I hate to say it, but maybe his brother was involved in that too."

She stared at him and swallowed. "I have negative feelings toward both of them because they wouldn't let me leave, … though I realize that I didn't know who Faheed really was. Hannah seemed to be very content with him, but I wanted to take her away, for both of us to escape, but then she died." Tears of sorrow and guilt stung her eyes. "So I was good with never knowing Faheed." She raised both hands. "Looking at it now, I feel as if I didn't do enough due diligence."

"It doesn't seem you could convince Hannah to leave him anyway."

"No, and I tried," she muttered. "I did. I tried to get her not to marry him in the first place. Then I tried to get her to leave him. He tolerated it for a while, but she seemed to be perfectly happy. So eventually I just ran out of arguments. What could I say? She was not even listening, and I didn't have any real ammunition to use against him in terms of bad behavior. He never hit her. He never seemed to hurt her in any way. He always treated her like a princess, which was exactly what she wanted."

Royce just nodded and didn't say anything.

She asked him, "Are you seriously thinking that maybe Saheed had something to do with her death?"

"I don't know. Some of your photographs are of him too."

"That's true. I was taking a bunch more of him because, well, he really threw me off. Something was just so slimy about him."

"But not about Faheed?"

"Because of my sister, I saw him in a different light, not necessarily a better light but a different one for sure. Saheed … makes my skin crawl."

"Good enough. Did your sister feel the same way about him?"

She nodded. "Hannah didn't like it when Faheed was away and when Saheed was left in control. It's not that he ever crossed any boundaries with her. I think Saheed had too much respect for his brother's property at that point in time. Still, Hannah told me that Saheed was always undressing her with his eyes." Royce winced at that, and Heather nodded. "I get that for another guy such a description could be seen as just being a ladies' man. But, to most women, it's got that sexual predator feel for us."

"Oh, I understand perfectly," Royce replied. "I'm wondering still if that isn't partly what this is all about. Maybe Saheed coveted what his brother had."

"He does covet what his brother has," she murmured. "I've seen that in him a lot, but I haven't ever seen him get an opportunity to do something about it."

"And yet maybe we just haven't seen it. Maybe it's still in the planning stages, but Saheed can't quite bring himself to do it."

"Maybe," she murmured, staring at him, lost in her ugly memories.

Royce pointed toward the kitchen. "We have toast or cereal for breakfast."

She blinked at him several times and then nodded. "Toast will be fine."

He nodded and again pointed out the mess on the counter. "Help yourself."

She laughed, as she got up. "After being in captivity for months, I tend to forget about doing these things myself. Hannah and I couldn't do anything, literally. The servants were there for everything, which my sister adored of course. I felt very uncomfortable at first, but then I got used to it. Even so, it was weird to think that these people are there just to cater to you. While I was a prisoner, I couldn't take a walk or do anything on my own. The housekeeping staff came every day. Bedding was changed every day. They did all the work. … It's a very privileged lifestyle."

"Which is why your sister enjoyed it so much," he noted.

She nodded. "And yet it seems wrong now." She put on two pieces of toast and poured herself a second cup of coffee, leaning against the counter as she waited for the toaster to *ding*. "We get to leave today though, right?"

"Yes, we're leaving today," he confirmed, with a smile. "So far we've managed to keep our location here a secret. So we'll just take a private plane to Holland, and, from there, we'll take a connecting flight to England."

She nodded. "I guess that's fine. I just want to get back on English soil again." Then she hesitated and asked, "What about my lack of paperwork?"

"That's one of the reasons we're following Jonas's instructions. MI6 is dealing with your paperwork. He has validated the documentation, so it's just a matter of getting you back home again and getting copies for you."

"Sure, but, until then, if I get separated from you guys, I'll be in big trouble."

"So remember that."

"I'm not planning on running from you," she declared in exasperation. "You guys are my ticket home."

He burst out laughing. "And we should remember that too, *huh*?"

She rolled her eyes at him. "You're a nice man, and I wouldn't insult your intelligence by saying that I'm only here to get home, but obviously I am here to get home safely."

"Don't worry. We get it," he said, smiling, "and you've been very good at handling the stress that's come your way so far. Keep it up, and we'll get out of here, hopefully without any more headaches."

As she buttered her toast, his phone rang. He answered it and frowned. "Yeah, Terk. What's up? … No, we're supposed to be leaving today. I know she'll probably be asking for an update on the guard."

Hearing that, she winced because the one thing she hadn't done was ask for an update. She'd been so stuck in her own worries that she'd forgotten about him. As she turned to Royce, hearing the change in his tone, she got worried.

When he disconnected, he sat there and stared at her.

"What's the matter?" she asked hesitantly.

"The guard didn't wake up."

"He's dead?" she cried out.

He nodded slowly. "I know for a fact that I didn't hurt him enough to die from, and he was alive and well when they took them into hospital, while under security, but now they're treating it as a suspicious death."

She shook her head in denial. "But he shouldn't have died."

His stare was grim, and he nodded. "No, he shouldn't have. Yet the hospital is treating it as a suspicious death. Don't worry. MI6 will get to the bottom of it."

She sagged into the chair beside him. "Are we really thinking that this was Faheed?"

"I'm not sure whether it was Faheed, his brother, or somebody else in the entourage who was tasked with the job, but, from Faheed's point of view, your guard failed in an unacceptable way."

She felt the color leaving her face, and she nodded. "Yes, that is exactly how he would view it." She shielded her eyes for a minute, as she tried to hold back the tears.

"It's not your fault," Royce whispered.

She lifted her head and glared at him. "If it isn't my fault, whose fault is it then?" she cried out.

"Those assholes are to blame. You know very well that one of them killed him," Royce stated, staring at her intently. "It's likely they are sending a message to you."

"What message? If they catch me, that'll be my fate?"

"It's pretty compelling, as messages go, and, given that somebody who failed got this treatment, then I guess it's possible," he murmured.

She asked, "There was absolutely no way he died of a heart attack or something else?"

He shook his head. "It was a drug overdose. He was already comatose, so he didn't commit suicide, and it was injected at that, so somebody else did it. We left him unconscious, but he was alive. Then he was supposed to be under guard at the hospital, so there is no way he could have taken any drugs himself. It was definitely murder."

She swallowed hard. "I just feel terrible. He didn't deserve that."

"Neither did you deserve to be kept a prisoner. Neither did your sister deserve to die early. You need to get it through your head that the guard made choices that put him in that position. Don't forget that he was part of a group who was keeping you as a prisoner," he repeated. "I understand that you're grieving because you feel you had a hand in his death, but you are not responsible."

"I guess that's another way to look at it." She shuddered. "I just wish it hadn't happened that way."

"I get it, but he knew full well what the consequences could be in that job too. Rest assured, he would have known that, the minute he failed, his death would likely be the outcome. The local authorities were trying to keep him safe, but they should have been more vigilant. They had been told that his life could be in danger."

"Why didn't they protect him?" she asked, staring at him in growing anger. "That was their job to do. They had him in custody. They should have kept him safe."

"Yes, they should have," he agreed, with a nod. "But people don't believe that someone would be so bold as to walk into a hospital and try to do something to a man under guard. Yet it only takes a momentary lapse in attention to pull that off. Plus, we know that money talks, and Faheed has plenty at his disposal. That's for the hospital and the local authorities to look at," he pointed out. "Our job is to get you out of here. The fact that the guard has been taken out now means that nobody can tell stories, and that's both good and bad. We don't want anything to do with it. We just need to get you out of here now."

His phone buzzed again, but this time with a text message. He checked it and nodded. "Terk is sending a ride for us."

"*Terk*," she said, her tarot cards jolting at her waistband. "That's the name I remember from before. Anytime I hear it, it's so familiar in my mind. But"—she frowned at him—"I don't know why."

"Terk asked me to work this case, and he is the person who works with …" He stopped and shrugged, unsure how to say it to sound less cuckoo. "I guess *psychics* would be one word for it."

"I prefer *intuition*," she replied. When Royce frowned at her, she tried for a nonchalant shrug and failed.

"Sure you do, but you also read tarot cards, don't you?"

She flushed and stared at him. "Yes, but how the hell did that even find its way into your intelligence notes? It's not common knowledge." In fact her cards were now heating up. Not in alarm but something else. It took her a moment to realize what it was, … an *awareness*.

He laughed. "Believe me that definitely works. Reading tarot cards, particularly if you're any good at it, is basically another form of—"

She jumped right in. "Intuition," she stated firmly. "It's another form of intuition."

He grinned at her. "Are you so against having any abilities?" he asked, with a hard emphasis on the word *abilities*. "To the point that you'll knock the fact that they even exist?"

"I'm not knocking the fact that they exist," she clarified, "but it was drummed into me from a very young age that it's not something we talk about. And, in no way could I let Faheed know about them. At least …" She stumbled over her explanation. "At least not how much I used them. He would say they were a bad influence. But they aren't. Not for me."

"I agree with that," he said, with a smile. "However, you were utilizing your special abilities, whether you like it or not, and you were utilizing them for Hannah's benefit, were you not? And your own."

"Hannah was getting almost despondent toward the end. … And I don't want you to think that she took her own life because that wasn't it. She'd had a very rare argument with Faheed, and she was quite perturbed by it all. I would use the cards to sort out a pathway for us from Faheed's prison, but some days I got no messages of any kind. I don't know why. I felt … almost bereft. Then, when I lost my sister, I was exactly that. And again I've never noticed such a lack of intuitive knowing as I have during my captivity. It's almost as if a favorite toy has lost its joy. Not that the cards have failed me but that I have failed the cards."

"Did she tell you what the argument was about?"

Heather shook her head. "No, I think it was just normal marital stuff, although she was different afterward. And never really recovered."

"Maybe it was the fact that he wanted a divorce or he wanted a change or … anything that she couldn't offer him."

She stared at him. "She didn't mention anything specific to me, so whatever it was … I have no idea."

"Do you get any mail from her or anything?"

"Hannah sent a lot of mail," she said, with a laugh.

"Mostly after that fight though. She loved hand-scripted letters. Of course she wrote emails, as well, but it wasn't the same. She loved to write letters and to mail them. She loved to get them too. I called her a traditionalist."

Royce nodded. "Any idea who she might have mailed a letter to recently?"

"No, I don't know." Then she frowned. "I didn't think about it before, but that seems so odd when she didn't have any friends."

"That's what I was getting at. You say she didn't have friends or family, just you, and yet she sent letters. Did you mail them?"

She shook her head, staring at him. "No, I didn't. How was it I didn't even see that as an odd thing for her to do?"

Heather seemed lost in her own mind. "Odd or not, it does bear some closer scrutiny," Royce stated.

She nodded slowly. "She didn't do it all the time, but more so in the last six months. It was as if she had a new hobby," she murmured, staring around the room.

He continued. "Any chance she would have put anything in those letters that would be damning?"

"No, I don't think so. She was very happy."

"Up until the fight with Faheed, which was when?"

"A month or two before her death," she admitted. "It was mostly because of that one fight, I think, and I did ask her about it, but she always just gave me this gentle smile and said, *Everything's fine.* Yet clearly it wasn't. You know how you get that feeling inside that yells, *It's not fine, that I'll never be fine again.* I didn't have any way to reassure her. Regardless, Hannah just repeated how everything was okay, so what could I have done? It's not as if I told her, *Hey, you're lying. Tell me the truth,* because then she would just get her back up and be upset with me."

"Did she show emotions?"

"No," she muttered, staring at him in surprise. "Not very often. … Dammit." She got up and paced the kitchen. "You're making me second-guess my whole life with my sister. Was she drugged? Depressed? I don't know anymore."

"I'm not trying to upset you," Royce began. "I'm just trying to get you to think back, so we have an idea of what was going on in Hannah's world right before she died."

"I don't know," Heather whispered. "It was odd, but she kept reassuring me, and I let her because I wanted to be reassured." She sat down beside him suddenly, as if a statue had been pulled down by its own weight. "I'm a horrible sister."

"Back to that misplaced guilt again. Listen. If Hannah wasn't willing to share with you, what else were you supposed to do? I won't say she brought this on herself, but obviously she was in a headspace where either she was content to stay burrowed in her cocoon or that cocoon was blowing up and she wasn't yet capable of expressing what the problem was or of seeking a way to get out of it."

Just then Rick walked in, poured himself a coffee, and gulped it down, hot and steamy.

She gasped. "How is it you aren't burning yourself?"

"I need the coffee," he said grimly, as he looked over at her in concern. "Did you guys hear the news about the guard?"

She nodded and whispered, "It's terrible. They didn't have to kill him."

"The fact that they did was either a message to all that failure is not tolerated or that the guard knew something, and they couldn't afford to let it get out."

"It could be either of those, or both for that matter," she murmured. "Faheed is not the kind to accept failure in any way, shape, or form. He is a hard taskmaster, as is his brother."

"Of course." Rick shook his head. "The brother seems to be an ever-present constant in this equation, isn't he?"

"He's an element for sure," She walked over to the counter, cleaned up the mess from her toast, then asked Rick, "How soon are we leaving?"

"Soon." He threw two slices of bread into the toaster and looked over at Royce. "Did you eat?"

Royce nodded. "Yeah, I got something earlier. We've just gone over these questions, not that it was a whole lot of help—except for a couple idiosyncrasies about Hannah that were kind of interesting." He quickly explained about the handwritten letters as well as the disagreement she'd apparently had with Faheed.

"Do you think she mailed them out?" Rick asked Heather.

"I think so. She handed them off to one of the servants to mail, and I saw them putting stamps on them, so it seems possible that they did send them."

"Do you have any idea where they went?"

"No," she replied, "I don't, which, ... which ..." She fell silent, unable to even express what could have gone wrong in that department. "Maybe I saw something that'll come back to me later."

"Let's see if we can track down where those letters went and what might have been in them. I don't know that it's important, but it would be something that could explain her mind-set at the time of her death."

She nodded grimly. "Yes, we need to. Apparently I don't

know anything, so whatever you guys can find out will be more help than anything I can offer."

Rick studied her and Royce, and Rick's gaze went back again to her. "Problems?" he asked.

"No, just an awareness that maybe I didn't know my sister as well as I thought."

"Ah, well, you aren't the first person to say that, and you certainly won't be the last," he murmured. "When it comes to this business, people are people, and they share only what they want to share, and choose not to share anything they don't want to," Rick explained. "So just make peace with it." With that, he looked back at Royce. "I'll pack up." Then he quickly disappeared.

She looked over to see Royce already packing up the laptop and the paperwork in front of him. "I feel as if I should be doing something," she muttered, looking around the room.

He smiled. "Go ensure you left no sign of being in your bedroom."

"I can do that." She hopped up, raced to the bedroom, quickly picked up little bits of laundry she had and folded them. Then she made the bed and headed into the kitchen to wipe down all the counters and surfaces. She asked, "Does somebody come in here and clean?"

Royce nodded. "Somebody will, but it may not be for a day or two."

"Okay, I've wiped down everything as much as I could. And this is the clothing that I wore coming in here." She held up the small pile in her hands.

Rick walked past and slapped a plastic bag on top. "Put it in here."

Within a matter of minutes, they walked downstairs to

the garage as their car pulled in. As she got into the car, she seemed anxious. "This feels …" She stopped. "I don't know how to say this without it being alarming. Leaving here feels scary because, with the guard dead, that seems to have upped the ante."

"It only ups the ante," Rick replied, twisting from the front seat to look at her before he started the car, "if you know something they want to silence you about. They're covering their bases."

She stared at him, bewildered. "If you're asking me if I have anything to share or to tell you that would bring him down, the answer is no. I've given you the photos, but I don't even know that they're relevant or if they implicate him or his brother in any way. I don't know anything about it," she declared. "Honestly, all I can tell you is the little bit that I've already shared with you."

At that, Rick nodded and turned on the engine. "Good enough. Let's go."

THEY WERE ALL in the car for the ride to the airport. Royce's gut told him that the energy around them was too still, too calm. That worried him. He sensed a storm brewing underneath the surface.

Heather broke the silence. "So you guys are wondering if Faheed or Saheed or some hired gun had something to do with Hannah's death?"

"Right, that does keep you grounded, doesn't it?"

"Yeah, but not in a good way," she muttered. "I've been racking my brain over my staff, trying to see if anybody there would have had a part in this, and, of course, the answer is yes. I can name three people off the top of my head."

From the driver's seat, Rick looked up at her in the rear-view mirror. "What was it that made you pick those people?" he asked, genuinely curious.

"For one, Dan's got a gambling habit. He's divorced. His wife walked away from him a few years back. He got kind of desperate there for a while. I lent him some money, and he got out of trouble, but I think he's back in trouble again," she explained. "He's damn good at what he does for the family business, but he's unstable and dangerous to have around because of the gambling."

"Very unstable and very dangerous," Royce murmured, getting instant energy flashes over the guy's name and situation. These erratic flashes were happening more and more and might be helpful, but, he couldn't count on their value, not without a second confirmation or some evidence to prove it all. He quickly tuned back into the conversation going on around him. "So he would have to be damn good at that job if you kept him around."

"He is," she murmured. "Yet it feels as if I'm watching over him all the time."

"And the others?"

She sighed. "Okay, another guy has three ex-wives, so he's paying alimony and/or child support to all three of them. He's forever broke, smokes a couple packs of cigarettes a day, and drinks a bottle of wine every night," she murmured. Then she laughed, "And yet I don't know that he would do anything wrong from a moral perspective. I just know that, if somebody could get him out of his financial woes, he might just jump on it in a heartbeat."

Rick muttered, "Yeah, he sounds ripe for somebody willing to accept a lot of money for a little bit of info."

"Absolutely," Royce agreed, as more but faded flashes hit him but less powerful this time. "Give us the full names of these people." When she hesitated, he shrugged. "We'll just do some background checks to ensure no private meetings are happening with any of these people. So you said *three* people. Who is the third?"

"Right, then another suspect is … Maria."

"So, who is Maria, and why would she be on the list?"

"Honestly she's probably not a suspect but her leaving was odd. She started off as an employee. I got to be really good friends with her, but then she quit and walked away from all of us, including me. I've lost track of her. I never understood why except that she wanted to be shut of us. I wondered if she had gone to work for our competition or something, but that's purely a judgment call on my part."

"Remember that thing about *instincts?*"

"Yeah, I know." She groaned. "It's hard for me to ignore the instincts thing. You told me that I wasn't allowed to contact anybody, but, if I were allowed, she would be the one who I would contact because I have this horrible feeling that something's wrong."

At that, Royce nodded, getting no flashes of insight or visuals on this person. "Give me her full name." And when she did, he asked, "Why do you think something's wrong?"

"*Instincts.* … I know it'll seem wrong, but it feels as if she's not there anymore—as in not alive anymore."

"Okay, that is a very interesting and specific instinct," Rick noted, looking at her in the rearview mirror. "It may not be anything, but it's easy enough to do a background check on these people."

"I also want to check on two others." And she quickly gave them those names.

"Why these two?" When she hesitated, Rick twisted around in the driver's seat and barked at her, "Really not a time for secrets."

"I understand, but I don't want to destroy their personal lives if I don't have to."

"We need to know what is it about these guys that has you thinking that whatever we'll find out would destroy them."

"They're having an affair with each other. They're both married to other people, and they both have families."

"Ah. Interesting people you keep on staff." Royce eyed her curiously. "And do you hire an investigator to find out this information, have a company spy, see the evidence for yourself, or … use the cards?"

"Not the investigator but all the others to some degree. When I started doing a lot of this, when taking over more and more of the company, I talked to my father about some of these problems. He told me that, as long as they kept working, … as long as it didn't affect the company's name or our net profit, he would keep them employed because he figured that it would be less harmful if he kept them close than if he had a bad relationship and they left in a temper, in which case they would quite likely try to destroy us."

"Your father's gone, isn't he?"

"Yes, unfortunately he passed away about six years ago now. Took me a while to get into the groove of taking over fully because management is one of those things that you think you can learn quickly, yet experience over time really gives you that edge. My father was very good with people, and I'm not sure I'm anywhere near as good."

"Doesn't matter whether you are or not," Royce stated. "You're younger, and you haven't had the experience he's had, so you need to cut yourself some slack."

She burst out laughing. "According to you guys, I should cut myself slack all the time."

"What's wrong with that?" Rick asked.

She shrugged. "I don't know, maybe nothing. Just, with all that's been going on, I should have seen or felt or at least understood what was happening and found a way to stop it."

Royce pointed out, "We're back to *instincts* again, right? Because we've kept that fairly low-key up until now. You haven't mentioned feeling off or about Hannah being drugged, right?"

"No," she replied, staring out the car window. "Believe me that I'm … I'm wondering about all of that now too."

"So, let me ask you something. Is there any chance you were drugged too?"

She stared at him in horror. "I don't think so. Why?"

"Because your instincts have sharpened considerably the longer you're with us," he explained, with that ironic tone of voice. She just blinked. "Think about it. You're telling us about these staff members now as clear as day, detailing the potential problems they could present and why they might be vulnerable to interference from an outside source," he noted. "You couldn't do that at least to some degree yesterday."

"I don't know that it's due to drugs," she clarified. "I think it was more shock and trying to figure out just what I was supposed to say and what I wasn't." Then she winced. "Although I will admit to feeling off for a long time, but then I had a lot of reasons for that."

"True," Royce agreed, "but I still wonder if you were given something on a regular basis that might have kept you … *docile*."

She flushed. "You mean, like Hannah?" At that, she felt Rick's look in the rearview mirror. She explained, "Royce brought that up this morning—or was it last night?" She gave a wave of her hand. "Royce wondered if my sister had been drugged on a regular basis to keep her from causing Faheed any trouble."

"Do you think so?" Rick asked.

"No, I wouldn't have *thought* so," she conceded, "but really what do I know? My coffee was prepared for me every day. If I asked for tea, it was given to me. If it was drugged with something tasteless, I would never know, would I? And because I was so upset about Hannah's death, my doctor— and I'm using that phrase lightly—definitely gave me something to calm me down. I didn't want to take it the first day, but everybody was urging me to. Then I didn't take it again after that, but I didn't tell them."

Royce shook his head. "It would still be in your food or drink though, knowing you might be palming the drugs. All of which makes me a little suspicious that maybe this doctor was accustomed to doing that because it kept Faheed's women the way he liked them."

"It's possible." Heather grimaced. "I just hadn't really thought about it until you brought it up."

"Now that you have your instincts firing up again," Rick began, "what does it tell you about what happened? No overthinking it, just tell me what your gut says."

CHAPTER 7

S HE SAT BACK and, out of sight of the rearview mirror, pulled out her tarot cards. It didn't take long for her to stare at a card that intuitively meant *betrayal*. Seven of swords. It had a lot of meanings but came up often with questions regarding Faheed. The answer turned her stomach, as she cast her mind back to mornings she woke groggy and disoriented, just putting all her symptoms down to grief and fear of her imprisonment. "My gut says I've been taking drugs without realizing it. Lots of times I didn't take the medicine I'd been given for one reason or another. Yet I was so numb with grief that I was pretty well falling into the same pattern anyway, enough that could make them assume I was taking it regularly."

"And that was to your benefit. They thought they had control over you, and the longer it went on, the less they expected resistance from you and certainly not an escape attempt. They didn't have heavy security on you, as they didn't expect to need it. Then, when you did escape, I'm sure it was a complete and total shock."

She sighed. "A couple times Faheed's doctor asked me if I needed anything to make me sleep, and I just told him that I already had stuff that I took every night." She got lost in thought. "It never occurred to me until I became a *prisoner* that he had any underlying reason for asking, but it did make me wonder. And then I remembered all of that just going away again." At that, she groaned out loud. "They've pretty well just been keeping tabs on me and drugging me up as needed, haven't they?"

"Possibly, but, because you weren't taking it all the time, that gave you an opportunity to get free of it. Even though you may not have realized that you weren't taking something, you were still following your intuition, and that kept you alive and sane anyway. Still, I wouldn't be surprised if you weren't consuming something in your coffee or tea every day."

In the background, as she put away her cards, she muttered, "Asshole."

Rick nodded. "Yeah, it also says a lot about his need for control. Again we have to ask, was it Faheed's need for control or was it his brother's?"

"I don't have an answer for you there," she murmured. "I want to believe it was Faheed, but I don't know that for sure. He could be the one pulling the strings though."

"Why do you want to believe it was Faheed?"

"Because you're starting to make me think that he did have something to do with Hannah's death, and, if that's the case, I want him punished. If it was his brother, that one's already slimy and nasty. I don't know that I could think much worse of him anyway. But to think that Faheed would do that is an act of betrayal that goes much further into my *What's wrong with this world* scenario that I can't, … I can't even begin to think that in *any* world such a thing would be acceptable."

"It's not acceptable," Royce confirmed. "You and I both know that, but, for somebody who's done it time and time again, he may just not even care. Maybe he has that under control. However, if he just found out that he couldn't get Hannah's company, which she had already given to you, Faheed may have lost control over his better judgment."

"Regardless," she muttered, as she sat back, "I want to get to the truth of it."

"You need to keep honing those instincts of yours," Royce suggested. "The drugs have worn off, but it would be lovely to know that you're fully functioning and that whatever skills and abilities you have are solid and dependable."

"For your use or mine?" she asked, with a wry look.

"Until we get you safely back home again, for all of us," he stated. "Remember that anything you can do to help us keep you safe is a huge blessing. We'll do the same anyway."

"Wait. … Does that mean you guys have abilities?" she asked, raising an eyebrow.

Royce smiled at her. "We both work for Terk. What do you think?" he asked, with a chuckle.

"I think you do, though I get the sense that you don't talk about it much. Since I think it's pretty amazing that we even got away in the first place, I'll continue to trust you and to hope that we can get the hell out of here safe and sound. Then I can get back home again and sort out my business, So I guess you're right. In the meantime, if you take down Faheed, along with his nasty-ass brother, I will be in your debt forever."

Royce nodded. "Let's see if they're guilty first, but there's enough photo incrimination of them being in close contact with killers, drug lords, and mafia members that it'll be quite the caseload anyway. Don't worry. A full investigation will happen."

Rick parked at a small airport, and all three of them exited the vehicle. Royce immediately put his arm around her shoulders and hugged her to him, nonchalantly taking in his surroundings.

She looked up at him. "Do you really think that somebody who's looking for us will be fooled by this little charade?"

"No. Still, if they're not looking too closely, all they'll see is a happy young couple."

"Ah, meaning, we'll blend into obscurity."

"Just one more relationship in a world gone crazy full of them," he noted cheerfully.

She snorted at that. "You do have a sense of humor."

"I do," he agreed, "although it's not as if you've had a chance to see much of it."

"Maybe not," she admitted, with a note of sadness in her tone. "And it would be nice to see you or to meet you under different circumstances."

"We can certainly arrange that," he replied, with a cheeky grin. "I'm not sure what you're doing in a couple days, but I know I would be interested in a dinner date." She laughed. "If nothing else, it will give you something to look forward to."

"I won't argue that," she replied. "Considering enough uneasiness is going on in my world right now, that's probably something to at least keep in mind, as one reason to move forward."

"Hey, you've got a lot more reasons than a nebulous date with a guy you just met," he pointed out. "Keep in mind your work, your freedom, and all the best that the world has to offer. Then there's your company."

As soon as they walked inside the private hangar, the pilot came to them.

"We'll be in the air in fifteen."

Royce nodded and turned to Heather. "Are you okay?"

"I will be when I'm safely back in England," she muttered, unable to ignore the vibrating tarot cards tucked in their box and hid in the waistband of her leggings. Whether they sensed danger or sensed her nervousness, she didn't know. The end result was the same and put her on edge. She wrapped her arms around her chest and looked around nervously.

ROYCE COULD SYMPATHIZE. He needed to get them back home again, but they would have to make a stop in Amsterdam first. That would unnerve her a little more than anything, and he wasn't sure she remembered that part.

The stopover happened soon enough. When they landed, a team of government officials were there to greet them. She moved closer to Royce, hating the immediate panic trying to take over. "Am I in trouble?" she murmured at his side.

"No, but again we're at a disadvantage with no travel papers. We're talking to MI6 to get this all sorted."

"*Great*," she muttered, with an eyeroll. "I was hoping the inquisition didn't start until I got back on home soil."

"It will, but they're providing us some security to ensure that you have a safe overnight visit."

"Why overnight?" she asked. "I would be totally okay to continue straight home again."

"I've told them that, but we can't control the weather. A pretty-ugly storm is coming between here and there," he shared, "and a lot of flights have been grounded, ours included."

"Of course. Why would anything be easy?" She shook her head. "Sorry, I'm not trying to be a bitch. I just …"

"It's all right. You're not, and I understand."

"It's almost as if you're too understanding," she noted, looking at him sideways.

He snorted at that. "I'm not sure there is such a thing. Yet it is needed, if we are to keep our heads in stressful times."

"Right," she conceded, "and this is what you're trained to do, versus me, hence the mess."

"Not sure that we're trained to do anything along this line of peacekeeping," he noted, with a laugh. "Yet we definitely don't want to get into any more trouble before we get home."

"I agree with that," she muttered.

As soon as they were allowed, they were escorted to a hotel, where they were given connecting rooms. Royce didn't like the look of that either. As he walked into her room to see her crashing on the bed, he asked, "Are you ready for a nap?"

"That and food," she said, yawning. "I really don't want to be here, but apparently this is where we'll be. I don't want to say *prisoners*, but … that is what it feels like."

"How about we go with *guests* instead? We'll be guests for a while but just overnight, providing the storm passes and we can safely get back in the air."

"It's expected to, isn't it? The storm passing, I mean."

He shrugged. "Expectations don't always work out, especially where the weather is concerned. So I prefer to just work on that whole premise that everything will be fine, yet be prepared in case adjustments are required."

"Sure," she muttered, and then she sighed. "Can we order in some food? Can we do something?" she asked. "I'm obviously not suggesting shopping or going out in public, and I'm content with staying hidden for the time being. But any activity would be so much better than this boring wait."

"I don't love the fact that you're over here in this room on your own." She looked at him, wide-eyed, and he shrugged. "A part of me says it's not safe."

"Feel free to bunk in with me then," she offered. "I have absolutely no death wish, and, if you don't think it's safe, I'm happy to listen, providing you fix it."

With that, she rolled off the bed and headed into the bathroom. He waited until she came back out, her face washed and looking marginally better, but the whole process was wearing on her, and he understood that. Her energy fluttered as if running on empty too. She needed a chance to recharge. They were almost to the point of being back on home soil, and that's what she was waiting for. Still, Royce couldn't count on Faheed *not* following them. "Did Faheed know anything about your business?"

"Sure, we talked about it a fair bit, but it seemed to be more of a curiosity. He was particularly flabbergasted that a woman would be *allowed* to have control of a company, for one thing," she noted, with a wry smile. "In his world, such a thing just isn't possible. I think it might have been what he and my sister fought about, but I can't be certain." When Royce didn't say anything, she sighed. "He was just playing me, wasn't he?"

"Depending on his end game, he could have been just doing his research and possibly thought the company might be in trouble if it was run by women. Hannah likely didn't give him a great impression of women in business," he added.

"He kept asking me about my second-in-command."

At that, he turned slowly and looked at her, the energy of the comment buzzing. "Was that one of the five people you asked us to check out?"

She frowned at him and slowly nodded her head. "Yes, why?"

"A man?" When she nodded again, it made the tumblers in Royce's brain *click*. "Which means that would be someone who Faheed would be comfortable talking to, or at least comfortable approaching."

"I suppose. Back to that, are we? I sure don't want to think that somebody in my own company had something to do with this."

"No, I'm sure you don't, but burying your head in the sand won't help us solve this." She glared at him, but he just smiled. "Again, not trying to be difficult, but we can't fix what we don't know about."

She slumped into place, and, when a knock came on the front door, he stepped over and let Rick in. She looked at him and muttered, "I guess you guys are prisoners too."

Rick winced at that.

"We're guests, remember," Royce chimed in.

"Right, so we're guests with no privileges."

Rick laughed. "Yeah, that's about the size of it. This weather may well pass by morning, so there's a good chance we'll be in the air not long after that."

"That would be awesome," she said, "and, so far, nobody's asked me any questions."

"I'm not sure they will. This is very much under wraps right now. They're doing this as a favor for MI6."

"Lovely. I'm glad to know that MI6 has such a long reach. However, it does remind me that other governments and other people have a long reach as well."

Rick nodded. "We're still investigating the people in your company, with priority on those you identified, but we don't have any answers yet."

"No, I'm not expecting any answers, especially anything that would make me doubt my own staff," she stated, then winced. "Until Royce brought up something."

"And what was that?" Rick asked, looking over at Royce and then back at her.

"We were just discussing the fact that Faheed doesn't approve of women handling anything and often asked me questions about my second-in-command. That's Dan, and he was one of the five names on the shortlist."

"And you're thinking what?"

"I'm not thinking anything," she declared. "I want to believe that he is exactly who I think he is and that he's loyal to me, and I will continue thinking that until I'm shown otherwise. But I'm sure the two of you are wondering whether Dan could easily be bought off with a bribe or with a promise of a better position, such as taking over the company. Royce asked if the fact that he is male would make it more likely that Faheed would choose him to discuss these issues, and, of course, the answer to that is absolutely yes. I can totally see Faheed doing precisely that."

"And, if he wanted that company, which I understand from you that he does, then it's also quite possible that Dan's been approached already."

"I don't want to talk to him about it long distance. I would much prefer to talk to him in person," she replied. "That's not something that I really want to just guess at, and I would much rather see his face when I ask him. Of course Royce doesn't want me contacting the company just yet because of Faheed."

"Of course. We also haven't had any luck so far in figuring out who Hannah was writing to all that time."

She stared at him, blinking several times. "Right, I'd forgotten about that." She shook her head. "She had no friends, so where did the letters go?"

Sensing only truth in her energy, Royce relaxed more. She really didn't know about those letters, neither had she questioned it. Was that because she subconsciously didn't want to know or because of the drugs? "That's one of the curiosities that we'll have to get to the bottom of," he shared. "Not that there's anything dark or dangerous or ugly about it, just that it's a curiosity. So we do need to figure it out."

She nodded. "I'm tired and worn out, but I also need food. I obviously won't get more clothes while we're *guests*," she noted for emphasis, "but it would be nice if I could get a solid night's sleep so I'm better prepared for tomorrow."

At that, Rick looked over at Royce. "I suggest we order in."

"That's what we were just talking about too," Royce said, with a nod. "I also don't like the fact that she's in a room all on her own, so I will stay here with her."

Rick didn't say anything, just nodded as if it made perfect sense to him.

That was a good thing because no way Royce would take no for an answer on that point, not given the ongoing prodding from his own instincts.

"Do we need to set up four-hour shifts?" Rick asked.

Royce grimaced. "We should."

Rick stared off in the distance. "I agree with not leaving her alone, so, for added security, I suggest we all stay in the same room." Then he frowned over at her. "Actually ..."

Royce nodded. "Yes, I think you're right on that too."

"Hang on a minute, he didn't say anything yet," Heather noted in exasperation.

"I know, but I just read his mind." Royce laughed at her gasp. "And I suggest we do it now."

"Agreed," Rick replied.

She threw up her hands and asked Royce, "What are you two talking about?"

CHAPTER 8

"WE ARE CHANGING rooms," Royce noted, "on the sly, so nobody knows."

She stared at him blankly. "Not even the Dutch government? Not even MI6?"

"No, not even them."

"Okay, fine." She hopped to her feet, grabbed her single plastic bag, and added, "Good thing I travel light."

They just smiled at her. Rick said, "Give us five." He looked at Royce sideways. "You want to do the honors?"

"Sure." And, with that, he walked to the front door and slipped out.

"What does that mean?" she asked Rick.

"He'll find a room that is unoccupied for us to go to."

"I thought I heard the hotel say that the place was full."

"It might be full as far as the books go, but that doesn't mean all the rooms are occupied."

"Why wouldn't it mean that?" she asked, clearly confused and staring at him. Rick just laughed. "I don't understand," she said. "Why wouldn't it mean full?"

"Because they hold back a certain number of rooms all the time, for unexpected visitors, for owners, for various clients who are either regulars or who will pay a lot more money to get a room without a reservation," he explained, with a smirk. "It's all about supply and demand."

She didn't like where he was going with that. "Seriously?"

He nodded. "Of course. It's standard operating practice."

She frowned. "That seems highly illegal."

He laughed. "Making a living isn't illegal, and offering VIP treatment to those in a position to pay more isn't illegal either. It might be unethical and irregular, but that doesn't make it a crime."

"Maybe it should be," she stated, still staring at him. "If I was here earlier and got a room, then came back a little bit later to book a second room for a friend, and they were almost all out and charged me a premium rate, that seems to be a rip-off."

"And yet if you really needed that room, you would be happy to get it," Rick pointed out. "So, while you might think it's a rip-off, and maybe it is, you would still be happy to take it and to pay the premium rate. I've certainly seen it happen more than enough times to make me believe it's a common practice. If it's not the standard practice at all hotels, I've seen it happen enough to make me think it's worth a shot here."

"Interesting," she murmured, then shrugged. "So, what you're really saying is that, even if the hotel is full, Royce should find us an empty room."

"Exactly."

"But how?"

He laughed. "Just leave that to him." She frowned at him, and he shook his head. "No, I'm not telling you. That's up to Royce. Let's just say that you're not the only one to have strong … *instincts*."

"I know he's got strong instincts," she stated for emphasis. "Yet I highly doubt that finding a room requires his instincts. Now he did need those instincts when he found me, … bouncing from window to window to see if anybody was inside."

"Is that what it seemed to be from your point of view?" Rick asked, a grin on his face. "Did he bounce from window to window?"

She raised both hands. "I don't know. He was just … suddenly there."

"How did you react?"

"How do you think?" she muttered. "I was absolutely stunned to see him, but, as soon as he was gone, I realized what a godsend it was. Since I didn't know how to help myself out of that situation, I tried to put myself in a position where maybe I could at least get free somewhere and find him later."

"I wonder how you would have found him?" he asked, studying her carefully.

"Maybe I wouldn't have, although the rooftop deck was a brilliant idea, if I do say so myself. Why do you ask?" When he just shook his head, she frowned. "You're prattling on about that energy stuff again, aren't you?"

His grin flashed. "Hey, that energy stuff has saved us many times."

"I'm not surprised," she murmured. "It's pretty wild and wonderful, depending on what you can do."

"Have you ever done anything, outside of tarot cards?"

"No," she murmured, "and I usually just do them for fun."

"*Usually*," he repeated, pouncing on the word. She glared at him, and he chuckled. "Believe me that I know an awful lot of people who would have had you bring your tarot cards out long before now, just to see what kind of answers you would give us on questions right now."

"Maybe, but these are my tarot cards, and I'm the only one who's ever handled them," she shared. "I certainly wouldn't take kindly if somebody else did."

"Interesting," he noted, studying her. "I've heard that before, how owners of tarot cards can be quite possessive."

"I don't know that it's possessive as much as they become tuned to our own energy."

"Ah, that makes sense."

Since he'd brought it up, she asked, "Do you know others who do tarot cards?"

"I do. Quite a few of them, and they all have a caveat that tarot cards are fine, but Ouija boards are not."

"I used a Ouija board," she said, with a smile, "until it was taken away from me. I presume you approve."

"I do. I've seen some pretty rough things happen with Ouija boards. Doorways get opened, and, the minute that happens, it's pretty damn hard to close it, and those things—people, spirits, whatever, that come out from that open doorway—are not anything to mess with," he muttered. She stared at him, and he nodded. "Yeah, I get it. It's fun and all that good stuff, but it's also dangerous as hell."

"I haven't had any negative experiences," she stated, "so what you're saying surprises me. Although I have had a long affinity with tarot cards, so the Ouija wasn't a big focus. I only used it when the cards would tell me to."

"Interesting. As much as I want to ask how the cards tell you something"—he stopped and raised one eyebrow—"I somehow feel you'll say you intuit the answers."

Silence came.

He chuckled. "Right. That's what I thought. I've also

known some people who were very good at Ouija boards, but that's because they were true mediums. Thus, when people came through, they had the ability to pass on messages. One in particular comes to mind. She could shut them down, which is a very valuable trait. However, we also had a case where a murdered spirit walked in and controlled the medium. We had to fight tooth and nail to push her back down."

"It still sounds like fiction," she muttered.

"Yep, but for somebody who's handled tarot cards, you know perfectly well how little fiction is involved."

"Yet most people would be horrified to hear you say that."

"I'm not most people," he said instantly. "I have seen some things in this world, and people do unbelievable things. You have absolutely no idea how incredibly messed up this world is out there."

"I always wanted to know more about the various energy workers," she shared. "It's not exactly something you can talk about or deal with very openly. I knew of a woman doing a bunch of research way back when on energy workers, and I thought about contacting her, but I never did."

He laughed at that. "Don't suppose that was Dr. Celia, was it?"

She looked at him in surprise. "I think it was. Why?"

"She's Terk's wife."

Heather stared at him in delight. "You're kidding? I would love to meet her," she shared warmly. "She was doing work that was very close to my heart."

"It might be close to your heart, but it's definitely her field," Rick noted. "We all refuse to be tested by her, which aggravates her to no end."

"But that doesn't mean that the work she does isn't valuable."

"It is valuable. She just has to find somebody as a test subject who won't be worried about other people finding out what they can do," Rick explained. "We've all come too far in our specialized world to let anybody in that deep."

"She must be totally frustrated with you guys then." Heather stared at him. "I would have thought it was a trust thing."

"Oh no you don't," he began. "You don't get to throw that in my face. It's not about trust. It's knowing that she's a researcher who will publish her work," he clarified, shaking his head as if he wanted to get rid of something evil. "If we knew for sure it would never go anywhere outside of our team, that would be a different story. But it's not because this is what she does, so we know perfectly well that she has to publish her results. That's a part of any projects funded by grant money, and that's her job," he stated, with a laugh. "Knowing those parameters, a few people have worked with her, and lots of others just smile and tell her no way."

"The fact that you can even tell her that and still keep peace and quiet in the family is huge."

"It is, but again that's where the trust part comes in," he stated, smiling at her. His phone buzzed a few minutes later with a text, and he pulled it out to read it.

She got up and came closer. "Did he find one?" Heather asked Rick. He looked over at her, one eyebrow raised. She shrugged. "It's him. I know that."

"How do you know that?"

She frowned, not liking the look he was giving her. "If I say *instincts*, you'll probably laugh at me."

"Nope, I sure won't," he replied comfortably. "It would

make me feel a whole lot better if it was."

"Was what? … Instincts?"

"Yes, because that would mean that you turned yours on."

"Yeah, I'm not sure what's going on in that sense," she muttered, as she looked around. "Every time I sleep I kind of wake up still in a half-groggy state."

"Oh, I'm pretty sure that he was giving you something, a light sedative. Something to keep you a little bit calmer, a little bit more controllable," he said, with a smile. "And I'm not so sure that it's all out of your system."

"So you've mentioned before," she noted, then motioned at his phone. "And?"

"It was Royce, and he has found something. We're supposed to leave this room with all your belongings and ours, and follow his instructions."

Snatching up her bag again, she walked to the door. "Let's go."

He laughed, walked over to her bedroom, and quickly locked that door, then headed to his bedroom, where he grabbed his bag and Royce's. Then together, the two of them walked to the stairs.

"Stairs, not elevator?" Heather asked.

"Stairs," he confirmed. "Most people don't take the stairs because they prefer the comfort and ease of an elevator," he noted. "So we'll encounter the least amount of people if we use the stairs."

She nodded at that. "And it goes along with being healthy."

"Health nut?" he asked her.

"I'm not a health nut, but I try to be conscious of it and make little changes that can make a difference."

"Little changes?"

"You know, park farther away in a parking lot or have greens more than anything else. Although here, I can tell you that diet-wise it sucks."

He laughed. "When you're on the run, food is food, so we can't worry about it until we get to where we have a choice. Right now, our choices are limited, so you'll have to just do what we do and deal with it."

"Of course," she said, "but, if nobody knows where we are, how on earth are we supposed to get food?"

"Oh, don't you worry about that." Rick chuckled. "Our people have ways in and out."

She rolled her eyes. "Good, because I'm craving a steak." He raised one eyebrow at her, and she nodded. "Medium rare, with a baked potato and lots of greens."

"Anything else?" he asked, amusement coloring his tone.

"Yeah, with peace and quiet to eat it," she muttered.

"I think we've got that handled too," he said, with a big smile. "We'll just have to see how our new accommodations are first." And, with that, he led her up four flights of stairs.

By the time she reached the fourth landing, he was holding the door open for her. "I need to get in better shape." She struggled to catch her breath. "Are you guys always this fit?"

"Yeah, but we also haven't been living under a great deal of stress the way you've been of late," he pointed out. "It plays havoc with your health."

"I'm totally happy to be walking away from that nightmare," she said. "It's not exactly the kind of life I had hoped to live."

"Nope, and we're getting there," Rick replied. "Just remember that. We're getting there."

She continued down the hallway, and, as they came around the corner, Royce held open a nearby door for them. He smiled and waved her inside. She quickly dashed inside, seeing a much nicer suite than they had been in before. "Wow," she whispered, looking around. "Are you sure it's okay that we stay here?"

"I'm positive." He flashed her a grin. "Don't worry. I didn't steal it."

"No, but I'm not sure what kind of magic you had to pull to get it for us. They could have given this one to us in the first place, but they didn't. So chances are it's either way more expensive or they had a reason for it."

"Doesn't matter," Royce said smoothly. "It's ours now."

And, with that, he closed the door behind them.

AS SOON AS Heather was inside, Rick announced, "I'll be back in a second," and he stepped out into the hallway.

Royce stood close to the windows, his phone out. "She wants food," he called out to Rick as he went to close the door to the suite.

"Yeah, I got that earful on the way up. Red steak and the works. You?"

"Make that two more of it all."

"That'll be delivered there then. I'll be back in a little bit." Rick looked around and nodded. "Nice choice. It's really quiet up here."

"It's definitely a more expensive offering that we probably wouldn't have been given on our own." Royce had a laugh. "But it's all good, and it's ours for the night."

"What if we have to stay longer?" she asked.

"I hope we don't for your sake, but I'm sure I can arrange to have it for one more night if need be."

And, with that, Rick took off.

Royce turned from the window and smiled at her, as she sat on one of the big couches and asked, "So, do the accommodations suit you, milady?"

She laughed. "This is the level that I'm kind of accustomed to, at least when I'm traveling with Faheed," she murmured. "But I was totally okay with the other room too, particularly if it didn't come with strings."

"This doesn't come with strings," he stated, smiling at her. "Not everything does."

"I'm starting to think maybe everything comes with strings of one kind or another," she muttered. "Yet I hope you're right. It would be nice to have some things in life not always be so mercenary and materialistic." She looked around and asked, "Where has Rick gone off to?"

"To get food," he replied instantly.

"Maybe to order it from room service, but I doubt that's everything he's up to," she declared, with a bright smile. "Although I did tell him that I was getting quite hungry."

"He took notes, so he'll go get three times your order." She blinked at him, not quite understanding. "We'll just have the same thing," he explained. "It makes it easy."

"Good, I hope you guys like steak."

"Love it, all red meat."

"Of course," she said, with a laugh. "Don't suppose I could have a laptop, *huh*?"

"Sure you can," he replied, as he pulled his out of his duffel bag and handed it to her. "I can just work off my phone for a little bit."

"How can you do that?" she asked.

"We're sorting out research, so you can have the laptop for a bit. I know that Rick's coming back with food soon, so I'll just keep working in the meantime." When his phone rang, he walked to the far end of the room to take the call.

Terk didn't bother with a customary greeting, just shared what he had found. "We've checked out the top three names you gave us from her company. All three of them are in some degree of financial trouble, in particular Dan, yet he seems to be the most stable. His gambling problem is in trouble again quite severely, though we don't see any signs of communication between him and Faheed or Saheed either. However, we're still looking. The guy with all the ex-wives just got a loan, apparently from a family member, to put him into a better position. We found Maria. She's changed careers and didn't want any contact with Heather after leaving. She said something about wanting to complete change including her friend group, but we will keep looking. She may be in another country, for all we know."

"That's good," Royce noted, "so chances are all three may be off our list."

"I would like to think so," Terk began, "though I'm just not sure who else might still be on this list, so I don't want to take anybody off just yet."

"Agreed. Heather did say that Faheed had grilled her quite a bit about her number two in command, which is Dan, and she felt if anyone would be approached, it would be Dan. One, he's male, and, as her number two, he would be in the know on a lot of the details of running the company," Royce explained.

"Good, so we'll do a deeper dive into Dan. Where are you now?" Terk asked him.

"We've just changed locations within the hotel," Royce

replied. "I arranged a place quite a few floors away, and we have placed an order for room service back at our assigned room. Meanwhile, Rick has gone to secure additional food for us as well."

"Good, I'm glad you changed rooms," Terk said. "We can't be too careful here."

"Exactly, and nobody appears to think that she's in any trouble, but she doesn't feel the same way. And, if we can get her to feel a little bit more comfortable, she might remember a few more things. We are wondering if Faheed might have been lightly drugging her and possibly Hannah too. Oh, and the thing with her sister sending out handwritten letters, any joy on that angle?"

"Not yet," Terk replied. "Rick did tell us about it, and we've started looking, but, so far, there isn't much to find. We don't have any way to track letters, outgoing or incoming, not without an address, so that could be hard to do."

"Right, they were headed to England, we think."

"How do you know that?"

"Heather remembered this as an afterthought, after I updated you on all the original answers she gave on my follow-up questions. She watched the maid affixing a stamp on one of the letters and caught that much of the address on the front of the envelope. Hannah wouldn't say anything about the letter, just smiled and went about her business. One more of those things that her sister didn't want to share with Heather."

"Seems her sister didn't necessarily share anything."

"I'm not sure she did. Heather's also wondering if her sister was kept lightly sedated and docile through other medications as well, but we brought up that idea."

"That would fit with Faheed's MO, wouldn't it?" Terk

asked thoughtfully. "The man didn't want resistance, and women were meant to be seen and not heard, so keeping them in a drugged state would have been right up his alley."

"I'm not sure that it was a constant thing, or just whenever Hannah may have protested something she didn't like in her life. I don't know," he muttered. "And it could even have been something that caused the supposed heart attack. Heather mentioned that her sister had always had health problems but didn't elaborate, other than to add that Heather had always suspected a good share of it could have been Hannah just seeking attention. When you consider that she was young and at least reasonably healthy prior to her death, it does make you wonder if somebody was giving her something, under the guise of keeping her calm, and that becomes even more likely."

"Probably doing it off and on for the duration of their marriage."

"Hannah also wouldn't talk to Heather about anything personal or private. She would just basically shut the door, so we don't really have any way to know what their marital life was like. That would have been basic things a sister would typically share, but Hannah didn't talk. Maybe she wasn't allowed to talk, couldn't talk, or didn't want to talk. We don't know. It could be any of the above. Heather mentioned that Faheed and Saheed both had random women when they wanted them, and Hannah didn't like it but had apparently made peace with it and wouldn't discuss that either."

When the call ended, Royce walked back over to the couch, where Heather was sitting with his laptop. "I see you have a few emails."

She lifted her head and stared at him, blinking several

times. "God, just being out of circulation for a while has my whole life exploding."

"Major problems?"

"Not that I've seen yet," she replied. "I do have very competent staff, but it looks as if we have orders that were canceled, orders that shouldn't have been, and I'm still trying to figure out why."

"Just ensure you don't respond," he cautioned.

She looked up, startled, then asked, "Do you want to tell me why? I've just been drafting a few replies, though I've not sent them."

"Create them if you want but don't send them, not until we're back in England."

Swallowing hard at that reminder, she sighed. "Good timing. I didn't even consider that." She shook her head in disbelief. "God, how quickly this all went out of my head. It's embarrassing."

"You just got busy and caught up in your own world," he said, with a smile. "No need to feel bad about it."

"I do though," she muttered. "You specifically told me not to contact anybody, but, from this distance, it didn't even seem that an email met that standard, so I just was going full steam ahead. What an idiot."

"You're not an idiot, but we sure don't want anybody to know anything about your whereabouts or how and when you'll be arriving. That has to be kept from everyone."

"Right. In that case, I'll close out of this email, and I will deal with all of it when I get back. That will be tomorrow, right?" she asked, staring at him intently.

"Hopefully, yes, given Mother Nature's willingness to get rid of all the mess out there." As he spoke, he pointed out the window, where the storm could be heard raging on.

She stared at him. "It's not the first time I've considered that we, as a society, are so lucky that we aren't caught in all these storms and that we do have facilities to hide out in, versus our ancestors, who had a much different life."

"Exactly," he agreed. "Yet, in the old times, we still had assholes who wanted to take it away from us."

She winced because, once again, it was a reminder of things that she was trying to forget.

He added, "Also, there's no update on the letters that Hannah was sending or receiving."

She shrugged. "It's one of those curiosities, but I don't really have any answers. I hope we get them at some point."

"Me too, and you're right. It's a curiosity. I want to get to the bottom of it, but, if we don't, well, sometimes we just don't get all the answers we want." Regardless, the letters would bug him. Particularly if Hannah was murdered. The letters meant something to him. "What about your sister's personal things?"

"Faheed has all of it."

"You weren't offered anything as a reminder, a keepsake, or something?"

She snorted. "Saheed gave me one of her hair clips, as if I should be pleased that he did that much." Royce pondered that, frowning, but he didn't say anything. "I guess that's not normal, is it?" she asked. "I didn't even think to ask. I mean, she had been married to Faheed for five years. It was her new life, separate from me."

"That goes along with everything else that you know about your relationship with her and also your sister's with Faheed, doesn't it? Keeping you calm, keeping you in control, just lightly medicated, so everything's good."

"*Great*," she muttered, staring out the window. "It infuriates me to think that's what I was reduced to."

"But you're not anymore," he reminded her, knowing inside she was recovering just fine. Her energy was smooth, still gaining in health, as he could see the darker bands softening lightly. The drugs were finally being washed through her system.

She took a deep breath and nodded. "No, not anymore," she whispered. "And, for that, I owe you a debt of gratitude. I could be dead by now."

"Maybe you would have been fine," he said, with a wave of his hand. "Maybe we're assuming behaviors, motivations, or other things about Faheed that aren't founded. So, let's try not to judge him until we know more."

She snorted. "Too late," she muttered. "I've already judged him and found him to be a very crappy human being. But then, so is his brother, and frankly I don't know if one is worse than the other. I also don't know if both are involved in something nefarious. What about the other wives?" she asked him. "I don't think—or at least I don't want to think—that Hannah knew she was one of his four wives."

"Would it have mattered to her?"

She winced. "I prefer to think it mattered, but again I don't know."

"All I can tell you is that he's been married four times, and in each case the wife died, leaving him a fortune."

"Yes, so I've been told, but I need to know why, how, and what is going on. You really think that's what he was planning for Hannah?"

"I have no way of knowing," he admitted, "but, when you think about it, your sister's death fits the pattern, hoping he would get your family's business. What is it worth?"

"Around one hundred million dollars," she replied. "However, I haven't looked at the bottom line in a while.

We were inching up over $80 million last time I checked." When he stopped and stared, she nodded. "As I said, my father trusted me with the company, and that's another reason I'm feeling horrifically betrayed at the moment. Surely I would never have abandoned my father's trust nor left the business without proper oversight in place."

"No, you wouldn't have," he agreed. "You know that inside yourself, which is why this outrage is hitting you even harder, because you know perfectly well that's not something you ever would have done without interference."

She took a deep breath. "Yet somehow I feel as if my father is up there, staring at me in horror."

"I don't think he would do that. I suspect he would tell you to take it easy before you join him."

"Ouch." She frowned at him. "That's a shitty response."

"Your father trusted you, so trust yourself," he stated, sitting down beside her and picking up her hand. "I get that you'll look at men in a very different way after this."

She shook her head. "Not all men, that's for sure. Yet I do admit that anything to do with Faheed makes me very nervous."

"Did he make you nervous before?"

She nodded. "When Hannah first married him, I was very perturbed. However, he treated her so well, and she seemed to be so happy, I just couldn't make an argument for how I felt about him out of it. She was obviously very well taken care of." She looked around the room. "How long will the food be?"

"Not long." He studied her intently.

She raised her hands in frustration. "I'm fine."

"Are you?"

"Yes, I will be," she murmured. Then she gave him a beaming smile, adding, "As soon as I get food."

CHAPTER 9

HEATHER TRIED TO put up a good front, but it still disturbed her to no end to think that in those last many weeks since her sister's death, Heather had fallen more and more under Faheed's control, or at least his family's control, albeit by drugging her. She paced their newest hotel room, her tarot cards clutched in her hand, as she contemplated her past. She now knew without a doubt that's exactly what happened. She just didn't know if it was Faheed's idea or his brother's.

She had to stop thinking about it, about the possibility that Faheed had drugged her to keep her *docile*—to use Royce's term. As each day moved along since her rescue, her brain was clearer. That alone gave more credence to the possibility she'd been controlled by drugs all that time. Would Faheed have just upped the dosage if she'd fought more? Or just given her an overdose whenever her usefulness had expired?

Still, something was off about his brother, Saheed, and she wanted him to be the bad guy because of it, but she didn't know that he was. Something strange was going on here. She looked over at Royce. "Does the brother have diplomatic immunity too?"

He smiled at her. "No, in theory, he does not, but he's part of Faheed's household. Thus, if Faheed can get him out of the country, it's certainly something that you would struggle to fight. Remember the American diplomat and his wife who killed a teenage boy and just left that country to avoid repercussions?"

"*Right*," she grumbled, "and that sucks for that poor boy's family."

"It absolutely does. That diplomat's wife killed somebody and got away with it, never facing the consequences. How unfair is that?" he asked.

She got up and started pacing. "I'm trying to control my emotions over this. I'm trying to be reasonable about it all, but I do think you were right. Faheed must have drugged me over the last few weeks. I don't think it was an issue before Hannah died, at least I don't think so. I was still in control of my feelings back then, as long as Hannah was happy. So I focused on dealing with emails and running the company."

"It's totally possible and likely reality," Royce conceded cautiously. "I hate to say it, but grooming is something that happens in a very subtle way, and you don't necessarily know that it's happening."

"Meaning?"

"Just that, when it came to making decisions, looking for advice, or anything along those lines, Faheed would gradually become the one you would turn to."

She sucked in her breath. "Now that makes sense because he tried it several times. A couple times I just got angry and wouldn't discuss it with him, which I know pissed him off. He was talking about my sister's controlling interest and how she should have it back again. I was not cooperative," she murmured.

"And that could have been enough to set him off," Royce noted. "You know Faheed and Saheed have a certain expectation of obedience, and when you don't fall in line …"

"You get what, drugged?" she asked in disbelief. "Who does that?"

"Men who want ultimate control," Royce replied. "Men who have the power to take what they want and to take out the people who are bothering or stopping them." He stared at her in concern, yet she needed to hear it. "So, just acknowledge that they exist and that you got caught up in it, and so did your sister. The jury is still out as to whether Faheed or even Saheed killed Hannah or not. Hopefully we will find out, but, for now at least, we don't know for sure."

Heather grimaced. "My worst thought was that she took her own life, but it just didn't make any sense because I knew that she was happy with him."

"Do you think she was really happy, or was it just on the surface?"

Heather gave him a haunted look. "I've asked myself that question many times, and I don't have an answer," she whispered. "I wish I did. I wish I'd pushed it in the weeks before, just to see if she was doing okay. But it seemed as if everything was normal, and, now that I look back, it's almost as if it was *too* normal. Is there such a thing?"

"Sure."

She pondered what she could see in the rearview mirror, so to speak. Her cards vibrated warmly in her hand. "Looking back, I sensed she was waiting. When I asked her how she was doing, she gave me this big smile, then said that she was doing just great. Immediately she would change the subject, and we'd have tea or coffee or something. She liked to watch old movies, old romance movies." Heather groaned, with a shake of her head. "I hated them, but Hannah put one on to shut me out, and she was putting them on a lot."

"So, I guess the question at this point is this, knowing that and looking back, do you think they might have had marital problems?"

She nodded slowly. "It would make sense if that's what was triggering her behavior. Yet another thing that would make sense was if he kept increasing the drugs a little more. She was prone to migraines and was constantly taking medication. So it could have easily been tampered with," she murmured, "if he wanted to."

Royce hesitated before asking, "I hate to ask, but was she expected to produce an heir?"

She looked at him and then shook her head. "No. Just the opposite, in fact. She wanted children, but Faheed was adamant that there would be no more children, … unless it happened by accident. In that case, he would take it as Allah's will. Plus, she was instructed to maintain birth control."

"Which would have been hard on her as well."

"It was."

"Any chance that she didn't take it—even once maybe?"

She stared at him. "I don't know. It's possible, I guess. I just don't know. Why? What are you thinking?"

"I'm just wondering if Hannah did something that would have triggered Faheed, provoking a decision to take her out. Was she becoming tiresome? I hate that word, but you know what I mean."

"Again I don't know," Heather stared at him unhappily. "Are you sure there isn't any food now?" she asked. "This conversation is incredibly upsetting."

He checked his phone and then smiled. "As luck would have it, Rick is here now."

She stared at him, just as they heard a knock on the

door. She bounced to her feet and raced to the door, but Royce's sharp voice snapped through the silence. "Wait."

She froze, then turned and looked at him, fear instantly coming over her.

"Don't ever open the door," he declared. "Just because it *should* be him, doesn't mean it is."

And, with that, he walked up to the front door to their hotel suite and made a tapping noise on the door. Then came a response from the other side, another series of taps. He opened the door to see Rick, with bags of food on the floor and a full trolley in front too. Rick was dressed in the hotel uniform jacket. Royce quickly let him in, and Rick took off the hotel jacket and smiled at her.

"Hey, I hope you were enjoying your time while I was out working," he teased, as he motioned toward the trolley. She frowned at him, pointing back at the delivery trolley. Rick explained, "We ordered it to our old room, so that people would think we were there. Once the delivery was left inside our former hotel room, and the hotel people left the floor, I collected it."

"Were you in the room at the time?"

He nodded. "Of course. I had to make them think we were there."

"Right. I never would have thought of that," she muttered.

"And you don't have to. That's what we're for."

She sighed. "Still, it feels weird."

"Doesn't matter," he said, with a big grin.

"What are the bags on the floor for?"

"You ordered a certain amount of food, but I figured that we wouldn't want to draw attention to ourselves by ordering very much more, so I brought some snacks for those of us who will stay up during the night."

"Right. So, you're back to the four-hour security shifts again?"

"Yes, we are," he confirmed. "That's the way it'll be until we get you back to England."

When he pushed the trolley forward, the smells hit her stomach, and it started growling.

He looked at her and laughed. "I guess that's good timing, *huh*?"

"You have no idea," she muttered.

Very quickly they were all seated around the table, with large platters of food in front of them. She cut into the steak, and it melted like butter in her mouth. She moaned as the first bite popped into her mouth. Then she just sat back and relaxed.

"I'm sure you must have eaten well with Faheed," Royce said.

She nodded. "Mostly I did. My portions were rationed, as were my choices. If I wanted something he didn't agree with, he made it known to me to just eat what was in front of me."

"Like what were you denied?"

"Oh, potatoes, cakes, pastries, bread even. Faheed felt women are supposed to be slim and trim and could never go off on our own and order whatever we wanted because we couldn't be trusted with such a decision." Royce and Rick didn't say anything to that and just stared. She shrugged. "Gilded cage, remember?"

"Sounds like prison to me."

"Which I'm really starting to realize more and more as I come off whatever drugs he had me on. So that is most likely the exact same state Hannah lived in throughout the years of her marriage to Faheed." Heather felt the realness of it, as soon as the words were out of her mouth, and it hit her hard. Heather had been too close to becoming her sister.

Not anymore.

WHILE HEATHER AND Rick crashed, Royce took first watch and quickly sat down at his laptop to do a deep dive into the other dead wives of Faheed, something he knew that Terk's people were working on as well. Yet it occurred to Royce that they didn't know how Faheed had met Hannah—or how he had met the other wives. Royce also wondered if there had been any local investigations into their deaths. Instincts prodded him that more was there. But what? The information was a little sparse. He contacted Jonas, looking for more.

When Jonas phoned him shortly thereafter, he asked, "You guys settled in for the night?"

"Yes, two are asleep. I'm on watch," he muttered. "She's pretty nervous, wants to get home."

"Yeah. It's too bad we had to stop you guys midway, but that's just the way it is," he replied, his tone light.

"We think Heather's been drugged since her sister's death, not exactly sure why. We know the how, starting with meds to help her grief after her sister's death, then continuing the drugging without her knowledge, probably via her food and drinks."

"What would be the purpose of that?" Jonas asked.

"Our bet is Faheed was making a bid for Heather's company." Instinctively it felt right to him.

Silence came from the other end. "Why?"

"Greed, of course."

When he shared the name of Heather's large whiskey company, Jonas agreed. "Makes sense. They have a hell of a product."

"With Hannah's death, Faheed assumed Hannah's share would go to him as her husband, but it doesn't, as stipulated by the father's will that it has to stay within the family, followed up and confirmed in Hannah's will. Turns out Hannah had already signed her voting proxy over to Heather earlier as well, so it's all under Heather's control."

"Interesting," Jonas muttered. "Yeah, losing access to that kind of wealth probably stuck in Faheed's craw pretty well, wouldn't it?"

"Not to mention the fact that women can't do business in his mind-set, so no way he would have allowed his wife to maintain control. He discussed Heather's hierarchy of employees several times with her, and she's afraid that he's contacted at least one, if not more than one, to try and take control. Plus, Heather believes Faheed is trying to break her father's will."

"That would suck," Jonas noted.

"Yeah, you need to contact Terk to get updated information."

"Yeah, I will," he replied, his tone dry. "There is such a thing as, you know, information sharing."

"It's all evolving, and now we're getting some clarity and putting it together," he explained. "So, I'm just trying to keep the status quo from what I know on my end."

"Appreciated," he said briskly. "I'll send you the files that we have on the other marriages."

Once they ended the call, it took about another eight minutes before the files came in. Royce sat here in the darkness, sipping coffee as he read through the files on the two other wives, from Faheed's second and third marriages. Both were of American origin. One had been living in Sainte-Marie of Martinque when he'd met her at a museum. They had spent a year there. Then she began to travel with him and married him. Her cause of death was supposedly choking on something. Another accidental death, which of course made Royce's back go up with suspicion.

Her family wasn't much of a factor. She did have cousins or other relations who had been given some initial payout, presumably to prevent any hue and cry, not that anybody in that position was likely to even know to do anything against a rich diplomat.

The other wife was an American out of Texas. She had been working in Switzerland as an au pair at the time, when she caught Faheed's attention at the opera. It had been a whirlwind romance, and she and her unborn child had died in childbirth.

At that Royce sat back, wondering why Faheed's first wife was the only one to bear children. Did Faheed not want any future children? His first wife gave him three sons and one daughter, all adults now. Maybe Faheed felt he was too old to be a father again or just that he had his heir and a spare, via the first wife, and called it quits on any more.

Even saying it that way made Faheed a jerk because he should have cared for all his children, no matter how many or how late in life. Maybe he did. Yet in each instance where Faheed's second, third, and fourth wives died *accidentally*, Saheed, the brother, had been, as he always was, close at hand. That made Royce even more suspicious. He quickly sent Jonas an email, asking for information on the brother.

When Jonas phoned him back, he asked, "Are you really

thinking Saheed's involved?"

"According to Heather, he's quite slimy."

"That's a pretty descriptive term," he noted, with a laugh.

"In every instance the brother was in those countries with Faheed and was around at the time of each subsequent wife's death. There could be some professional jealousy going on here between the brothers. *Something* is going on there."

"It's quite possible," Jonas conceded thoughtfully. "We have looked at him in the past, but he doesn't have a criminal record. We don't have anything really, though we found some suggestion that he was accepting bribes for contracts."

Royce agreed. "Unfortunately that's a common problem in the diplomatic field."

"Right. So, then what?" Jonas asked.

"Then we keep looking," Royce muttered.

"The physician who attended the wife's death who died with her child in childbirth met with some backlash, questioning whether everything was done to save her and her child."

Royce asked, "Do we know the sex of the child?"

"Female," Jonas replied.

Royce winced. "Faheed has adult children, three sons and one daughter at this point. They probably would not be happy to welcome any more siblings."

"Realistically it shouldn't matter to them either way, considering Faheed's marriages were his choices in his life," Jonas suggested, "but I know what you mean. Anyway, if we have confirmation that the same physician was attending both wife number three and Hannah up until their deaths, that is suspicious as well. I'll do another check into him,"

Jonas offered, "and any other medical personnel who are still there in Faheed's entourage. Did Hannah have any regular nurse or someone like that?"

"I don't know. Is it customary to have a medical team traveling with Faheed's entourage?"

"Yes, absolutely," Jonas confirmed. "Some of these people don't even blow their own nose. So, yeah, I will look into it," And, with that, he disconnected.

It boggled the mind to think that people were so dependent on the services of others for the simplest things in life, but it wasn't for Royce to judge. If the same doctor and possibly an attending nurse were on staff at the death of wives three and four, that upped the ante as to who were the guilty parties in all this.

When Jonas phoned back only five minutes later, he announced, "I just got a report on the doctor on my desk. He was not allowed to practice medicine in the US."

"What for?" Royce asked.

"Malpractice, with several lawsuits still pending against him. He dodged the law for quite a while. He's supposed to be an exceptional doctor but didn't always follow the rules or legal avenues and did surgeries he didn't have approvals for."

"So, if Faheed wanted something, like to let these women die for example, that would suit this out-of-bounds doc totally, wouldn't it?"

"It would. He's not licensed to operate in England at the moment either."

"Any chance that he came over with him?"

"He comes over all the time," Jonas said. "From what I am seeing here, he's been a part of Faheed's personal entourage for a while."

"And there's no way to stop that?"

"No, of course not. If he's not practicing medicine on any English citizens, then it doesn't really matter. The diplomat is perfectly capable of hiring whoever he wants for his own personal household."

"Right, and that probably explains how they're accessing the drugs as well. So, we have a dodgy doctor, a scary brother, a husband who keeps gaining the inheritances of all these wives at a very rapid rate. This is such a cluster fuck, and we cannot do anything about any of it. … Hang on a minute, the one wife out of Sainte-Marie, I thought she had no immediate family. How would Faheed have benefited from her death?" he asked.

"Back then she'd just inherited the family's fortune out of England," Jonas shared, as he rustled papers around. "Seems she was born in America, so she's a dual citizen. Anyway her parents were killed in a plane crash. She was estranged from them and was hanging out somewhere in the Caribbean when she found out. I'm not sure how she met Faheed. Or who knows? Maybe he just heard about the family deaths and their fortunes and decided to introduce himself."

"Yeah, that would be possible too. Particularly if he was hunting for a particular kind of wife—rich and docile. Which I would imagine he was, considering that he had already buried his last one by then. According to what Heather said, her sister didn't know about the last two wives, just the first one."

Silence came on the other end. "Seriously?" Jonas asked.

"Yeah. According to what Hannah was supposedly told, Faheed's first wife died in a car accident years ago, and so he didn't want Hannah driving. He wanted to ensure that she stayed safe. So he arranged to have her driven wherever she wanted to go."

"That's convenient."

"Right. It allowed him to keep track of where she went, when she went, and who she met, so Faheed doesn't have to worry about anything or anybody coming in between them."

"Meaning that Hannah couldn't have a lover without somebody knowing."

"Exactly. I guess that's why I'm still wondering what the hell was up with those letters." He frowned considering what they knew so far. "According to Heather, she and her sister had been very, very close—up until that marriage."

"Did Heather mention how Hannah met Faheed?"

"She was visiting someone and went as their guest to an art show. Hannah was an artist but had no urge to go public with her art. Yet she enjoyed the arts, and the gallery had a big opening night and then an after-dinner party for the featured artist. Hannah was in attendance, and Faheed apparently fell hard for her. Or appeared to fall for her."

"Okay, good enough," Jonas muttered, "I will do a follow-up with anybody else who is a regular in Faheed's entourage. Of course we can do nothing while they're not on British soil. I wonder if they would come over to talk to Heather. Maybe we can set up a trap to bring him over, under the guise of Heather wanting to see him or to show him the company or something," Jonas pondered out loud.

"At this moment, she would freak out completely if we suggested such a thing," Royce declared. "She just wants to get home safe and sound and not have anything go wrong at this stage, like losing her family's very successful company to Faheed."

"I get that," he muttered. "I was just thinking out loud, trying to figure out what we can do to get this guy."

"What about other countries?"

"We're in contact with the countries where all the women were killed and to a certain extent the countries where the women themselves came from, since their citizens have died," Jonas replied. "This is definitely an international situation."

"But we don't really have any way to contact him," Royce pointed out.

Jonas asked, "What about Iran itself?"

"What about Iran?" Royce asked. "We both know all too well that Faheed has denied any wrongdoing and has been backed up by his government. Yet you can expect every country to say the same thing about their diplomats."

"Unfortunately we see that time and time again, don't we?"

"Yes, we do."

And, with that, Jonas rang off for the second time.

As Royce lifted his head from his laptop, Rick appeared, standing in the doorway to his bedroom, rubbing the sleep out of his eyes. "Was that Jonas on the phone?"

"Yes." Royce then brought Rick up to date.

Rick frowned. "So, with each wife's death, Faheed basically inherited a family business, which would help legitimatize anything he was doing in his mind, even give him an excuse to step in because he would improve things for them. He meets them, hooks them, and, within a couple years, he's overtaken these companies."

"Sounds about right."

"How long was he married?"

"The first one he was married to for seven years and produced three sons and one daughter. She died afterward in a car crash."

"Ouch, she was just a broodmare, having four kids in seven years."

"Exactly. The concern at this point in time is if the good doctor, who lost his license to practice in the US, seems to have been attending the family all these years and maybe helped each wife to die from natural causes. He has an advantage as a medical doctor to get close to the women."

"Right, so even if we do prove wrongdoing, we don't have any way to prove that it was Faheed and not his hired help."

"Exactly. I hate to say it, but it's damn smart on Faheed's part. He can always claim complete ignorance, and a jury will definitely let him off the hook, without even second-guessing things."

"Not only will they let him off," Rick added, "but he probably won't even get that far because you can't prove his involvement over anybody else's. This will take a lot of time to sort out. … You ready to get some sleep?"

"Yeah, I've done what I can do right now," Royce noted. "If you come up with any new information, let me know." He looked down at his watch and winced. "I better grab some sleep now, and we should plan to head out early. The weather has at least calmed down some."

"Good. Go grab some sleep, and I'll see you in a bit."

With that, Royce got up and headed to the empty bedroom.

CHAPTER 10

EATHER WOKE UP, bounded out of bed, had a quick shower, and redressed in the same clothes she'd been wearing, which made her cringe but, hey, that's what it was. She pulled a tarot card and found the Sun card staring back at her. A great omen. With a lighter heart, she walked into the main room of the hotel suite. She smiled when she saw a trolley of fresh food. "Who got to go play manservant this time?" she teased.

Rick looked up and smiled. "Me again. Sometimes the routines are just too perfect, and you get into them, and it's hard to get out of them," he admitted.

She heard the shower running in another bedroom and nodded toward it. "Did he get some sleep at least?"

"He did," Rick stated cheerfully. "We both got a few hours."

She nodded. "Anything is better than nothing right now. Please tell me that it's a go and that we're leaving soon."

"It is a go," he said, laughing at her antics.

"Great, that is fabulous news." She sat down, lifted the lids off the food platters, rubbed her stomach, and shared, "You have no idea how much better I feel, now that I really get to eat." She quickly served herself pancakes, scrambled eggs, and sausages, then turned to Rick. "Did you eat?"

"I had some, and I'll get some more in a bit," he muttered. "Just trying to do the paperwork, so we can get out of here."

"Oh, right. I suppose you have red tape to take care of, don't you?"

"Absolutely, particularly when you don't have the right papers. So we're traveling under an immunity clause," he shared, with a laugh. "When that kind of stuff happens, believe me that there's paperwork."

"And yet would there have been paperwork for a diplomat to fill out? Would Faheed have had to do that, or would his secretary have taken care of it?"

He frowned at that remark. "Did he travel with a secretary?"

"Yes, Ana, his secretary, helps out. Plus a manservant. His name was Bingham, and he used to do some administrative tasks too."

"Then either of them probably handled these things as well. I don't know if Faheed ever did very much of anything himself. He didn't seem to be a man interested in working, or did he?"

"No, he sure didn't," she said, as she forked up some sausage. "Yet he was always there, always into everything, but he delegated the actual work."

"That makes sense. It seems the richest people find others to do the work for them. Who knows what he delegated to whom. We understand a group traveled with him, and it included more people than we think."

"There were always more people than you would think, and a lot of them switched out," Heather shared. "I've been involved in some of his travels with my sister, particularly when she was going through a low period. She thought she was pregnant and wasn't, and that started a big fight with

Faheed. But, regardless of that, the other people would be there one day but wouldn't be the next. Then you would turn around, and somebody else would have just flown in with documents or whatever that Faheed needed or wanted at the time."

He nodded.

She continued. "For these people with access to a lot of money and power, you don't realize how their worlds function, once they become accustomed to a certain life-style. … I never really understood it, but I do know a lot of people danced to Faheed's tune."

"Did his brother have the same power?"

Heather frowned. "Not nearly the same—at least overt-ly. Yet, if people had problems with Faheed, they went to Saheed. So Saheed had some sway over Faheed or just did some secret workaround to ease tensions."

"So Saheed had no real power," Rick concluded.

She shook her head. "I'm not sure that Saheed *didn't* have power. You say he had none, but, from my perspective, he had plenty."

"Yet he had no position of his own."

"Ah." She pondered that and then agreed. "That's true. He had no position of his own and was employed by Faheed, so, in that sense, you are correct."

"So did Saheed work for the country of Iran?"

"I don't know," she replied, pondering that. "Of course you're not getting any help from the Iranian government on this, are you?"

"They would likely say it's a witch hunt, claiming the accusations amount to nothing. That it was to be expected, since he was a virile man, and he tended to enjoy frail women, hence the problems."

She stared at him in shock, and Rick put up his hands. "Don't get upset or worried. I'm just ad-libbing. Did Iran say any of that? No, they didn't. And I don't know that they would have. I was just guessing, based on experience. Still, do we ever really know what people will do?"

"Exactly. I'm surprised to think that my sister would have come under that same umbrella."

"And yet she would have, wouldn't she?"

"Yes. Now that you've stated it so clearly, she absolutely would be deemed as frail, but I can't say that I appreciate it. And, if Faheed's marking me with the same brush, that would make me very angry."

"But he isn't, not in that sense particularly. You are anything but frail. He's just marking you for your capital assets."

She winced. "I do have a will in place," she muttered.

"What'll happen now that your sister is gone, and you can't leave everything to her? Who do you leave it to?"

She frowned at him, then shrugged. "Charity. I've got a foundation being established, and a board of directors will be in place. The profits are to be sent to my selected charities." She really hadn't thought it through though. "It's fairly complicated, and I haven't gotten all the details worked out yet. However, with my sister gone, and no one else in the family to leave it to, I wasn't sure what else to do."

"I like the idea of charities," Rick said, with a nod. "You just need to ensure that your board of directors doesn't take everything for themselves first."

Silence came, as she winced. "That is some of the stuff I'm trying to lock down. Plus I was wondering about making provisions for some staff members."

"Would Dan be one of those?"

"No, Dan would *not* be one of those. Yet employees who

have worked there for thirty or forty years," she added, "are ones who I'm more concerned about."

"I'm pretty sure Dan would be more concerned about himself."

"I would hope not," she murmured. "He makes a very good wage, and his options are not limited, compared to other people there."

"Nobody makes enough though," he stated, staring at her intently. "You do realize that, right?"

"Of course nobody makes enough," she admitted, with that wry look. "That goes back to that whole topic of greed, doesn't it?"

"Yep, and, for all we know, your sister was murdered over it." Her breath sucked in hard at that, and she stared at him. He realized the insensitivity of his statement and whispered, "Jesus, I'm sorry."

"No, you're right. It is quite possible. I just don't want to think about it, but that doesn't change the fact that I can't ignore it," she muttered. "It's just pretty rough to think about right now."

"Sure, it is," Rick agreed. "Sisters are very special, and you spent a lot of time with her, especially at the end, it seems."

"I'm grateful for that too." She stared off in the distance. "I might not have had that opportunity, and that would make me very sad, losing that opportunity, not getting it back again," she muttered.

Rick just smiled. When they heard the shower stop, she looked over at him. "Do you think that somebody in my company might really be involved in some way?"

"I don't know that yet," Rick admitted, "but we'll get to the bottom of it."

She nodded. "I want to think none of them are involved, but you guys are making me very aware that the world out there is not the way I want to see it."

"No, it isn't, but that doesn't mean that you can't make it better than it has been up until now," Rick suggested. "So keep that in mind too."

She smiled. "That was a very diplomatic answer."

"Hey, just trying to keep you happy," he said, with a smile.

"I get it," she agreed, "but it still sucks."

"Sure, it does, but you've come a long way, so let's keep that going." He hesitated, then added, "Do you use your cards to answer any of these questions?"

She sighed. "While a prisoner I tried, even when my sister was alive, but honestly, it's the only time I worried that my cards and I were no longer on the same wavelength. I used them and could get some answers, but they weren't defined, not as crisp as when I used them before."

"Drugs," he noted flatly.

Wincing, she nodded. "In hindsight, I think so. The readings are clearer now than what I was used to getting before and maybe even stronger—as in I don't always need to pick a card to hear the answer."

"Interesting." Rick frowned and looked as if he would say more, but a bedroom door opened, and Royce walked out.

She smiled up at him. "There you are," she said warmly, loving the sight of him. Something was growing between them, but she had no idea just what or if it was only on her side, but she hoped not. And maybe she was just so damn happy to have escaped and to not be alone right now. She hoped her judgment was better than that. She sent the question to her cards, pulling out her deck, and flipping the top card. Then she looked up at Royce. "How was your night?"

"I had a good night," he said, with a smile. "How about you?"

She shrugged. "It was okay. We're moving in the right direction now. That's what I care about."

Royce looked over at Rick. "Any update?"

"Yep, we're leaving in a bit." He looked at his phone and added, "In about forty minutes."

"Oh good." Royce nodded. "In that case, food first. Then we can pack up and head out."

As she headed to her room to collect her few possessions, she glanced down again at the card she'd pulled.

The Lovers.

WITH HEATHER IN the back seat of their newly arrived vehicle, courtesy of Terk, Rick drove, and Royce took the passenger seat. They left in the early morning hours, heading straight for the private airport. They hadn't checked out of the hotel, but she figured the local government would know exactly what was going on. If not, they could contact MI6. As soon as they hit the airport, they quickly boarded a small plane and lifted off almost immediately.

As soon as they were free and clear and the seatbelt sign went off, she beamed at Royce. "I didn't think we would make it here," she exclaimed, laughing. "It's been such a hard journey already that I figured something else would screw it up for sure."

"We're here, and we're free and clear, it seems. So, all we

have to do is get home and land," he stated, with another smile.

She nodded. "When can I contact my company?"

"Not yet," he replied instantly.

She checked his energy and determined his response was more about safety than instincts. Regardless it was the same answer. Elements were at work here that she needed to respect. She frowned. "Are you guys still thinking that it's all connected?"

"We're not so sure that it's connected as much as a possible link to some proof to hold Faheed or Saheed or one of their people accountable."

She winced. "Fine. I'll stay off communications for now, but I do need to get into the office. I saw enough on my emails last night to know that I need to handle some important matters, and I need to do that fast."

"I hear you," Royce said. "Hopefully today, but it won't be early. It may not even be by the end of the day. If things get really ugly, it may not be until tomorrow. Yet nothing we can do about it, and we don't want to jump the gun. We need to put everything into play, keep it in play, and hope that, by the end of today, this is done and dusted."

She smiled and settled in to enjoy the rest of their flight. "Now that would make me happy."

Royce looked over at Rick to see his gaze going back and forth from Heather to Royce. Royce just shook his head. "Don't even go there." Hell, Rick had better not go there.

Royce already had enough confusion in his own mind. Something about Heather's energy almost synergistically matched to his own. No one else saw energy in the same way he did. Maybe someone at Terk's castle did, but Royce hadn't met anyone who saw the energy waves quite the way he comprehended them. Yet here was someone who he could see a shift, ... a sliding, ... almost a melding of her energy to his. They certainly liked each other, but this was different. There was almost a fatedness to their union that made him somewhat uncomfortable. He'd always been someone in control—especially of the major decisions in his life. Yet here was something he wasn't sure he had any sway over.

"Too late," Rick declared, abruptly interrupting Royce's thoughts. "Will you guys follow up on this when you hit England?"

Heather replied, "Sure, why not? He's the most interesting man I've met for a long time." Rick looked at her with a wounded expression. She rolled her eyes. "Oh, please, enough with the puppy-dog eyes. We both know perfectly well you have somebody waiting for you when we touch down."

"I do, and believe me that I can't wait to see her."

And that maybe was the crux of the matter for Royce. He didn't have anyone. He was pretty damn sure that the woman he hadn't realized he'd been waiting for was sitting right beside him.

CHAPTER 11

THEIR FLIGHT TO London was anticlimactic. They ended up at a small private airport, and government vehicles came with men in black suits to pick them up and to carry them away.

The initial sight of the men made Heather pause. She glanced over at Royce and murmured, "Is this what you expected?"

He gave her a grin and nodded. "Something along these lines, yeah," he murmured. "They're nothing if not into theatrics."

The MI6 driver and his partner in the passenger seat shared a knowing glance. Then the driver shot Royce a look in the rearview mirror.

Royce just smiled.

Heather sighed. "I suppose I have to go in for questioning or some such thing," she said, hating that she sounded grouchy and ungrateful. Still, she was tired and wanted time at home, preferably alone. Although the thought of being on her own wasn't as comforting as she thought it would be.

"You have to expect some questions," the driver replied. "A lot of effort was expended to help move this process along."

She winced and shook her head. "I sound like an ungrateful bitch. That's so not me."

"And that's okay," Royce added, putting his hand on hers. "You've also been through an awful lot lately. Stop trashing yourself."

"Easy to say but not so easy to do. Too bad you're not my fairy godmother and can make that happen with a wave of your wand."

"Hell no, I'm not worth a damn in a skirt," he quipped.

His remark was so unexpected that she burst out laughing. He grinned at her, and she realized he'd done it on purpose. She sighed. "So, we're back to your being one of the good guys." He raised an eyebrow and didn't say anything. "You are," she repeated in a persistent tone. "Yet I get it. You probably don't want to be called that, but …"

"Don't like being called what?" he asked, frowning at her. "Did I miss something?"

"A nice guy," she clarified. "You probably don't want to be called a nice guy."

"Sure, I do," he said. "You could call me a hell of a lot of worse things."

"Here I thought men didn't like it. I thought it was a phrase that upset them."

"Doesn't upset me," he muttered, turning his attention again to the road.

Now Heather noted a little too much commotion on the road. "What's going on?" she asked.

He shot her a look and then gave her a bright smile.

She shook her head. "Oh, no. I've come too far to ignore the warning signs."

"Good," Royce stated, "because that means those instincts of yours are working."

She frowned at him and looked outside. "Everything's still so damn fuzzy. I was hoping clarity would return faster."

"We can't talk about everything here," he whispered to Heather, catching the driver's glance in the rearview mirror once again.

She sucked in her breath, her gaze shifting to the world passing by. She couldn't sense anything. Yet her cards were heating up in the waistband of her leggings. "Something's wrong, isn't there?"

"Let's just say, we've picked up a tail."

Her gaze locked on Royce's. "From the airport? That would mean that somebody knew ahead of time that we were landing."

"It would, wouldn't it? But then you would be amazed at what kind of money people will pay for information and get it quite easily."

"Even from Jonas's office?"

"I wouldn't be surprised." He gave a dour chuckle.

"What's so funny, damn it?" Heather asked.

"Jonas will be absolutely thrilled to find out he has a mole, a snitch," Royce declared cheerfully. "Cleaning house is always fun."

She shook her head. "I don't think you should be having as much fun with all this as you appear to be."

"Hey, there's not nearly enough fun on the job as it is," Rick added.

Heather was frustrated to see a grin on his smug face as well.

"Don't take that away from Royce." Rick's mocking voice was that of a little boy, and she found herself laughing too.

"I know you're doing your darndest to keep me occupied and distracted and not aware of what's going on around me," she shared, "but I do need to know."

"If you've already figured that out," Rick stated, "I'm not doing a very good job."

She smiled. "I'm really not foolish, and I do understand that we have a whole different set of problems over here, but I thought I would be safe from Faheed here."

"I'm not saying you're not," Rick pointed out. "Still, he's probably been keeping an eye on us."

"Which would imply that he knew where we went."

"It would, indeed. Remember that our operation rescued you out of Finland," Rick shared, "and I'm sure Faheed has already recognized that it had *military* written all over it."

She muttered, "Meaning government."

"Yep, meaning government. You are a British citizen, and MI6 tends to *not* like it when things happen to their British citizens."

"*Great*," she murmured. "The question is whether Faheed will leave it alone now or come after me."

"Does he have any reason to come after you?" Rick asked.

She shrugged. "Not that I know of, except that he wants my company."

"And it's a big successful company worth megamillions," Rick noted comfortably. "So, I guess the question really is, how far does he want to push it?"

"I'm pretty sure he's not stupid when it comes to these matters, and the fact that he came very close to getting his hands on it once may very well keep him pushing for the prize."

"And possibly his brother too, right?"

She nodded. "I wouldn't be surprised, but I do love to hate on him."

Rick chuckled at that. "Always need to be nice to the

ladies if you want them to not hate you."

"How about just being nice, period," she murmured. "As long as you don't come across as being a full-on asshole, life becomes pretty easy for all of us."

"Got it," Rick said, amid a fit of laughter.

"I guess that comment's for me." Royce looked from one to other, and a grin took over his face.

She snorted. "As if you need any lessons in relationships." He studied her, but she shook her head. "No way you don't have somebody in your life."

"Actually I don't, and I haven't had for quite a while." He shrugged as if it were a non-issue. Beside him, Rick started to laugh, clearly tickled at something. Royce glared at him, and she finally caught the look between them.

"Am I not even allowed to ask a question?" she muttered. "May I remind you that you've asked me thousands of questions."

"It was hardly a question," Rick clarified, still laughing. "More of a fishing expedition. And don't insult me by denying that."

She glared at him. "You do know that it's good to be quiet sometimes." At that, he burst out in even louder laughter. She sighed and settled back. "You guys are very irritating."

"I thought we were nice guys," Royce teased, with an injured tone. Then he added, "Don't worry about Rick. He's just in a happy marital state, and he wants to see everybody else be that happy."

"I won't argue with that," she said. "Wouldn't it be nice if there was such a thing as a happy marital state?"

"There is," Rick stated instantly, "but you have to find the right partner for that."

Just then the vehicle took a hard left, and she was slammed against the passenger door. "Ah, crap," she cried out. Almost immediately the vehicle took a quick right. She grabbed onto the door handle to stop herself from sliding back and forth, her gaze going from Rick to Royce and back. Then her tarot cards heated up too. And so far they'd never been wrong. Even now they bordered on hot. That was a typical sign of danger. A warning, so to speak. "Please tell me this is all part of the plan."

Rick smiled and nodded. "It is now."

She groaned. "We really are being followed, aren't we?"

"Our driver is doing standard evasive maneuvers, trying to drop the tail."

She stared out the window, trying to see behind her but couldn't really see anything. "It's so hard to know," she muttered, as she stared all around. "Why would anybody even bother trying? That's what I don't get."

"The fact that anybody is even looking for you is what interests me," Royce stated. When she shot him a look, he smiled. "The fact is, you're back in your hometown, you somehow survived that nightmare of captivity with Faheed, which was obviously very well done, so much so that you don't really know you've been being gaslighted or drugged."

She winced at the truth of his statement. "As much as I hate to hear you say that, I don't even know how much of what my sister ever told me is true now. If she was also kept drugged into a happy state, maybe she truly wasn't happy. Maybe all that time it was the drugs talking, and I don't know shit."

"Maybe not," Royce acknowledged, "and I think it's one more reason why we need to find out who that handwritten mail of Hannah's went to."

She turned to face him. "You really think it's that important?"

"It's an anomaly," he declared, with a shrug. "An anomaly that I can't begin to make heads or tails of, so, for me, yes, it's *that* important."

She pondered that and then shrugged. "How do we find out?"

"I don't know yet, but that will be something we need to work on. Did she have any friends in the company?"

She frowned at him. "We're back to that? She didn't have any friends, remember? The family business wasn't even a part of the equation for her. She didn't work there even years before I got her voting rights. Business just wasn't her thing. Hannah has always been more of a loner."

"Maybe so," Royce said, "or maybe she had some friends you didn't know about."

"In that case then don't ask me," she replied in exasperation, "because, if she did, and I didn't know about them, I can't answer the question."

Just then the vehicle took another hard right, sending her flying again. Royce reached out, wrapped an arm around her, and pulled her up close and buckled her into the middle seatbelt "Here. I'll help you from getting hurt on these corners."

"How come you aren't being tossed around?" she muttered, glaring at him.

"Because I see them coming, and I had my seatbelt on," he shared, with a laughing tone.

She sighed and snuggled in closer. "We will get out of this, right?"

"Oh, absolutely," he vowed, looking down at her.

As the vehicle continued its erratic movements, Heather

grew uncertain and more nervous. She reached for her ever-trusty tarot cards and gripped them for security. When Royce looked over at her, with an eyebrow raised, she just smiled and pulled them out enough that he could see.

He whispered against her ear, "What good will that do you right now?"

She flipped open the box, and, as she held the deck tightly against her, she pulled out one card from the center of the pack. When she stared down at the Death card, her gaze shifted to the men around her. In an urgent whisper she asked Royce, "Do you know who is tailing us?"

He shook his head, his gaze on the card. She flipped it over and put it back into the deck. "Does that mean what I think it means?" he asked her.

"No, not necessarily," she clarified, "but it does mean that the path we're on right now is not good."

"Not good how?" Rick asked, looking over at her sharply.

"We're heading into … something ugly."

At that, the driver snorted. "*Great.* Are you the boss now? Do I take your word for it, just because you said so?"

"It's not just because I said so," she declared, looking over at Royce and Rick urgently.

Rick leaned across the seat to the driver. "Change of plans now."

The driver glared at him. "I have orders."

"And I just changed them." Rick held up his phone and pointed to the map on his screen. "We're going here." With a last glare, the driver took a series of hard turns and came to a stop inside an underground garage. Then Rick barked orders in their faces, "Move, move, move."

She was quickly hustled out of the vehicle. They wanted

to take the elevator, but she was adamantly against it. Rick and Royce aligned to her side. The two MI6 men stared at her, shook their heads, and stepped up to follow them as well.

"Your funeral," the driver noted. "We have seven flights to go."

She winced at that, but no way she would back down now. Then, with Royce and Rick at her side, she moved at a slow and steady pace up the stairs. She was tired, but she wouldn't let them know, not after having insisted.

As she got up to the target landing, the two MI6 men stepped in front, opened the stairwell door, checked, and then motioned for her to step through. They led the way down to an apartment on the left-hand side. As soon as the door was opened, she was pushed inside and came to a dead stop, her mouth open, even as she tried to protest.

Two masked gunmen stood there to greet them, instantly taking down the two MI6 men. Royce and Rick stood still and raised their hands. The gunmen didn't attack them, but the guy nodded to his partner, who began tying up the two unconscious MI6 men. Meanwhile the head guy held his gun on another man, seated in a chair.

"You were right about one thing," Royce muttered behind her. "This won't come to a good end."

"Yeah," she replied. "I always find that's the way it works. Even when we change plans to avoid the ending, we don't like what finds us anyway."

"You could have pulled that card a little earlier, you know?"

She quickly pulled a new card. "Well, our destiny has changed." She held up the Fool card.

"Good or bad?" Royce asked.

"Just trust and keep putting one foot in front of the other, but expect the unexpected."

"So the jury is out. *Great.*"

"I should have been pulling cards the whole time, but I wasn't thinking to utilize them in this way. I just used them to keep Hannah happy and for fun." She shrugged, staring at the two gunmen standing before her, united again and pointing their guns at everyone. Stepping forward, she asked, "So, what the hell is this all about?"

If Royce was surprised at her question or her actions, he didn't show it. The gunmen moved Royce and Rick forward, their hands still in the air. One of the gunmen motioned them to move off to the side, away from Heather. "Pull out your weapons," the head guy barked.

"We're unarmed," Royce declared. The silent gunman promptly searched them to confirm this.

Meanwhile Heather stared at the man sitting there, guns held on him. Instinctively she knew who it was. "Are you Jonas?"

He gave a clipped nod.

"Nice to meet you," she said, with a smile.

He just stared at her with a narrowed gaze.

Heather thought Jonas was probably wondering what she was up to. She wasn't up to anything. That was the problem. She walked closer to Jonas, when one of the two gunman raised his gun to her. She stared at him and snapped, "Do I look like I have a weapon?"

He snorted. "Doesn't matter if you look like it or not, we don't trust anybody."

She didn't say anything as she was quickly searched, but she certainly didn't have a weapon. When she pulled out her cards, the head gunman snorted, grabbed them, and tossed them on the counter in the nearby kitchen. She felt that sense of loss immediately.

She hated that feeling and absolutely detested being separated from them. Of course that should have said something to her a long time ago about what power she held over them—or what power they held over her. She didn't know, but she knew that her instincts were always much more sharpened and fine-tuned when she had them on her person. That said a lot about how she was feeling now, which was a whole lot more in control, right up until he'd taken away her cards. She walked over to the kitchen counter and picked them up. When the head gunman glared at her, she shrugged. "What? You're worried about a set of tarot cards?" she asked, laughter in her tone.

He motioned for her to sit down, but his subsequent words were a whole lot nastier as he told her to shut up.

She didn't say anything but sat down beside Jonas. She knew things would get dangerous very quickly. She just didn't know which way it would break.

She studied Royce and Rick, realizing that they were by far the most dangerous men in the room, even unarmed. The two masked men may have had guns but that wouldn't stop Terk's guys. She didn't know in what way Royce and Rick would act; she just knew it would be something deadly and fast. She stared at Jonas, noticing the huge welt on his face. "Did they do that to you?" she asked in a hard tone.

He gave her a look. "Yeah."

"Wow." She glared over at the two gunmen. "Not only are there two of you but you also have weapons, yet you still beat him up?"

"He didn't cooperate," said the other gunman in a bored tone, who had been quiet until now. "So, you should probably pay attention.'

She glared at him. "I'm really not very good at that. I've been kept prisoner for way the hell too long."

He studied her with interest. "So, you really are Heather, *huh*? Hannah's sister?"

She nodded, staring at him. "Ah, so Faheed sent you?" she asked.

The gunman who had ignored her question hadn't shown any recognition of Faheed's name. She stared down at her cards.

"Put them away," he snapped. She looked at him and shrugged. "If you want to keep them, you won't bring them out again."

She found it interesting that he was so unnerved by them, but she had seen a similar reaction from other people in the past. She found that response more of a curiosity than anything else. She put them away, looked over at Jonas, and frowned to see that his head wound had started to bleed. She noted that her cards were vibrating slightly at the dangerous circumstances, but they weren't hot and screaming. So the danger hadn't reached explosiveness yet.

She got up, walked over to the kitchen, pulled some paper towels off the roll, dampening them at the sink. With a dry one in her other hand, she returned to clean Jonas's head wound. She stood by him, bending closer to blot the blood flow. He frowned at her in surprise, as even the gunmen didn't appear to know what to do with her. She just shrugged. "This situation doesn't mean we can't be nice."

"I don't really give a crap about being nice," the one gunman snapped. "Now sit down and stay down."

She handed the towels to Jonas, yet remained standing. "If you can keep a little pressure on it, the bleeding should stop soon."

He nodded and took the towels.

"What makes you think he'll even be alive long enough to worry about keeping his wound from bleeding?" the obvious leader asked, with a hard snort.

She turned to him. "I know these men. They don't have to be assholes just because you have an agenda that these guys somehow got mixed up in."

"What do you mean, somehow got mixed up in? You really don't think that he was responsible for all this headache?" The head gunman waved his weapon at Jonas.

"Of course not," she snapped. "I'm not exactly sure what this is all about myself. However, if it's got anything to do with me, then it's all Faheed's doing."

"I don't know any Faheed," he snapped right back, then shook his head. "Why do you keep bringing up this Faheed?"

"Why do you need to hide behind a mask?" she asked.

He shook his head. "Just mind your own business." He waved his gun again. "Sit down and shut up." When she sat down and glared at him, he snorted. "You know, for somebody who is facing a gun, you really don't know when to be quiet, do you?"

"I shut up when you told me to," she pointed out, with a shrug. "The fact that I got up to deal with his head wound doesn't mean I didn't follow your orders."

He glared at her, and she stopped talking but was watchful. She looked over at Jonas to see an odd look in his gaze as he studied her. He didn't seem to know quite who and what she was. However, if he dealt with Terk's team much, then Jonas probably thought Heather had all kinds of abilities that she did not possess. She certainly didn't want him to get the wrong idea and to think that she had any way to get his sorry ass out of this because she didn't. Still, she was certain that Royce and Rick would pull off some rescue.

She looked over at the guys, with an encouraging smile. At that, Rick just rolled his eyes, and Royce's lips twitched, as if he thought her response was funny. "So, do you want to tell us what this is all about?" she asked the gunmen.

Immediately the gunmen turned their weapons her way. She snorted. "Fine, fine, shoot us all. It's not as if we'll do anything about it."

The head gunman relaxed slightly at that reminder. "Exactly, you won't do anything about it, so just shut up." He bellowed on the *shut up* part.

Then it hit her. She asked the gunmen, "Are we waiting for somebody?" The head gunman glared at her yet again. She sat back one more time and realized she really didn't want to know who they were waiting for. A part of her really did, but, if it had anything to do with her family, with her company, then she really didn't. She sighed as she sat here, thinking about it. "I don't think I want to know."

The head gunman ignored her. However, as she went to open her mouth again, his gun raised in her direction. "Ha, I wonder if shooting me will get you what you want?" she asked in a conversational tone. "Because either way, my company sure as hell won't go to anybody connected to this nightmare."

Of course she was bluffing because, although she'd a will in place and had begun the charity foundation setup, she certainly hadn't gotten the final paperwork finished yet. So that brought her back even closer to this being Faheed's nightmare. "Faheed certainly won't get it," she muttered.

"I don't know what company you're even talking about, so I don't care," the head guy stated in exasperation. "What the hell is your problem? Can't you keep quiet for even a few minutes?"

"You weren't talking," she said, "so I had to."

"No," he bellowed, "you don't. You can just shut up."

"Then tell me what I'm here for. Why are you holding me, and what the hell is your problem with me anyway?" she asked, glaring at him.

He groaned and looked over at Royce. "Is she always like this?"

Royce shrugged. "Pretty much. She's just nervous. She's been through a lot already, including being held prisoner for some time. So finding out that she's now a prisoner again, not to mention having absolutely no idea what's going on, is just making her a little more upset. You get used to it."

"You better shut her up," he bellowed. "I can't wait until we're done with this already, so I'm not putting up with her mouth."

Royce added, "Maybe you should tell me what we're waiting for, and we'll do what we can to help you through this. Obviously she wants to survive."

"She does?" the gunman asked him. "Maybe she will. But you don't want to survive?"

"I would love to, but it depends on who and what you're after, as to whether that's in the cards," he replied.

The head gunman gave him a wolfish smile. "I'm glad you understand the situation, and so does your buddy here. But, as for this guy," he said, with a wave of his gun at Jonas, "I still don't think he gets it. He thought he could resist, but, of course, it's futile."

Just enough ego filled his tone that she glared at him. "Really? So, the two of you overpowered a man without a weapon, even though he's obviously way older than you." At that, Jonas stiffened at her side. She instantly rounded on him. "It's true," she snapped crossly. "So don't get in a snit about that." He just stared at her, as she turned toward the gunmen once again. "So, how is it that you can be proud of this job?" she muttered. "I hope you're getting paid a lot of money."

"We are," the second gunman stated impatiently. "Now, if you don't shut up, it won't be nearly enough money to make up for putting up with you."

Rick and Royce shared a knowing glance, and Heather caught a glimpse of it. She also felt her tarot cards heating up but in a good way. She even felt a surge of energy hitting her in waves. It was profound. Frowning at this new event, her intuition simply said, *Your friends are helping.*

Encouraged further, she smirked at the gunmen and added, "I hope you got paid upfront." When she saw the head gunman instinctively draw back his free hand and form a fist, she nodded. "Oh, I see how it is." She glared in his direction. "You guys beat up women, don't you? They don't shut up when you want them to shut up, so *boom.* You just give them a cuff across the side of the head."

He stepped forward and asked, "You want one?"

"No, I really don't, but now that I've got your number, I know what kind of little piss-ass cheater you are."

"I'm not a cheater," he said in outrage.

"Sure you are. You're the guy who uses force to get what you want, and that makes you a cheater because you don't think most women have the same physical force available to them, which makes you a power bully. Just bullies in the sandbox," she stated, sitting back and glaring at them. "You won't even tell us what this is about."

At that, the gunman walked over to Rick. "Make her

shut up."

Rick shrugged. "I can't." Then he smirked and nodded toward Royce. "He might be able to."

She glared at Rick. "Why would he make me shut up?"

At that, Royce walked over, picked her up in his arms, and walked back with her, holding her close as he set her on her feet. The gunmen broke into raucous laughter. She glared at Royce, but he gave her a strong headshake, and she backed off once again, glaring again at the two gunmen.

"See? That's all you are, bullies. That little display of strength from Royce is all you recognize. You don't care about the fact that I have a brain, as well as wishes and wants and desires. Do you really think I haven't had my fill of people like you? For all I know, Faheed killed my sister. So, if you're associated with him in any way, rest assured I will see to it that you guys pay."

"We don't know any Faheed," snapped the head gunman. "We're dealing with Englishmen here, not foreigners."

Such a nasty tone filled his words that she believed him. "Oh, that's interesting," she muttered, frowning at him. "In that case, you don't want me to leave before *the Englishman* arrives, right? You might not get paid in full, right?" And, with that, she turned and walked to the front door of the apartment.

Even Royce, who reached out to grab her, missed. She was there before the gunmen even had a chance to blink. She had the door open and was stepping out into the hallway, when the second gunmen reached her. She turned on him, spitting mad. He raised the gun in his hand, as she cried out, "No." Then she gave him several hard kicks to his shins, followed up with an elbow to the eyeball, and plowed him one in the nose with her fist.

She heard the *crack* of his nose as it broke, but she was too busy crying out in pain to note her success because her own hand hurt so badly. When Royce joined her in the hallway, he stopped in astonishment to see the gunman on the ground and her sitting there, crying out and holding her hand. He grinned, walked over, and picked her up, giving her a whopping kiss. "We'll have to teach you how to give a proper punch."

"Really?" She glared at him. "You think I didn't do okay on my own?"

"You did, but you're not supposed to hurt your fist in the process," he added, with a smirk.

Rick picked up the still moaning gunman in the hallway and brought him back inside, where Jonas stood, holding a gun on the head gunman.

Heather looked over at Jonas with satisfaction.

"Not sure what your game was," Jonas admitted to Heather, "and believe me that nobody else knew the playbook for your attack either. Yet apparently you're pretty darn effective."

She shrugged. "I'm hardly effective enough," she muttered. She walked over to the one standing gunman, and, in a surprise move, she smacked him hard across the face.

Royce joined in and knocked him out, then announced, "Rick and I can carry our prisoners out of here, but somebody needs to revive Jonas's men here. They need to walk out on their own."

Jonas interrupted, "I've got more men on the way, so I suggest you stick around. Just make sure these two are out for the count and secure them to the bathroom plumbing."

Royce and Rick took care of that, then searched their pockets for any IDs.

WHILE EVERYONE WAITED for more of Jonas's men to arrive, Royce was more worried about Heather's edginess and stressed energy. First, he grabbed some ice from the freezer and wrapped it in a kitchen towel. He had her put it on her hurting hand, as he gently wrapped her up in a hug and whispered, "It's okay. We've got them, or, should I say, you got them. It's all right."

She sagged against him, quietly in thought now.

Jonas stepped up beside them. "I didn't expect you to save the day." She turned and glared at him, but he just smiled at her. "Hey, whatever works for you, I'm totally okay with it."

"Fine," she muttered. "But I want to know who these guys are, what they are doing here, and why?"

"They're down there because they can't stand," Rick teased, with exaggerated politeness.

She rounded on him, and he grinned. "We didn't get to see this side of you before," he noted. "I think I like it."

Royce did too. His grandfather would have called that *spunk*.

Color washed over her cheeks as she sighed. "I don't get mad often, but, when I do, I tend to cause a scene."

"Noted for future reference," Royce stated, with a smile sent in her direction.

Immediately Rick started to laugh. She turned on him again, and he held up his hands. "You've got no reason to be mad at me."

"No, I don't." But she felt her tarot cards burning again. She pulled them out, and this time pulled out the ten of swords. She frowned at that.

"What does that mean?" Royce asked.

"Nothing good, but *betrayal* is the word that comes to mind."

"Do the cards have meaning or do you give them a meaning?" Jonas asked, studying her curiously.

"Cards are intuitive," she explained. "You can say what you want and mock it at your peril, or you can understand that they have their own message, and it's not necessarily what the card itself is showing you but the message that comes in along with it … intuitively."

"So as in … psychically?" She rounded on him, and he held up a hand. "I figured I would get a hard reaction to that." He gave her a knowing smile.

"You're partially right," she conceded, "but most people don't particularly choose that word."

"Right," he agreed, "they don't, but that doesn't mean that I don't believe in psychics and psychic abilities."

"You have good reason to believe," Rick noted, staring at Jonas. "So, we found no IDs on them. So did you figure out who these guys are?"

"Not yet," Jonas grumbled.

"I've got their phones," Royce shared, holding both up. "We need to find out who they are, why they're here, and if they're after her or us."

"Oh, I rather like the idea of them being after you," Heather replied, laughing. "That would be a nice change."

"It would be," he began, "except that there's no reason for anybody to be after us. Therefore, it's more likely you they're after." She glared at him, and he smiled. "Just because we now have these two doesn't mean that others could still be after you."

She turned to Jonas. "Are you the one helping me get

loose?"

He nodded. "Yes, to a certain extent," he said, "but I'm also hoping that you can help us put away Faheed."

She pondered that. "It's not quite so easy. You know that, right? Faheed has a lot of support."

"He does, indeed, and that's making our job infinitely more difficult," he admitted, "which is why we need somebody on the inside."

"Somebody on the inside would have been nice, but I don't know anything, and I, for sure, am never going back."

At that, Jonas took a deep breath and dropped the bombshell. "Actually … Hannah was on the inside."

CHAPTER 12

AS BOMBSHELLS WENT, that was a big one. Heather stared at Jonas in shock.

Even Rick whistled, and Royce stepped up to Jonas's side, asking, "What do you mean, she was on the inside?"

"Those letters you asked about," he began, "were from her, and they were coming to me. To a PO Box that we had set up in the name of one of her old school friends. We sent letters, innocuous letters, back and forth. It was her way of getting a message out. She's also the one who warned us that you were in danger."

"So, we shared those details with you, including the letters, and you still denied it?" Royce asked, eyeing him with a flinty expression.

"Get over it. It's part of the job."

She dropped onto the nearby couch in shock, as Royce sat down beside her and held her close. She buried her face against his neck as she tried to process the information. She lifted her head and looked over at Jonas, bewildered. "Why?"

"Because she figured that she was being drugged, didn't think she had any way to get out of her situation, and wasn't sure she wanted to. … Something about the gilded cage or something," Jonas gave her a confused look. "She wanted to be there but felt strongly he had to be stopped. Does that make sense to you?"

She sobbed slightly. "Oh, yes, it does. But it would have been so much easier for her if we could have just put him away first."

"It would have been, but she also wasn't looking to fight for herself. Hannah was trying to get you to safety."

Heather just stared at him, as she struggled to begin to understand what he was talking about.

"Maybe you should start at the beginning," Royce suggested, pulling her back into his arms.

When she protested, he just pulled her back in again. "Please, we all need to understand this."

She sagged against him, realizing that this had been a blow to him too. She looked over at Jonas. "He's right. I need an explanation."

He nodded. "Your sister contacted us several months ago. She was very much afraid that arms dealing and murder-for-hire contracts were coming out of her husband's office. She shared that she absolutely loved him and didn't want it to be him but had heard enough to realize that somebody who used to work for MI6 had just up and disappeared one night. It was somebody Hannah had been getting closer to, almost to the point of being able to confide in her those suspicions of what was going on here, when suddenly the woman just disappeared."

"Are the MI6 missing an agent? That would likely be her. Faheed would not take a betrayal like that easily," Heather muttered.

"Hannah told me that you didn't know anything and that you weren't a part of this. Still, Hannah was pretty sure that, once she was gone—should there be no way for her to get out of this—that your life would be in danger next. She'd made the mistake of telling Faheed something about the way the company worked and how you were doing a hell of a job managing it. Apparently that upset her husband tremendously, and he looked into the details.

"He then found out that you not only had majority control—because Hannah had signed over her voting power—but that, in the event of her death, her shares would also revert to you instead of him, as stipulated in your father's will. He was so mad. Hannah realized that her hopes and dreams of being loved for herself were going up in smoke and that Faheed was just after her money."

Tears came to her eyes as Heather realized all her sister had kept from her. "Why wouldn't she have told me?" she asked.

"Toward the end, she thought that everything she said and did was being recorded—or listened to, at least. They had taken away her hair clips and even her reading glasses and replaced them with new ones, similar but different. She mentioned how they felt different too, somehow heavier. She could never really figure out what was going on but was under the impression that her every word was being recorded."

Heather stared at him in disbelief. "There was no way to write me a note or to do anything?"

"I think she was mostly concerned about keeping you alive. She also said something about the family business needing you."

"Says the woman who had nothing to do with the family business," she muttered. "She wanted nothing to do with any of it."

"Anyway, due to her, we started looking into this and found out that Faheed now has four dead wives," Jonas shared. "We didn't know what had happened to Hannah until suddenly an announcement was made that she had died of a sudden heart attack. We tried to get it looked at via the diplomatic office in public relations," he noted, with a wry look. "That doesn't work for shit."

"No, of course not," Heather agreed, "particularly in Faheed's case, when he wields as much power as he does." She sagged in place and looked up at Jonas. "So, she knew? She knew she was in danger and didn't do anything?"

"It's possible, yes," Jonas replied. "You yourself said that she enjoyed that lifestyle that Faheed gave her."

"Sure, but we had money. We could have made it so that she had a whole lot more than what Faheed gave her," she whispered, still stunned and unable to process all the implications.

"You thought she was off somehow during those last few weeks?" Jonas asked.

"Yes, she was. I just didn't know what it meant. I kept asking her if she was okay, and she would give me this really sad smile and say, *Yes, everything is fine*, but I knew it wasn't fine. I just couldn't get her to open up and to tell me what was wrong. I thought it was, you know, marital problems. God knows there was plenty to feel bad about there," she whispered. "This is not what I expected."

"No, but it makes sense now because how else would MI6 have had any idea of what was going on?" Royce noted.

"Faheed had four dead wives," she exclaimed. "Doesn't that trigger some kind of a global response?"

"Nobody follows anybody enough for that," Jonas stated. "Particularly since each of the deaths were easily explainable. It was just seen as a case of a poor man with terrible luck who maybe should choose heartier wives."

"*Right.*" She stared at him in horror. "How long had

Hannah been corresponding with you?"

"Months," Jonas stated simply. "We were trying hard to find a way to get her out of there. He'd been invited to England and still has an open invitation, so, if he shows up now, I won't be surprised."

"If he does show up, can we nab him?" she asked Jonas.

"Not without something seriously solid. Diplomatic immunity goes a very long way."

She blinked. "Even murder?"

He winced. "In theory, no. But, if he leaves the country before we've got him, that would be it," Jonas conceded. "And we would only go forward with an ironclad case, so I suspect he wouldn't stay in jail anyway."

She shook her head. "Meaning he would be released?"

"You have to realize that his own country can't handle that level of embarrassment either, and there's a good chance that they would ensure he didn't survive."

She winced. "Meaning they would assassinate him themselves?"

"That's possible, but I really don't want to speculate."

"No, you don't have to," she said. "It's very much the world they live in, isn't it?"

"It is, absolutely. They know very well that every day they are playing the game, they're fighting for their lives."

She sucked back her breath. "What else did she say in those letters?"

"That she suspected Faheed was running arms and that his brother was heavily involved as well and was possibly even more involved in the arms dealing than Faheed was. He was collecting as many businesses around the world as he could for the day that he retired from his job. Not that such a thing would ever happen because it was all way too convenient to protect him from his crimes."

"She didn't say anything about the wives?"

He shook his head. "No, she didn't say anything about the wives, though she did say that other deaths were suspicious that she didn't know anything else about."

"I'm sure there are lots of them," Royce muttered, massaging her shoulders now.

She nodded. "It'll never be just one. If they got away with it once, then you know how it goes." She just sighed and went on. "I'm still in shock that she never told me, that she never did anything to save herself."

"Did she try to send you away? Didn't she try to send you back to England?"

Heather nodded. "But I knew that she wasn't well, that she was off somehow. She was despondent and not her normal self, so I, … I stayed. I didn't want to desert her."

"And your remaining in Faheed's sphere probably would have sent Hannah into more of a spin. One of the last letters I had from her mentioned how she was afraid she was being poisoned and wouldn't be around much longer."

"Jesus," Heather exclaimed in a frustrated tone, almost hysterical. "Couldn't you have done something?"

"At that time you were all traveling constantly. Besides, there wasn't anything we could do without revealing that the intel came from her."

"Of course … and that would have either sped up the process or he would have had her locked up as being completely unstable." Heather had just so much to process, and yet all of it made a sick kind of sense. "It just hurts me so much to consider her going through all this alone and not thinking she could tell me," she whispered. "I didn't see any of it."

"No, but I think she feared, if you knew about it, you would go on a rampage," Jonas shared, as he motioned at the gunman on the ground in the nearby bathroom.

She winced. "Right, and I would have," she declared. "I would have barged into Faheed's office and raised hell."

"And you would have been dropped right where you stood," Rick declared, his tone harsh. "You must have known that. Otherwise you would have done something about it. Did you ever check your cards?"

"I did," she said, looking up at him. "All my instinctive answers that came through the readings were that my sister was deeply troubled, but, because I couldn't get her to open up, it didn't help me understand what was going on. I wanted to fight it all, but I didn't have a target."

"What about your instincts, without the cards?" Rick asked her.

"Again that's why I didn't leave," she whispered. "I just knew she was in trouble, but I didn't know how or what to do about it. Only after her death did I realize just how accurate my assumptions were, and then I found myself a prisoner," she stated. "I didn't think I was a prisoner before because I hadn't made any attempt to leave."

"Exactly," Royce agreed. "If you think about it, as soon as you would have made an attempt to leave, you probably would have become that prisoner you weren't yet aware of. As long as you didn't fight back, Faheed didn't have to enforce his will. However, the minute you put up any kind of resistance, … then he would have been forced to act and to hold you back."

"Bloody hell," she muttered. "Just when you think you know somebody, you find that you don't know anybody."

Jonas added, "We did ask her if she wanted us to put an

op into play to pull her out, but she told me no, … several times in fact. She repeatedly said that she was right where she needed to be."

"Wow." Heather stared at Jonas in shock. She looked up at Royce. "You didn't know?"

He shook his head. "No, that information was withheld from us too," he shared, staring at Jonas.

Jonas shrugged. "Come on, you guys know how it works," he replied. "Too often nobody ever really knows until something blows up." He looked down at their prisoners on the bathroom floor. "Speaking of which, we should have company soon."

"Is it the right kind of company though," she asked, "or the wrong kind?"

He gave her the ghost of a smile. "My kind."

"Yeah, you mean the ones who are still unconscious?" she asked pointedly.

He frowned at that. "I checked them, and they appear to be just knocked out."

At that, almost as if understanding that he was being talked about, the driver started to moan and rolled ever so slightly.

She bent down beside him and patted his shoulder. "It's okay. You'll be okay." He opened his eyes and stared at her in confusion. She motioned at the room around them. "You missed all the action though."

He slowly sat up, noticed his partner on the floor beside him, and then his eyes widened as he caught sight of the two strangers, handcuffed to the plumbing, who were also down. "Good God." He winced, reaching up a hand to his head. "I gather we were taken out as soon as we walked in."

"That you were," Jonas confirmed, "as was I."

The driver stared at his boss and shook his head. "So what the hell happened to switch this around?"

Jonas snorted. "She happened."

At that, the driver turned and stared at her in shock.

She shrugged. "Nobody ever sees the women as a threat," she stated. "We're just to sit up, to sit down, or to shut up. So, when we act in a way that they're not used to, they don't know how to handle us." Of course what she didn't say was she could feel—sense?—the positive energy coming from her tarot cards. She knew that would be one step too far for these people. Or maybe not.

Jonas noted, "Somehow I feel there's a whole lot more to that explanation."

"There is," Royce agreed, with a half laugh, "but this might not be the time to tell it."

She stiffened and looked at the door. "We have company."

"Good," Jonas replied, as he walked closer to the door. Then he stopped and looked at her. "Good company or bad company?"

ROYCE WATCHED HEATHER carefully. Her fingers shifted to the box of cards stuck in the waistband of her leggings, as she stared at the door. He could see the change in her energy as she got the answer she sought. Her aura smoothed from the ruffled edge to one draping like silk around her. She stared at the door and then gave a nod. "Good company."

"How do you figure that?" Jonas asked curiously.

She pulled out her tarot cards and shared, "They're vibrating in a good way."

Royce smiled at Jonas's instant snort of disbelief.

Jonas opened up the front door and let in his team. Immediately the gunmen were cut loose from the plumbing and were picked up and moved out. The driver lifted his unconscious partner and followed the others.

Rick turned to Royce. "I'll find a room for us." Then he promptly left too.

When the apartment was emptied except for just the three of them again, Heather looked at Jonas, "And now what?"

"What do you mean, now what?" Jonas asked. "We start at the beginning again. And try to find the person the gunmen were waiting for."

She groaned. "I really should be let off the hook of any questioning, considering you already had my sister feeding you whatever information you needed."

"She had very little access," he reminded her.

"I had even less," she declared, "so don't forget that."

"I'll remember," he replied. "I just need a little bit more information than what we've got."

"You'll need a lot more," she muttered. "Faheed's very smart. He won't get caught easily, and I don't know what the hell's going on in terms of his brother, but he'll be in the middle of it as well. Saheed is far too involved in Faheed's life."

Just then Jonas's phone buzzed. He looked down at the message and whistled.

"What's that?" she asked.

"Faheed and Saheed have both arrived in England. They just walked out on the tarmac. They have been cleared to visit London."

"Well, damn." She stared at him. "They must be coming

after me." She turned to face Royce, panic in her gaze.

He gripped her uninjured hand. "We'll be fine, remember? So far, this has all come out okay."

She glared at him, looked around the room. "Can we have it be not quite so close next time?"

Jonas glared at her. "Yeah, the plan was not to have any of this happen," he snapped, "so it won't happen a second time."

"You couldn't help my sister. You couldn't stop them attacking you, holding you at gunpoint. You don't know who these gunmen are working for. You couldn't stop these gunmen from finding me too," she muttered. "So how am I supposed to trust you the second time around?" He had been in the act of walking toward the front door, but he stopped and glared at her. She shrugged. "You want my trust, but I really want my safety first. I already know what these guys can do." She shook her head in disgust, "My sister is a testament to that."

He nodded and quickly left.

She stared over at Royce. "Are we leaving?"

Royce smiled at her. "Yep. I'm expecting Rick to call at any moment. But what would you like to do?"

"Go to my house and spend the night in my own place, after getting out these clothes and into a hot shower. Maybe get some food and a good night's sleep. … Then go to my office. So much needs to be done."

Rick rejoined them, and Royce nodded, then spoke. "Sounds like a hell of a plan. We're good to go."

"What about Jonas?" she asked.

"He left us behind, so we're on our own timeline, at least for now," Royce said. "You ready to skip?"

She laughed and raced to the front door.

CHAPTER 13

AT ROYCE'S AND Rick's insistence, Heather went in through one of the rear exits to her apartment building. It was mostly a fire escape and not a common entrance or exit. Thus, if they wanted to keep her arrival secret, this was the better option. Not that she cared at this point. So much had been going on that she just wanted to get home, which was tantalizingly close, yet seemed so very far away.

Rick and Royce were being ultra-cautious, and she appreciated that. Still, by the time she was finally inside her apartment building, then stepping into her own residence, she felt the tears threatening. "God, you can't imagine how many times I wondered if I would ever get back here."

Immediately Royce placed an arm around her shoulders and held her close. She wanted to sob and also to rail against the injustice of it all. She had had no time to process everything that Jonas had revealed about her sister, and Heather acknowledged that she needed that processing time. However, just to know in this moment that Royce was here for her meant so much. She didn't want to build up any expectation that he would be here for her forever by any means, but it was so damn nice that he was here for her right now.

When she finally stepped back, she looked up at him with a gentle smile. "Thanks. Sorry for being such a wet sponge."

He shook his head. "After what you've been through, this is nothing. Don't be so hard on yourself."

"I keep thinking about Hannah. Even this place reminds me of her too," she began, as she turned to look around. "We spent a lot of time here, before she married him."

"Is it your place or your sister's?"

"Essentially they're the same thing now," she replied. "It was mine beforehand anyway. Anytime she came into town alone—which obviously wasn't a thing after her marriage, but, before that—she stayed with me all the time. She had a boyfriend prior to Faheed, and it looked as if they might have gotten married for the longest time. Then she caught him cheating. He laughed at her and called her all kinds of horrible names and said he wouldn't get stuck with that for the rest of his life. I wanted to go punch him out, but she dissuaded me against it by telling me how he wasn't worth it. In a way, she'd been right. He wasn't. But, boy, it sure makes you question everything and everyone around you."

"Which is too bad," Royce noted, "because all the world is not always so shitty. It's not full of only shitty men."

"I know that." She sighed, leaning back to look up at him. "You and Rick are the exception to the rule, aren't you?" she teased.

Rick smiled, as if acknowledging her mention of him in this otherwise very personal discussion with Royce.

Royce raised his eyebrows. "I hope it's not so bad out there that we need an exception," he clarified, "but I do understand why people would look at it that way."

She didn't say a whole lot to that, but he was right. She still had this sense of things being so *off* in so much of the world. She could only hope it wouldn't end up being quite that way in reality. Yet her recent experience hadn't been very positive. She stepped away from the guys and took a moment to look around her apartment. Suddenly she let out a *whoop*.

Royce laughed. "I gather you're happy to be home."

"Yes," she declared, as if, for the first time, finally realizing that she was here. She walked around, turned on her desktop computer, opened up her blinds, and stared out of the window to the city below. "I have such a feeling of relief," she shared, as she turned to look at both men, her gaze going misty. "Thank you, thank you, thank you."

Rick just nodded, as he walked toward the kitchen. "You got any coffee?"

She laughed. "I often wondered if you were eating anything or just surviving on coffee."

"Coffee will keep me alive when a lot of other things won't," he said, tossing her grin.

"Coffee should be in there. Help yourself." Within minutes she heard cupboard doors opening and closing, and she laughed. "He really makes himself at home, doesn't he?" she asked Royce.

"It would seem so." Royce laughed. "You did tell him to."

"I know, and I hadn't really thought it through, but yeah. He's fine."

At that, Rick poked his head into the main living space and asked, "A pot for everybody?"

She nodded. "I may or may not have enough, but, yeah, go ahead and make a full pot, even though I'm exhausted."

"So?" he asked. "What's that got to do with it?"

She rolled her eyes. "We're not all invincible like you."

"Meaning?" he asked.

Hopefully he was only feigning confusion. She sighed. "Meaning that I'm likely to stay awake if I drink coffee."

Rick shrugged. "It won't keep me awake." Then he disappeared into the kitchen.

She heard the fridge opening moments later and shook her head, then called out to him. "There won't be any edible food. I haven't been here for too many months."

"That just means we'll have to order in then," he called back.

She looked around, then walked into her bedroom. "Do you know what this means?"

Royce walked in behind her. "What does it mean?"

"It means I have clothes," she exclaimed, turning to look at him, a big grin on her face. "I can have a shower whenever I want, and I can dress in clean clothes."

"That you can." He chuckled. "Apparently that's important too."

She rolled her eyes. "Absolutely everything about having and living with true freedom is important. How can you guys get anywhere if these things are not important to you?"

He just smiled, understanding that her question was rhetorical.

"Would you mind if I have a shower now?"

"No, go for it." He looked around at her bedroom. "Nice room. It's really pretty but not in an overpowering sugary way."

She stared at him, as he viewed her home but from his perspective. In a way this was his first indication as to who she was like here in her own personal space. The room was elegant, decorated in cream-colored tones, but had a touch of a royal purple accent all over the place. The bed was a queen size because she couldn't stand small beds, and it faced the beautiful view outdoors. "It's not very fancy," she muttered, suddenly doubting herself.

"Fancy?" he asked, looking at her. "Why do you need fancy?"

She shook her head. "Right. Somehow you always say the right thing and make me feel like an idiot." She laughed at her earlier remark. Then she pushed him out of her bedroom. "Go, so I can get a shower. Then I'll be out in a few minutes for coffee."

"It should be ready by then," he said, with a big grin.

She rolled her eyes at that. "Figure out what you want for food, and we'll order in," she suggested.

As he turned and walked out, she was already tossing her dirty clothes into the hamper, absolutely ecstatic and overwhelmed to just be home again. So many times she hadn't been so sure that she would accomplish this. She stepped in under the steaming hot water and cried out mentally to her sister. *I made it, Hannah. I made it. And I'm so sorry that you didn't too.*

Immediately her tears started to flow because her sister wasn't here with her. Hannah had obviously had some inkling of something being very wrong with Faheed. Otherwise she had no reason to contact Jonas. To even think that Hannah knew how to do that boggled Heather's mind. Her sister wasn't stupid. She just never had any interest in the family business, never had any interest in that side of things.

It had always been Heather's thing, not her sister's. That didn't make it right or wrong. It just made it what it was. Now as Heather cried, listening to her sobs coming from her heart, she felt the full weight that her sister was truly gone, as was the rest of her family. Heather was now the last one left alive. It was a sobering thought, particularly when everybody had done so much to build up the business all these years, expecting a long-lasting legacy. Yet to see herself now all alone, carrying that ultimate level of responsibility, representing her family? Well, it was pretty … daunting. She wasn't even sure she was up for the task, although she was pretty darn sure that her father would tell her off immediately for even having such a negative thought process. Still, it was hard to think of anything else right now.

She let the hot water wash away her tears. By the time she was done, she felt a whole lot better. She would miss her sister every day of her life, but nothing could be done about that now. Heather would have to think hard and long about why her sister hadn't shared anything with her, especially when it was obvious that Hannah needed help herself.

Maybe Hannah truly didn't want to believe that this would be the end result? Heather just didn't know. It seemed to be such foolishness on Hannah's part to leave her own life up to chance. Faheed had many, many things going on in his world, but none of them were terribly nice, particularly if you considered that he'd kept both Hannah and Heather as prisoners. But, even considering that, Heather refused to let it bring her down right now.

As she stepped out, exhausted through and through, she dressed in comfortable loungewear. With a towel wrapped around her head, she stepped out into her living room. Both men looked up, and almost identical grins crossed their faces at her getup. She pointed a finger at them. "Don't say one word," she muttered. "After all I've been through, you're lucky I've got clothes on." Realizing what she'd said, she groaned. "I suppose you can't just forget I said that, right?"

"Hell no, feel free to do whatever you need to do. That's

all right with me. I'm here to help." Royce teased, laughing.

She shook her head. "Very funny. I'm just so tired right now and still so emotional. It all keeps hitting me in these never-ending waves."

"And it will for a while," Rick noted, looking over at her. "Just when you think you've dealt with it, something will remind you of her, and it'll come back all over again."

"That's already what happens with my parents as it is, and it's one of the reasons my sister and I stayed so close, as there was just the two of us," she shared. "It was a sobering realization while I was in the shower just now that it's just me now. I'm the last one in my family."

"What about aunts, uncles, extended family?"

She shook her head. "No, none of that either."

"I'm sorry," Royce muttered. "It is hard when you're the only one left."

"It is," she whispered. "I know I'll get through it, and everything will turn out okay, but it's, … it's daunting."

He didn't say anything more, just nodded, and she really did believe that he understood. He didn't always say a whole lot, but he seemed to get it, and that was worth more than she could say because not everybody else would. It seemed as if fewer people in her world ever truly got it. They were always more about themselves than anything else.

She sniffed the air, smiled brightly, and looked at Rick. "All right, so how's the coffee?"

"It's not bad," Royce replied, with a chuckle, "considering it's Rick's first time using your coffee machine setup."

She winced at that. "Good point. Sometimes getting the right balance can be a little tricky. Yet, when we really need coffee, none of that actually matters, does it?"

"It's all good," Rick said, looking up from his laptop.

She stared at his laptop and nodded. "Yeah, that's what I need to do. Please don't try to stop me from contacting my company now. I need to send out emails and check up on lots and lots of stuff."

"I won't," Royce claimed cheerfully. "As a matter of fact, you need to let everybody know that you're back at the helm, in case some issues are going on behind your back."

"Oh, I'm sure there have been," she declared, gritting her teeth. "I've been thinking about those guys who caught Jonas. The only way they would have known that I came back into town was if Faheed mentioned something to those gunmen, or if they found out through a leak in Jonas's world. Yet the gunman stated *Englishman* so …"

"It could have come through Faheed's middleman to your company. We're still trying to track that down now, and frankly it's a bit of a mystery. If Jonas has a leak, he won't be a happy camper. He already couldn't do anything to save your sister, but don't think for one second that it's not eating away at him all the time."

She winced. "I never did let him off the hook on that, did I?"

"You don't have to. Hannah contacted him, or at least it landed on his desk. He's the one who kept up a relationship and had to deal with the letters coming in, but knowing that she was at the other end of that was hard on him."

"Of course," Heather acknowledged. "I didn't even think of that."

"You don't have to think of everything, you know," Royce pointed out once more, as he stared at her. "Sit down and dry your hair. I'll get you a coffee."

And he was up off the couch before she even had a chance to argue. What could she say? He was already here, helping in so many ways, and it was easy to let him continue. She thought about her sister and how Hannah would probably have agreed with that. Still, Heather wanted to run into the kitchen and take the coffee away from him, just to ensure that she didn't become too accustomed to being waited on. That brought back the memories of the gilded cage with Faheed.

Yet refusing Royce's friendly help was certain to make her look foolish in this context. Not something she particularly wanted right now. When he returned, she smiled and thanked him.

"Problems?" he asked, studying her when she took the cup from him.

"No, just more of a realization of the lifestyle my sister accepted. She was very happy and content with it. And she let it be that way. It didn't work out too well for her, did it?"

He stopped and held up a hand. "Okay, I missed something, and I don't know what triggered what you're saying."

She groaned. "I'm not making very much sense right now, and I get that. I'm sorry," she whispered. "It's just that my sister wanted to be waited on hand and foot. That was the life she wanted. She didn't run her own bath. She didn't brush her own hair. She didn't do anything along that line, and to even consider that she could be responsible for cleaning up her room or scrubbing a toilet was laughable. That was something she absolutely adored, the lifestyle I mean."

"I can imagine it's something that might be easy to get used to."

"And that's what I'm saying. … When you said that I should sit down and that you would get me coffee, I realized just how easy it is to get used to that. As Hannah's sister, visiting her, I was in a way treated as a revered guest, almost doled out like, *Hey, you too could have this life,* you know?"

"Did she dole it out though?"

She pondered that. "She extolled the virtues of it early on, but I can't say that she ever forced me to accept it."

"I would think not," Royce agreed, "especially not once she became aware of the underbelly to that very lifestyle."

She nodded. "An underbelly that I don't think she fully wanted to see."

"Would you?" Rick asked. "Hannah had made all these adjustments and found herself sitting in this beautiful life, servants at her beck and call, yet her beloved husband, the person who makes it all happen, is also the most likely to blow it all up. Would Hannah really want to see the truth of that? Would you?"

She winced and shook her head. "No, and I'm not sure that Hannah really believed Faheed would ever go this far," she replied. "That's what I want to think anyway."

Rick nodded. "I'm pretty sure she believed that he loved her and that whatever marital problems they had toward the end could just as easily have been the fact that she realized this wasn't quite the paradise she had hoped it would be."

Sipping her coffee, Heather deliberately didn't go any further with the discussion. It was the only way to stop the tears from pouring down her face. It would be months—if not years—before she could finally see her sister's actions for what they really were, an attempt to save Heather's life, after having already accepted that her own life would be forfeited. That acceptance of her sister's self-sacrifice made it so hard because surely there must have been some way to have helped her too.

Heather knew that these men would have helped, although she had no idea how. Hannah was legally married to Faheed and had been very happy up until that point in time. So what could anyone else have even done? Heather was at a loss on the whole thing.

With a sigh, she added, "I think that's a really good topic to just leave until later." The men agreed, after seeing her resolve and hearing the finality in her tone. She then put a hopefully sincere smile on her face and asked them, "You're still here, and I'm not sure what's happening at this point. Can you fill me in?"

"We're waiting to hear from Jonas and Terk."

"Why?" she asked bluntly.

"You still haven't answered any questions for Jonas, and he did expend an awful lot of effort to get you back again."

She winced. "Right, so I still need to talk to him. I was kind of hoping that maybe I could avoid that part." Both men just stared at her, and she had the grace to look ashamed at least. "Fine, apparently that's not in the cards."

"No, it's not, but it doesn't have to be as horribly traumatic as you're imagining it to be."

She just stared at Rick. "You did not just say that."

He burst out laughing, then shrugged. "Okay, I did not just say that."

She sighed. "Fine, so after Jonas, then what? Am I just free to pick up my life and carry on?"

"Do you think you'll really be free to carry on?" Royce asked her. "That's the question."

She winced. "So you really think Faheed will come over here and get me?"

"He already is here. Remember? Once you have your legal protections in place, then it would make no monetary difference to him if you're alive or dead. Then you should consider whether he wants to get back at you for having outsmarted him."

Frowning, she sighed. "He really doesn't like losing. That's for sure. But I also can't see him thinking I'm a big-enough fish to be bothered with. In a way, I think he saw the writing on the wall when he realized he couldn't get to the company through my sister's half."

"Do you think he would have let you run the company?"

"He certainly might have for the first little bit, that grooming bit you mentioned before, but then I would have had nothing but trouble with him," she murmured. "Even though he wouldn't have had any voting rights, I don't think it would have taken him very long to make some arrangement so I wasn't around or able to do it."

"I don't think so either," Rick agreed. "I think he would have cheerfully arranged an accident or something else that rendered you incapable."

She nodded. "So, another thanks to you for saving me from whatever that end would have been. It still sends chills down my spine."

Rick shook his head and tossed a whole pile of restaurant menus on the coffee table. "I found these in your kitchen."

"Right." She stared at the menus. "I do cook, you know?" They just stared at her, and she smiled. "Okay, so not very often, and I don't have any food here anyway, but I do know how."

"*Uh-huh.*" Rick chuckled. "Let's just say that I don't want to trust it tonight."

She wanted to take offense, but there was really no point, considering he was correct, so she smiled at him. "That's probably a smart idea. You guys pick whatever you want, and just make sure there's lots of it."

"Are you going to eat?" Rick asked her.

"I will, and I'll probably get up and refill my plate several times and eat some more," she muttered. "Even if it's only out of relief."

"You'll eat what you need to eat," Royce noted comfortably. "I trust in my body to eat what it needs."

"Yeah, we women have a tendency to eat our emotions," she pointed out, with half a laugh. "So that's not necessarily something I would care to trust, since right now my emotions are all over the place."

AFTER THE PIZZA had been consumed, she curled up on the couch, yawning.

Royce walked over, sat beside her, and asked, "Why aren't you going to bed?"

She stared up at him and shrugged. "It feels wrong in a way, you know?"

He stared at her, not sure he understood what could be wrong about it. "Are you afraid they'll get you here?" he asked, looking to Rick and back at her. "Because we're staying."

"I understand that. I just—"

His gaze narrowed. "Are we talking about tarot card stuff again?"

"No, I haven't checked my tarot cards." She pulled them from her pocket.

"Do you feel as if you have to check them?" It wasn't likely the best time to broach this but ... "I'm pretty sure that they are more of a comfort to have around you than a tool. The answers you're looking for come on a psychic level, not from the cards. The cards are more like props."

She frowned, staring down at the cards. "I can sense things much better if they're on me," she muttered. "So, I generally keep them with me all the time. The good news is"—she held them up—"they're not triggering anything."

"That's good, I guess. I'm still not exactly sure how that works," Rick admitted. "They send you signals?"

"Not so much. I feel or sense signals in a way, when something is going on, but I just don't know how to say it out loud or even how it works. I feel heat, vibration, et cetera. I haven't tried to explain it before. I generally don't talk about it at all. Most people aren't open to the concept."

"Got it," Rick murmured. "It doesn't really matter, as long as something is happening, and we're moving forward."

Heather felt he was obviously trying to assess her without making it look like it.

Royce added, "Go and get some rest. We'll let you know if there's any trouble—and your own cards will alert you too."

She hesitated, then nodded. "I need to. I'm tired."

"Of course you are," Royce agreed, walking with her to her bedroom and waiting until she got into bed. "Will you be okay?" he asked, unable to shake the worry in his tone as he stared at her. She'd gotten very, very quiet earlier. He didn't know if it was because of the memories of her sister, memories of how close Heather had come to not getting free, or what, but it worried him.

She smiled. "I'll be fine."

"I know you'll be fine," he replied. "That's not the problem."

"What then? You're worried about me?" she teased.

"Yeah, I am," he stated. "In case you hadn't noticed, I've

decided you're pretty special."

"That's nice to know," she muttered, with a smile. "On the other hand, when this is over, that's a different story."

"You don't feel it's over, do you?" He glommed onto that instantly.

She stared up at him surprise and then slowly sat up. "I guess that's the problem, isn't it? I don't feel it's over."

Hearing part of the discussion, Rick walked to the bedroom doorway. "What do you think isn't over?"

She frowned. "Whoever hired those gunmen who attacked Jonas," she began, looking intensely between the two of them, "that part isn't over. And the fact that Faheed is in town. … That means that's not over either."

They both nodded. "Good enough. We'll keep watch as we have been, just in case somebody decides they should come to visit."

She stared at him. "Of course Faheed would know where I live."

"Of course he does," they said in unison, with a joint nod. "We did expect that."

"I didn't even think of it," she muttered, staring at them.

Royce grinned. "You don't need to. That's our job. Now go get some sleep, and we'll be ready if he does come."

She thought about it and added, "You know that he won't come in person."

"That's okay too. Now get some rest, just in case … we have to run," Rick shared, with a wry smile.

She groaned. "That's not even funny anymore."

"Sure it is," Rick proclaimed. "Besides, it is a joke this time."

And, with that, they turned out the lights in her bedroom and walked away. Royce looked over at Rick as they headed into the kitchen, but Rick held up a finger. Royce nodded, sat back down again, and waited. It didn't take too long, about ten minutes, before slow, steady snores came from her bedroom.

"What do you think?" Royce asked.

"I don't know anything about those tarot cards," Rick admitted, "but they give me the heebie-jeebies."

Royce snorted. "You? With the kind of work you do, you've got the heebie-jeebies? That is hilarious."

"I know, but this is different and not something I have any experience with," he conceded, with a boyish grin. "Believe me that it caught me by surprise, and I'm not that happy about admitting it."

"Fair enough. So, what are we thinking about Faheed at this point?"

"Oh, I expect he's going after her company, probably wants some showdown, and that'll be interesting. I don't know whether he'll attempt to talk her into going back or will do something else entirely, like try to convince her that he'll break the wills and get access to the company that way."

Royce stared at him. "That wouldn't be good and not impossible if he's got a good lawyer—or a sneaky one."

"No, it wouldn't be, but, with a fortune at stake, it could be tied up in the courts for years."

He nodded at that. "Plus, you're not allowed to benefit from a will if you had something to do with the death of the deceased."

"Which means we need to get as much evidence as we can, just in case Faheed tries something like that. I know Heather believes it's locked down, and he can't touch the company, but—"

"Lots of things can be bought with enough money and

power, so that's a definite concern," he muttered.

"What are we thinking about her staff?"

"I think she's right in that this isn't over with, and I hate to say it, but we still don't know how anybody knew we were in town. Some information was flowing, and whoever passed that information along is in this up to their necks. I'll start doing some more research into her company and her employees and even her board, plus contact the father's lawyer who drew up her father's will."

"Do you think that's wise?" Rick asked. "Contacting the lawyer, I mean."

"Yes, because, if he's into anything illegal on this, he needs to know that we're on his ass, and it won't fly."

Rick thought about it for a moment and then nodded. "Yeah, you've got a point there. If he has any intention of getting out of this alive, he needs to ensure he's on the right side of this. Let's hope he's not some shady lawyer."

"And yet her father's will was set up a long time ago," Royce noted. "So, it should be something that will hold."

"What we don't know is if it's ever been challenged. And I have a hunch a challenge from a guy like Faheed would be quite a bit different than what these estate planning lawyers usually deal with. And, if Faheed's coming over here to challenge her personally, that's a totally different story too."

Royce nodded at that. It was late, and he wouldn't get through to too many people, but surprisingly the father's lawyer answered. When Royce quickly identified himself, the lawyer was astonished.

"Where is she?" he asked suspiciously.

"Sleeping at the moment, having just dealt with a rather unpleasant afternoon, including an attack by several armed people when we were in a meeting with the British government," he shared.

The lawyer sounded genuinely shocked.

"We suspect there will be some challenge to both Hannah's will and her father's will in an effort to bring Hannah's holdings under Faheed's control."

The lawyer paused. "That shouldn't be possible. It was intentionally set up to be ironclad to keep the business in the immediate family."

"Faheed has an awful lot of clout," Royce explained, "so I'm just giving you a heads-up. We also know that somebody on this side has been helping him."

After a moment of shocked silence, he burst out, "Surely you don't suspect me."

"We're hoping it's not you," Royce declared, his tone hard, "because we have very little tolerance for that kind of thing. This woman desperately needs somebody she can count on in her corner."

"I have known those sisters their whole lives," he protested stiffly. "I would never do anything to hurt them."

"No, but Faheed is very big on influence, including kidnapping family members or using other forms of blackmail to compel people to do what he wants, when he wants, and how he wants," Royce stated equally stiffly. "So, protestations aside, we are perfectly aware that everybody can be compromised."

"That may be, but, rest assured, I haven't been," the lawyer snapped. "I'll definitely be on my guard, and now, if you'll excuse me, I'll go reread those wills."

"Can you file any kind of injunctions or anything to stop him?"

"I'll take a look," he muttered. "It never occurred to me that there would be any kind of argument. It was a very well-known fact that Hannah's share went directly to Heather. And she signed over control to Heather ages ago."

"As far we've gathered, both of those points are things that Faheed either didn't know of or thought he could overcome right from the beginning."

"I don't think he knew beforehand because he didn't ask me for any of the paperwork until recently."

"And you gave it to him?" Royce cried out in shock.

"Of course. But only what he was legally allowed access to, which were copies of Hannah's will. As Hannah's husband, he has the standing, so I had no choice but to provide it." At that, the lawyer hesitated. "God, he really will try to challenge it, won't he?" His tone took on various shades of concern, worry, even fear.

"Sure he is, and this is his fourth dead wife," Royce added, his voice harsh. "And every time he's received one hell of an inheritance. Do everything you can to ensure this asshole doesn't get Heather's family business." And, with that, he ended the call.

Still steaming, he explained to Rick about Faheed contacting Hannah's lawyer, looking for documentation on Hannah's will and likely more, although the lawyer hadn't confirmed anything.

"It would be expected that a surviving spouse would be calling, requesting legal documents," Rick pointed out. "That is pretty standard for anybody."

"Maybe so, yet it just adds more fuel to the fire."

"Since Hannah was Faheed's fourth wife, I would say that Faheed's lawyer probably was on it early, even before they met and married, just to confirm the wealth of the family estate. Maybe they found out early on that the father's will was unbreakable. Since then, with all that money tempting him, Faheed and his lawyer have been probably working their way in, trying to get that stopped. Maybe they only needed Heather to go missing for a few days for some loophole to open to make that happen."

At that, Royce bolted to his feet. "Do you think that's why he kidnapped her?" He quickly phoned the lawyer back. "Is there anything in there about if one of the owners, operators, is not seen or heard from in however long, it brings up something about mental competency?"

"Of course," the lawyer replied, "although I don't know about going missing for a short while. I think that's quite a bit longer than however long Heather was missing or at least out of commission. Everybody at the company was well aware that her sister had passed away."

"Was there ever any suggestion that Heather might have taken her own life out of grief?"

The lawyer sucked in his breath. "God, I hope not. You've got me absolutely paranoid now."

"So you should be because Faheed's already in England, and you can bet that whatever the hell's happening, he'll try it soon." And, with that, Royce disconnected again.

"This is game time."

CHAPTER 14

W HEN HEATHER WOKE up, she stretched out, aware she was in her own bed, and gave a happy sigh. Freedom had never felt so good. Realizing that the men were in her apartment somewhere, possibly waiting for her, she rolled out of bed, dressed quickly in clean clothes, then practically danced her way out to the kitchen, singing, "Good morning."

When she didn't get a terribly bright response in return, she stared at them in worry. "What happened?"

Royce looked up at her and sighed. "Good morning, sunshine. Glad you had a good night's sleep. I would say that, so far, everything's fine, and we're still working on it."

"Then why does it sound as if what you're working on isn't exactly going well?"

"It's not going badly either. There was a clause in your father's will that, if you were out of commission, deemed incompetent, or a few other things like that," he muttered, "then …"

She shook her head, but the look on his face had her sagging onto a nearby chair. "I understood that it was unbreakable," she whispered.

"It very well may be, yet a few *management of the business* loopholes are in there that make it a little different," he reminded her. "Even with your controlling interest, if you are deemed incapable of making these kinds of decisions to run the company, then someone competent can step in."

She swallowed and nodded. "That makes sense in a way. … I don't like it, but there was something about that in Father's will, yes."

"And that's what we're working on right now, under the premise that Faheed hoped to keep you either grieving or in such a state that you would be unable to return to work. Then he could step in as the likely candidate for management of the company. Eventually, with a little bit of time and help, he could set the stage so you didn't come back. Particularly with the drug issue."

She swallowed, thinking about how easily Faheed could have made that happen. "It's pretty depressing to think that somebody would have so little care for who you are and for everything you've done that they want to take it all away from you."

Royce just nodded, not saying anything, and waited.

"I need to contact my lawyer right away."

"We did last night." She blinked at Royce, and he shrugged. "Sorry, there was no time. He needed the heads-up that there could be some injunctions or challenges happening, even a challenge to the wills."

"*Great*," she muttered. "That is not the news I wanted this morning."

"Of course not," he agreed, "but, if we could prove that Faheed had anything to do with your sister's death, then it's also quite possible that he couldn't gain from her will after what he's done."

"Is that even possible to prove?" she asked. "There's no body. There's no nothing."

"I know. I know that Jonas is going back through the

letters that she sent, looking for anything that might help in this instance as well because he wants to ensure Faheed does time for her murder."

"And all the other women," Heather noted.

"Yes, and anybody else who might have been caught up in the same nasty net."

"I'm a little afraid that will be something Saheed gets thrown into, instead of Faheed paying the price that he owes."

"Let's work on one thing at a time," Royce noted. "It's too easy to focus on the details and to lose sight of the whole forest."

"I'm not losing my company," she declared passionately, feeling her cards heat up. Was it an omen, or were they just reacting to her emotions? Attached messaging or detached messaging? One thing she hadn't considered was her cards' ability to be a barometer for her energy. She couldn't consider it right now either.

Royce asked her, "What if they feel you haven't been there to hold it up?"

"But who would say that?" she asked.

"I don't know," he replied. Just then his phone rang, and it was the lawyer. Royce put it on Speakerphone and sat down beside Heather.

"I've just received a filing from Faheed's lawyer, saying that Heather's been found incapable of handling the business," he began briskly.

"That would be one of the expected avenues, seeing how he kept her drugged without her knowledge during that time."

"Apparently he also has employee depositions saying that Heather showed signs that she was incapable prior to this last visit with her sister, giving cause for concern. Now, of course, they're saying that Heather's totally incapable."

"Send me copies immediately," Royce snapped. "Talk to her because she's here right now and listening, as I put this call on Speakerphone."

"Really?" he asked hopefully, and then he hesitated. "How does she sound?"

She snatched the phone from Royce's hand. "Pissed off," she snapped. "My sister's been murdered. I was a prisoner, escaped, then I arrive in England and was held at gunpoint, all because some asshole is trying to steal the family company."

"That sounds …"

"Horrible is what it is. If you let this happen, it will be something that you'll take to your grave, as being a travesty against my family on your watch, and that's only presuming that I can't get at you first," she snapped once more.

"Hey, hey, hey," he said, trying to calm her down. "All I'm telling you is what came through this morning."

"Now tell me how the hell I'm supposed to fight that."

"If you hadn't taken off in the middle of the night— which is what they're saying because you were suddenly afraid of your life with totally no basis, and no way for anybody to prove your own competency—it wouldn't have looked so bad, according to Faheed."

"I took off because he was my captor," she yelled. "How is that even something I have to argue?"

He hesitated before speaking. "Look. I'll do what I can. If you have any pull with any judges or anybody who can help with this, you need to pull all those strings."

She ended the call, and, using the number that Jonas had sent her, she was put right through to him. "Anything you want from me, you can have, but you make sure that bastard doesn't get my goddamn company."

Jonas, his voice shocked, asked, "Whoa, whoa, whoa, what are you talking about?"

She put it on Speakerphone and motioned at the men to explain to Jonas, while she paced, furious at the sudden turn of events. She heard them talking about Faheed making his move to upset the applecart with the will and to use her *lack of mental capacity* in support of his case for taking over her family's business.

"That's an interesting move," Jonas muttered. "It also means that they don't know anything about Heather and the UK government. I've got lines to judges, and we can manage for now. So tell Heather to calm down. I'll get back to you." He disconnected.

At that, she looked over at them. "Do you think he has enough pull with the judges?"

"This is MI6," Rick reminded her, a wry tone in his voice. "If anybody has any pull, it's him."

She sank into a kitchen chair again. "This is what Faheed was trying to do the whole time, wasn't it?"

"And the longer you stayed, the more you made it all work to his advantage," Rick stated in a hard tone. "Good thing we got you out when we did."

She stared at him.

"I'm not making light of this," Royce began. "I'm also fully aware that people are doing the best they can right now to stop Faheed. However, it's also up to us to do our best too. Can you think of anything you can utilize against him?"

"I don't know," she wailed. "What am I supposed to have?"

"Your sister thought she was being recorded, and thus,

all discussions were being forwarded to him. Do you think he did the same thing to you?"

"Oh my God, if he did, that's how he knew where we were and our plans."

Royce nodded.

"So, MI6 didn't have a leak. It was me?" She reached up to the beautiful diamond hairpin she had gotten from her sister and removed it from her hair. "Jesus. This was my sister's, and Faheed gave it to me. No, wait …" Confused she studied it carefully. "No, it wasn't this one. It's close but slightly different. At least I think so. We were always swapping out hair clips." When the guys frowned at her, she shrugged. "I know she had a favorite couple that Faheed had given her and she gave one to me, but they were similar so we sometimes confused them. Faheed gave it to me after my sister's death though."

"When was this?" Royce asked, getting back on track.

She pursed her lips. "Around the same time as she passed away. I don't remember exactly. It wasn't exactly a priority for me back then."

"How early before?" Rick asked, hopping up and walking over to look at it more closely.

"Maybe a couple days before she died."

"Interesting." He took it, looked over at Royce, and nodded. "This could have a bugging device in it." He held it away from them, as if that distance would not record anything. Then he stepped farther away as he kept poking the top of it, as if that would disarm it somehow. He looked over at Royce and put his finger to his lips, then shoved it in his pocket, as Royce led her back to her bedroom and shut the door.

"Oh my God," she cried out, "it was me the whole time.

I was the one leading them to us." She stared up at him in shock. She'd been duped in so many ways. It both disgusted and terrified her. If she'd stayed, what else would Faheed have done?

Royce winced. "You didn't know."

"No, of course not," she muttered. "That's what happened to my sister too, isn't it?" She began to get furious all over again.

Royce suggested, "I'm pretty sure Hannah finally realized that she was in way too deep and that there wouldn't be any getting out for her, so she decided this was the way to go."

"Jesus," Heather muttered, staring blindly in the distance as the implications hit her. How had she not known? Then how would she have? It's not as if she'd asked the cards about a possibility so unbelievable to her at the time—even now. Plus, she had to keep reminding herself that she'd been drugged. She still felt the brain fog effects at times. "That is not what I want to believe."

"Yet this is the evidence we have in front of us," Royce stated, his tone turning harsh. "Now is not the time to stick your head in the sand. Use your cards, your intuition, that's fine, but stay here in the now, in the present. Focus."

She blinked, let out a deep breath, and nodded. "You're right." Her voice strengthened with conviction, sensing her cards in a supportive vibration, making her once again wonder if they were reading her energy rather than offering insight. Frowning at the thought, she glared at him. "Faheed won't get my company."

"And this gives us good ammunition."

"Not really," she warned. "He'll just say that I put it there myself. And likely use things like the Ouija board and my tarot cards as ammunition for my supposed growing mental instability."

"He probably will, but that doesn't mean he'll have any pull with it," Royce replied. "Remember that you're not alone anymore."

She blinked several times and then nodded. "I'm really glad to hear that," she whispered, "because it sure feels as if I'm very alone right now."

He walked over to her, pulled her into his arms, and just held her. She wrapped her arms around him tightly and squeezed hard. Something was so very substantial and reassuring about him. And he was offering the support and comfort she needed. A lot could be said about that.

She tilted her head back, tears in her eyes. "I really, really can't lose my family business on top of losing my sister too. It's all I have left. It's my family legacy. I will let them all down if I lose it."

He nodded. "I understand and suggest we go into the office today and see if anybody's surprised to see you there … and maybe not in a good way."

She stared at him and winced. "You still think somebody in the office was working against me?"

"I'm sure there is at least one," he told her, "and so are you. Especially if someone in the company is supporting Faheed's assertions of your incompetence to run the company."

She nodded. "I don't want to believe it, but I'm not sure how I can't now."

"And that's the problem. Once you start with this kind of deception, you instinctively know who it is, don't you?"

"I don't want it to be who's on my mind," she said, "but it's the most logical answer."

"Who is that?" he asked, and she winced. "I know that you want to wait until you know for sure," he added, "but we can't afford to take that chance now or to waste that time either."

She shrugged. "I have two choices that would be the worst and/or best cases in this instance," she began. "Dan's one of them, but so is Jenny."

"Who the hell is Jenny?" he asked. "She's not on our list."

"No, I was thinking of her when I went to sleep last night. She was in a relationship with Dan, and things blew up. That was one of the times where I told Dan to get his act together and to stop causing trouble. In that discussion, we more or less decided his relationship with Jenny was impacting his decision-making in a negative way. He broke up with her shortly afterward, and she quit almost immediately."

"Do you really think she loved him that much to retaliate over a broken relationship?"

"No, I think she hates me that much," Heather clarified. "I would have let her go soon anyway, but I was trying to put some distance between the time period when Dan broke up with her and when I fired her. Dan's drinking and gambling had become a huge issue that Jenny was contributing to, and I was just trying to find a way to get him back on track, then move her on, without upsetting everything at work," she muttered. "You know how that goes."

"You have to find the balance I suppose, or it doesn't make for being a good CEO," he reminded her.

"Nope, and don't worry. That was brought home to me a couple times," she muttered.

"By board members?"

"Sure, you're only as good as your last dividend, it

seems," she snapped.

He laughed. "True, so probably people on that board are in favor of getting rid of you too, I presume."

"I don't know." She frowned. "I wouldn't have thought so. I've always done well by them, but, people being people, maybe they thought it would be something of a boon to their bottom line if Faheed took over," she muttered. "I just don't know."

"I think it's time we go find out."

She nodded. "First I'll call an emergency board meeting for today. Then I'll change clothes. But you're right. Time to get to the bottom of this." At the doorway, she stopped and looked back at him. "When this is over, what are you doing?"

"I don't know," he replied, a slow smile taking over his face. "You got any ideas?"

"Oh, I've got ideas," she quipped, with a laugh. "I was thinking it might be nice to spend some time away from all this nightmare—alone together."

"I'm right there with you," he agreed, with a nod. "I have the time, since I don't currently have a full-time job anyway." He smirked at that, and her eyebrows raised. "It's contract work," he explained.

"Ah, so you could take off a few days and maybe stick around?"

"That is a really good idea," he teased. "But, right now, get ready for a showdown."

WALKING INTO THE corporate offices about an hour later proved to be a revelation for Royce. Surely Rick would have agreed as well, but he was off getting together a backup team.

At the sight of Heather, several employees came running, giving her hugs and condolences on the loss of her sister. Others were more reserved in their approach but appeared to be quite sincere in offering their sympathies for the situation Heather found herself in, and they didn't even know the half of it.

She smiled with grace, spoke to everyone on a first-name basis, which was quite a feat in Royce's mind, considering the number of people they had seen. By the time they made it up to her office, she had her CEO demeanor firmly in place, which he found fascinating to watch. She also released the stranglehold on her cards she kept in her blazer pocket. They were a security for her, but here? Not so much needed here. She was in her element.

He asked, "Where to first?"

"The meeting with the board of directors. They should be arriving within the next thirty minutes. I have a controlling interest, plus my sister also had her one-third interest, and that is under my control as well."

"Right, so Faheed really needed to get rid of your sister first and then deal with you."

"Looks like it," she snapped, "but that is something he will not do."

He smiled as she walked into her offices, where her administrative assistant came running. She threw her arms around Heather and burst into tears. The two women just hung on for a long time. "Why didn't you tell me? I would have come to help. You know that."

"I do know that," she replied, "but it's been kind of crazy."

The other woman just nodded and wiped away her tears.

It was obvious that they were close, and Royce just hoped that the trust Heather had for this woman wasn't something that would come back to bite her.

As they walked along the corridor, heading to Heather's big corner CEO office, another man flew out to see her, with shock on his face as he cried out, "Heather?"

"Hey, Dan," she replied, bracing to see him. She read his facial expression, then sighed. "It was you, wasn't it?"

He frowned at her, then looked around nervously. "What are you talking about?"

"Oh, I think you know," she stated. "I just don't understand if you realize the havoc that you've brought on through all this."

"What are you talking about?" he cried out, wringing his hands. "I really don't know what you're saying."

"You'll have an awful lot more time to think about it as we go forward. I'm sure of it."

He just blinked.

"Yeah, I know that you were working with Faheed, so that he could take over my company," she declared. "I still find that hard to believe, particularly after everything I've done to help you." As she continued speaking, her voice gained in volume. "Did you also have a hand in sending two armed men to kidnap me as I landed on UK soil?" He blanched at that question, and she nodded. "And, for all my help given to you, personally and professionally, that is how you repay me?"

He stared at her, his face working. Meanwhile, around them, the nearby employees gathered together and froze.

She gazed around at the people she'd worked with for years. Raising her voice, yet calm and cold, she announced, "For those of you who don't know, the information about my kidnapping was withheld in order to secure my release. My sister's husband, Faheed, decided that he should own my company, not realizing that, upon my sister's death, he would not get her shares." She stopped speaking, slowly making eye contact with her staff, one by one.

"I'm not exactly sure who all is behind his takeover bid and who all here are assisting Faheed and Dan, but multiple investigations on all levels are underway," she shared. "So, anybody involved in this will be discovered. Believe me that MI6 will find you," she snapped, her gaze hard.

"I've been to hell and back, and I've also had to deal with my sister's death, which I haven't yet had a chance to grieve," she explained, her voice coming out even stronger, not bitter, but the power in her tone was quite amazing.

Royce felt only pride and admiration.

She continued. "I will not tolerate this kind of blackmail to prevail within my company ever again. I do the best I can for everybody in this company, and, if you are not happy with me at the helm, take your personal things and get the hell out of here today. If you are staying, be prepared for a full-on investigation into your personal and private lives, should it be determined that you have had anything to do with my ongoing nightmare.

"From now on there will be enhanced security systems in place, with increased checks and balances, and sadly it will no longer be the same laid-back family work environment we've all enjoyed. Because these few people who have betrayed me have ruined it all. So, I have no choice but to make changes. I was kidnapped, and my sister was murdered, all so her greedy husband could get his hands on this company, my family's company, that we have worked for generations to build and maintain," she described bitterly.

"I simply will not tolerate anyone who participates in efforts to take my family business from me. I'll be in my office, waiting to meet with my board members. Whoever is leaving, go now. Will it stop the investigations into your lives? Hell no. But anyone leaving today is deemed as giving me your immediate verbal resignations, and you won't be part of the company going forward. I would appreciate that much honesty. You have twenty minutes to make your decision and to depart. Your parking access and business access will be shut down ten minutes thereafter. Don't expect any pay beyond twenty minutes from now.

As for Dan here, he's going nowhere but to jail. The questions now are: who is going with him and who is walking out? Don't doubt what I say. I won't leave a rock unturned until I get to the bottom of this nightmare. So leave now or stay. Either way expect an investigation and related charges. It will still be the same company to our customers, but, for employees, once trust is broken, it can never be repaired. New expectations must be set and reached. New rules that are fair and reasonable will be set and maintained. But this level of betrayal? ... Never again."

And, with that, she turned and stepped into her own private office and slammed the door.

Royce stayed behind to watch the shock on everybody's faces, as they tried to assimilate what had just happened.

True to form, Dan cried out, "See what I mean? She's lost it."

Royce took a step forward. "Considering you'll spend the next twenty years in prison for fraud, embezzlement, attempted murder, and God-only-knows how many other charges, you might want to control your mouth." His flinty gaze bounced off the confused sea of faces gathered around.

"Everybody who has been listening to the lies coming out of Dan's mouth should remember one thing. This is a man who lied, who stole from the company, who betrayed the person who has only tried to help him turn his life around. Then Dan accepted a bribe from Faheed, who then kidnapped Heather and drugged her. Then Dan arranged the attempt to kidnap her again making sure she'd never see daylight again. Once she escaped Faheed's prison, she was greeted within the hour of her landing in London with two armed men, wishing to kidnap her once again," he told them all, his voice hard.

"I am part of the special team who rescued her, but sadly her sister died before anybody even knew what was going on. Hannah was already fighting for her life before this ever blew up to the extent that people knew about it. So, anybody else here, who is planning to listen to anything that comes out of Dan's mouth, or who has taken actions based on anything Dan suggested, we will find you, and we will take the appropriate actions." The threat in his words was obvious.

Gasps and cries erupted.

He understood. For many this was the first they were hearing this story. His gaze moved from one to the other, looking for guilt, looking for anything that prodded his instincts. Several people had turned to look toward Heather's office. He checked their energy from where he stood. Beside him, everybody in the office froze as his gaze went from one to the next.

"If you happen to be part of the team Heather trusts and loves and you haven't betrayed her," he added, "you will be safe, but God help you if we find out later that you lied. As Heather told you just now, you're either loyal to this team, and you will give your all for it, or you need to pack up your bags and get the hell out while you can." He looked at his watch and announced, "You only have fifteen minutes left to make that choice, and then whoever's out of here is out of here permanently, and whoever is left behind had better have absolutely nothing to hide and better be prepared to go forward to assist Heather and MI6 in any way. Because a hell of a shakedown is coming."

"What if we stay, and she loses?" came a nervous question from the back.

"You mean, loses the court case that you guys seem to already think is happening?"

"Faheed was here this morning."

Royce looked over at the source of the words and barked, "Come on up, and tell me what you know."

A young man stepped forward. His energy was nervous but clean. He wasn't involved, yet he felt guilt.

Curious, Royce asked, "Who are you?"

"My name is Evan. I work in the brewery." He shifted from foot to foot and scratched his nose. "Faheed was there this morning."

"You let him in?"

He swallowed. "Yes, we did because, as far as we knew, he was part of the company now. Dan told us so." Evan pointed to him for emphasis.

Dan remained silent.

Royce shook his head. "Faheed's not part of Heather's company, never has been and never will be. And just in case that point got missed here, Faheed is also suspected of having murdered Hannah. And Faheed has been holding Heather prisoner against her will, drugging her, since her sister's death."

At that absolute point-blank statement, there was shock

all around, and tears from several of the women.

Royce nodded. "Should any of you think I'm here alone, you're wrong, and a whole SCO19, which is the US SWAT team equivalent over here, should arrive any minute."

At that, Dan made a squeak and tried to bolt for the exit.

Royce watched as Dan raced toward the nearest exit door. Just as he opened the door, Royce pulled the energy from all the employees, creating an invisible web, and watched as Dan slammed into it. For anyone watching, it seemed he stopped in shock at something on the other side of the door.

And there was something on the other side.

Rick.

The two men exchanged glances. And, for the first time, Royce heard Terk laughing inside his head. *Great timing and cool energy trick. Welcome to the team.* And, with that, Terk was gone from Royce's mind. Grinning at the possibilities opening up in his future and surprised at the excitement he couldn't have imagined prior to this, Royce released Dan into Rick's care, who handed him off to the armed government man behind him, saying, "The only place you're going to is jail, Dan. Attempted murder and kidnapping charges are just the start of it. Not to mention you were behind the men who kidnapped an MI6 man!"

Royce nodded. "Dan's one of the worst. He also just tried to turn everybody against Heather."

"No, I didn't. No I didn't," Dan squeaked out.

Another woman stepped forward. "Yes, you did, you lousy little liar. How could you do that to Heather or to Hannah? How could you do that to either of them?" Tears erupted from her eyes. She brushed them back impatiently.

"Hell, how could you do that to any of us?"

He started to blubber. "It's the gambling debts. I've got a problem and—"

Another person in the crowd added, "And yet Heather bailed you out time and time again. She gave you every opportunity to get help and to become a decent human being, but what do you do? You sold her out."

Before long a whole litany of charges were launched against Dan. When he was finally released to be transported, Royce turned to the rest of them. "What Heather needs right now is to know that somebody is in her corner, that each of you haven't tried to sell her out or contrived to kill her and her sister."

The place erupted as each person tried to talk over the other.

Royce held up a hand to regain control of the conversation. "It will be a while before Heather learns to trust at the same level that she did before. She's also grieving the loss of a sister, whom she dearly loved. … That won't be an easy process, nor should it be, but mark my words, this company will never be in Faheed's hands," Royce added in a firm tone.

"But he was already down there at the brewery," one of the thirty-odd people in front of them pointed out.

"Yes, I hope Faheed is still there. That should be interesting."

Just then the double doors opened, and, sure enough, Faheed strode in, barking out orders to people who were scurrying along beside him.

He stopped when he got in front of Rick and Royce, blocking his way. "Now who are you?" he snapped with such arrogance, his hands on his hips. "Better yet, what are you doing in my company?"

CHAPTER 15

THE INNER OFFICE door flung open. and Heather strode out in a controlled fury, struggling to command her emotions as she faced her nemesis. "It's not your company." She smacked him hard across the face. "Not only is it *not* your company, you murderous little bastard," she proclaimed, "but you killed my sister, and believe me that my lawyers will be all over you for this."

"Now you see," Faheed announced to the entourage behind him, his hand cupping his injured cheek, yet his eyes glinted with fury. "See what I mean? She's obviously overwrought."

"Yeah, I'll *overwrought* you," she warned.

Rick stepped forward. "We've already been discussing the lovely little mess you've got going on here with the people who betrayed her from within her own company, like Dan," he told Faheed. "Despite your best efforts, you can't do anything to get this company away from her."

"A good share of it belonged to my dearly departed wife," Faheed declared, "and I inherit everything that was hers. That's how the law works."

"Except in this case," Heather snapped. "I don't think you'll bypass the law when it comes to my company."

"Your company? You're a woman," he said, with a sneer. "You cannot own such a prize and no way can you run it."

"I absolutely can, and I have for many years now." She gave him a detached smile. "I obviously am very much still in control."

Faheed glared at her. "You are not a normal woman. You should be at home, tending to a husband and his family. Don't worry about business matters. The company is now mine. I've already taken care of the paperwork."

She stared at him, struggling to hide her fear. What was he up too? Her cards started to agitate. She took a deep breath, glancing at Royce, who studied Faheed as if seeing a new bug. Something was off. Something was seriously wrong, but what? She turned to look around at as many people in the room as she could.

"If a *normal woman* means bending down for your bloody pleasure at your will," she replied, "you're damn right. I'm not that. Neither are you a normal man. You're a tyrant, a bully, and a murderer." She was spitting fire, but her tone was calm and controlled, ... with a storm raging underneath it all. "Believe me when I say this. I am cooperating fully with MI6 on all counts."

Anger flashed on his face, as Faheed clearly didn't comprehend such resistance. "May I remind you that I enjoy diplomatic immunity?"

"Except for one thing," Jonas declared, as he strode in behind Faheed, with another whole team of SCO19 behind him.

"What is that?" Faheed roared. "And who are you?"

"MI6," Jonas replied, with a big smile.

At that, Faheed made a single motion to one of his own men beside him, as if to have Jonas removed from his presence, but Faheed wasn't prepared for Jonas holding up his phone.

"Faheed, I have your Prime Minister on the phone right now," Jonas shared to all gathered here. Then he spoke into the phone, "Go ahead with your message, sir."

And to everybody's amusement, the Prime Minister clearly stated, "Faheed, you are relieved of your duty as diplomat. You will not use diplomatic immunity to run amok in this world and certainly not while representing our country. You, your brother, and your entourage, will all report back here, if the British government sees fit to release you. At that time, we will talk about what happened with the various other incidents and complaints against you locally," he noted, the fury in his tone clearly most evident. "I can't even begin to tell you how much I want to talk to you, and, if you weren't in the UK, soon to be under lock and key, I would be coming over there to deal with you myself." Then came a *click*, and the Prime Minister of Iran ended the call.

Jonas stared at Faheed. "You do not have diplomatic immunity any longer, so you do not have any way of getting out of this right now," he explained, as he ordered them all to be taken away.

Faheed cried out, "No, wait." He turned to face Heather. "Your sister was nothing but a bitch."

She strode up to Faheed, and he reared back. "What's the matter?" she asked in a mocking tone. "Are you afraid this *woman* won't cower before you? Are you afraid this *woman* will strike you first? Are you afraid this *woman* will have something to do with putting you and your brother away for life? I sure hope so. ... I hope I'm responsible for making sure that, when somebody says jump in jail, it's *you* they make do their bidding, and you will no longer sit there in all your false finery, acting as if the world is your oyster." The storm within her raged on. "You deserve to be punished for what you did to my sister."

"Your sister was nothing, just a pampered porcelain doll."

"And that's what you wanted, wasn't it?" she asked. "That's how you wanted her, nothing but a completely acquiescent doll, which is why you kept her drugged without her knowledge. You are nothing but an arrogant asshole, Faheed, and you will not get away with this."

"I already did," he declared.

"No, you didn't. You—" She stopped and frowned at him. "That's why you had Dan send those armed men after us, wasn't it?"

He stared at her in surprise.

"You were looking for the listening devices."

For the first time, fear crossed his face. She crowed. "That's what was wrong with it," she exclaimed, as she turned to Rick. "That wasn't the hair clip that Hannah gave me some two days before she died. That's why I couldn't figure out why I had that one. Remember, Rick? Yet the hair clip I have was the one Saheed gave me as a memento. You need to check what's on that one." She faced Faheed with a sneer. "Oh, Faheed, you should communicate better with your brother. And isn't that a lovely little twist, Faheed? All those bugs that you kept on my poor sister, and she figured it out, and now it'll be *Hannah* who puts you away after all," she stated in delight. "That is Hannah claiming her own justice." And Heather started to laugh.

Rick pulled the hair clip from his pocket, where he had shoved it earlier. He asked for permission to use one of the nearby computers. Heather nodded and pointed to the closest one. Once he plugged in the hidden USB connector within the hair clip, he started playing the recordings on it.

Soon a conversation between her sister and Faheed filled the air.

Hannah's voice was clear as she cried out, "Why are you doing this to me?"

"I'm not doing anything to you. You're obviously overwrought," he stated in a calm, determined tone. "Besides, it's time, and I've had enough of this."

"Then just let me go," she whispered, tears choking her voice. "Let me go, Faheed."

"No," he snapped. "I will have that company for all my pain. Now drink this, dammit."

Then there were sounds of a struggle, and Hannah screamed. Thereafter her voice was muffled, and she was choking, as he repeatedly told her to swallow, as if pouring something down her throat.

Heather, the shock and horror evident on her face, had her hand across her mouth, holding back her cries, as she listened to her sister struggle and die on the recording device. She stared at Faheed, his face going gray as he listened to his own words and actions on the recording.

Next, they all heard a scuffle, and then Faheed must have pulled out his cell and made a call. He spoke again. "Dammit, Saheed, where were you? You should have helped me earlier. Now we have to fix this."

"If you would have let me do it my way," Saheed replied, "she would have been taken care of already, the same as the others."

"We can't be killing them all the same way," Faheed snapped. "At some point in time, someone'll start suspecting."

"Look at who you are. No one would dare come after you." A note of patronizing admiration filled Saheed's tone.

"You, my brother, are untouchable."

"Hardly," he muttered.

At that, the recording ended. The room went silent for a moment, then Faheed turned to look at his brother, clearly livid. "How did she get that recording, Saheed?"

Saheed stared back at him and shook his head. "I have no idea. The bitch probably stole it."

"You know exactly how I got it, Saheed," Heather declared. "You gave the hairpin to me. You asked if I wanted something to remember my sister by, *one last piece*, you said. The other hairpin I have, she gave me herself," she pointed out. "It will be interesting to see what is on that one. So, Saheed, did you not know that your brother was bugging Hannah with these hair clips? Did you just bug her clothes or her room or her purses? Or … maybe you've simply grown weary of doing your brother's bidding and arranged for him to take the fall for her death?" She laughed when she saw his face reveal his guilt, for any or all of it. "Not because you were going down with him, but so you could take his place. But, as we all just heard, that won't be happening either."

"I didn't kill her," Saheed declared.

"No, but you just admitted to killing the others."

He stared at the hair clip in fury. "It was supposed to stop. The device was supposed to stop before I entered the room."

"It didn't stop, and it caught absolutely everything we needed to convict you both," she stated triumphantly. Looking at Jonas, she asked, "May I?"

He responded with a nod.

Heather figured Jonas was unsure if he could stop her from whatever she had in mind anyway. She took a deep cleansing breath. "Faheed, former diplomat, you are under arrest for the murder of my sister. And you, Saheed, who terrorized my sister every day of her life, you are under arrest as well as an accomplice to Hannah's murder. I can only hope you will be put away for the murder of Faheed's other wives too."

CHAPTER 16

B Y THE TIME Royce led Heather back to her apartment, it was very late, and she was exhausted. It had been a hectic day—filled with boardroom meetings, interviews with local police, MI6, SCO19, plus calls with courts, judges, attorneys, as well as face-to-face discussions with company employees, and all kinds of other unpleasant dealings. At the end of it, Heather was free and clear. She was unquestionably back in control, happy to find that she had never lost control, and the attempt to wrestle it away from her had been terminated before it went entirely too far.

As she opened the door to her apartment, she walked in and muttered, "I'm going straight to bed."

"Good," Royce said, closing the door behind them.

She turned to him and asked, "Are you okay to stay the night?" He raised his eyebrow and smiled, and she sighed. "I know. We were talking about it, but …"

He nodded. "Go. Get some sleep."

She nodded gratefully in return, then walked into her room and closed the door, and he could almost see her collapse mentally. She was done in, but she'd represented herself well today. Her family would be proud to know that she stood up for everything important for the family business as well. Royce respected Heather so much, as she had fought well for her company and for her sister, all the time she was away as well as today.

As for Faheed, he was in trouble all over the place. Turns out several other governments wanted him as well, especially now that he was in custody. Royce was pretty sure the British government wouldn't let Faheed go anytime soon. He had a lot to answer for.

Royce was glad that Hannah's murder had been solved and the murderer caught with the best kind of evidence, Faheed's own words used against him. It was over and done, and Royce, for one, couldn't be happier. As he sat again on the same couch he had been on before, Heather opened her bedroom door and walked to him in a nightie. "Do you want to shower?"

He nodded. "I would love a shower."

"Good," she said, as she handed over towels to him. She still had her tarot cards in her hand.

"What's with those now?" he asked, tucking the towels under one arm.

She smiled. "I had them the whole time in my office," she shared, "trying to do some readings without everybody around. Believe me that they told me perfectly well who I could count on and who I could not."

"I'm glad to hear that," he said. "What do they say about me?"

She laughed. "Pull a card."

Reaching forward, he selected a single card from the middle of the deck. Flipping it over, he rested it on top.

She held it out and asked, "What do you think?"

And there in front of him was the card with a picture of two people entwined. He stared at it and looked up at her, one eyebrow cocked.

She nodded and whispered, "Lovers."

"Aha."

"The cards tend to be absolutely right-on with me—not with everybody, but, for me, they're a second skin."

"Interesting," he murmured. "Pretty sure Terk would want to know about those."

"Pretty sure Terk would say it has nothing to do with the cards and everything to do with my utilizing them as a tool."

He laughed. "I can see him saying that. You could always come and spend some time with me at Terk's place and get to know the rest of the gang."

"Will you go to work for them?"

"It's been discussed," he noted. "I'm not too sure what I'll do just yet."

"If you don't have a home at Terk's place, I can hardly come, can I? Besides, I need to be here," she pointed out, "particularly after everything that happened today."

"I know, and I didn't say I would live there at Terk's place. I'm not sure I'm up for that many babies."

"Rick was telling me about that," she said, her eyes widening. "That's a lot for anybody."

"It is, yet … they're all pretty happy."

"You could always stay in London and work for them as needed, whenever they had anything going on."

"And that's possible," he agreed, with a nod. "Not too sure what I'll do yet. I know Jonas was nudging around me as well, talking about business and optional work," he said, with a laugh.

"What about all the energy stuff that you guys do for Terk?"

"It's not as if Terk's place is very far away," he stated. "So, if I needed to commute between here and there, it would be fine." He looked over at her. "Would the traveling bother you, as that's part of Terk's ops?"

"No," she replied. "Although I do want you here more than gone away somewhere."

He laughed. "How about if you were traveling with me?"

"That's a different story." She smiled. "I have a lot to process over the next little while."

"You do, and that's fine with me. You have lots of time to process things. I will always support you in whatever you do, from running your family business to starting a new venture," he vowed, as he headed into the guest bathroom. "I'll go get that shower."

He stepped out soon afterward, a towel wrapped around his hips, wishing he knew where his duffel bag with his clothes in it had gone.

She looked over at him, and a slow smile split her face. "Now, that's a lovely way to walk into a lady's apartment."

He sighed. "I seem to have lost track of my clothes."

"What happened to your bag?"

"I'm not sure, I thought it was still here."

"Maybe Rick took it when you guys went into town today."

"Probably, since I was headed into the corporate world with you and Rick was off to gather the big guns. Still, I don't need clothes to sleep in. I'll roust up a new outfit tomorrow."

"Good idea," she said, chuckling. "Now, can we get some sleep? I'm so tired." Then she yawned yet again.

"You should have been in bed a long time ago," he noted. "You didn't need to wait up for me."

"I wanted to," she shared. "Just in case you had any doubts about where you're sleeping, it's in here with me."

And, with that, she led the way to her bedroom and her bed.

Royce hesitated in the doorway.

"Don't even think about it," she warned in that CEO tone she'd been using all day. "Yes, I know exactly what I'm talking about, and, yes, I know exactly what I want to do. I'm just too tired to do it right now," she added, her tone turning cross. "So, either get into bed or don't, but I'll talk to you in the morning." And, with that, she rolled over and closed her eyes.

A bark of laughter burst from Royce, as he walked over to her bed. "With an invitation like that, how could I ever refuse?"

She chuckled. "You can't, but I didn't expect you to anyway," she murmured.

As the mattress sank beneath his weight, she rolled toward him. Reaching out, he pulled her into his arms. "Now that is where you belong."

She smiled. "Maybe, at least for tonight." Then she slowly fell into a deep sleep.

He followed not too long afterward, waking several times, assessing intuitively where they were and how they were doing. Not registering any danger, he fell back asleep over and over again. By the time morning dawned, he felt as if he'd gotten enough sleep to survive another day. He opened his eyes to find her staring down at him. When he reared back, she chuckled.

"I brought you coffee and crawled back into bed to wait for you to wake up."

"Coffee?" he repeated. "In bed?"

"Yes, I figured it was my turn to wait on you."

"No such thing as turns in a relationship. We both wait on each other. We both try to make the day easier for the other one," he stated. "You've been in tough straits recently."

"I have been, but I'm getting back on my feet, so no need for you to look after me now."

"What if I want to?" he asked, raising an eyebrow.

"That's a different story," she whispered, giving him a cheeky grin. "I more than happily accept all the tender loving care coming my way. I just didn't want you to feel as if you have to look after me because I wasn't capable. For a while I wasn't," she acknowledged, "but thankfully I'm doing much better now."

"Good," he said, as he shifted to sit up slightly and picked up the coffee cup. "Did you get any sleep?"

"I did. I do have to go into the office today though."

He nodded, knowing that would be high on her agenda. "I'm pretty sure we'll have to deal with the government at some point today and a few other things. Like my clothes. Maybe Rick has them. I'll give him a call."

"What about Rick? Where is he?"

"He went home to his wife last night," Royce said, with a wave of his hand. "If Jonas needs him, they know where to find him."

She smiled. "There is a great deal of comfort in knowing that, when you run into times of trouble, there's somebody to call," she shared. "I'm still amazed that my sister had the wherewithal to contact or to get through to Jonas somehow. ... It still breaks my heart that she didn't see a way out for herself, or at least feel that she could stay alive long enough to get out on her own. I don't know what she was thinking honestly, but I can't do anything about it. I just hope she's at peace now."

"I'm sure she is, especially knowing that you're not up there with her," Royce stated.

Heather nodded, sipped more of her coffee, and then put it down. She snuggled up closer with him. Holding his cup to his lips, he took another sip. Then she put it off to the side, pulled the blankets back, and sat in his lap, facing him.

His eyebrows shot up. "Lady, when you get your equilibrium back, you're downright dangerous."

She chuckled. "You haven't exactly seen the real me quite yet," she admitted. "I've alternated between being devastated and whiny, or upset and heartbroken, but I haven't really been the much more *CEO-me*."

"You can be the *CEO-you* anytime you want," he replied, shifting beneath her.

She smiled. "That's exactly what I was thinking, so maybe you could try out the real me for a change."

"It's all the real you, the same one I've spent the last several days with," he pointed out. "All the different parts and pieces of you. I'm certainly not judging how you handled all the trauma you went through."

She leaned forward and crossed her arms on his chest as he slid down until he was mostly flat. "Back to that being a nice man thing, I guess." When he shuddered in response, she said, "I thought you didn't care."

"I don't," he said cautiously. "Unless it sounds as if it's becoming more of a label than anything."

She rolled her eyes at that and kissed him. "No, no labels," she said, "just a whole lot of appreciation for who you are." He reached behind her, his hands massaging the back of her neck and shoulders. She moaned softly. "Now that you can keep doing anytime you want."

"You've been through a lot," he admitted. "We could probably both use some deep-tissue massages."

She opened her eyes and asked, "Can you book us a

couples massage?"

"Absolutely. I'll look into it while you're at work today, if you want."

"Ooh, that's a good idea," she whispered. When his hands stroked down her back, she felt it through her thin nightie. She sighed. "I can't believe it's all over with."

"It is," he stated firmly. "There will still be hiccups, a few bits and pieces to deal with, but there won't be any more of the trauma level that you've already been through. That's over with."

"What about Faheed? Do you really think he'll go to trial?" When Royce hesitated to answer her question, Heather eyed him curiously.

Royce finally spoke. "I worry that, without protection, he won't survive jail. Whether their own government picks off the brothers, one by one, or they choose to commit *suicide*, I don't know which one will come first."

She pondered that and nodded. "I guess I can see that. It's too bad because a part of me wants to see him suffer for a very long time." When he gave her a smirk, she nodded. "I know. I know. I should be nicer."

"No," he countered, "don't ever feel as if you have to validate those feelings. Nobody would ever judge you for being upset over the senseless loss of your sister."

"Not to mention the other women," she reminded him.

"Exactly," he murmured. He pulled her down and gave her a light kiss, then a deeper kiss, and finally a kiss that left her gasping.

"Christ." She rested her head against his chest. "You pack a crazy punch."

"Crazy?" he repeated, rolling that word around in his mind.

"Powerful, deadly, knockout punch of a kiss. … Whatever you want to call it," she muttered, as she leaned down and gave him a kiss, her tongue dueling with his. When she finally lifted her head, she smiled at him. "I am so looking forward to this."

He laughed and rolled until she was tucked underneath him. "So am I."

He lowered his head to savor every inch of her lips and the sweetness of her mouth. By the time he began to trail kisses across her cheeks and down her neck, she was purring like a kitten in his arms. He couldn't believe they were here and happy and safe, and he didn't want anything to mar it. He took his time, enjoying absolutely everything about this wonderfully innocent woman, and yet he knew that she was a worldly corporate CEO too, now writhing in his arms.

When he finally shifted so that he was between her thighs, he looked down at her, and she smiled, pulled him closer, and lifted her hips. "Yes, please."

Then he plunged deep inside her, closing his own eyes as she closed around him, making him gasp in joy. And then he started to move. When she came apart in his arms, he couldn't do anything, so caught up in the same maelstrom that had driven her until he reached his own completion.

Shuddering, he climaxed in her arms before slowly sagging down beside her, pulling her into his arms and just holding her close.

She nestled against him, murmuring, "I wish I didn't have to go to work today."

He chuckled, held her even closer in his arms, and whispered in her ear, "Nobody said you have to go in first thing this morning though, did they?"

She laughed. "No, at least not for another hour."

"How about two?" he asked. "That sounds like a reason-able compromise to me."

"Oh? What do you think we'll do for the next two hours?" she asked in a teasing tone.

He leaned over, slid back down, and took one flush-pink nipple in his mouth and suckled deep. She heaved, her body arching beneath him, and, when he lifted his head, she gasped. "Absolutely two hours," she whispered. "We don't need to go in a minute earlier."

He laughed and resumed what he was doing. As far as he was concerned, he could do this forever. She was a very special woman, someone who connected with him on so many levels, and he was blessed to finally have found her.

EPILOGUE

TERKEL SAT IN the huge dining room, among several of his team. Terk, his arms full of babies, looked over at Celia.

She smiled as one of the twins stretched, smacking him on the cheek. "Kalen really likes your cheek," she murmured.

"Yeah, but it isn't Kalen. It's Daren," he murmured, as he kissed each baby on the top of their heads.

"Sounds like Royce completed yet another successful job, doesn't it?" she noted.

"Yes, he did a wonderful job on this one. Considering that he and Heather will both be here in a couple hours," he added, "I'm grateful we had a couple weeks in between jobs, so we caught a break on some things."

"Yes, it's nice to have at least some jobs that aren't so overtly dangerous. Some escorting and investigative work gives everyone a bit of a break on the stress element," she noted. "These ops that almost take my breath away are hard when I think that anybody could come close to getting killed. They are all our family, our growing family, and such a loss would just devastate everyone."

"Which is why we also won't go there," he reminded her. "That is not something we want to think about or to put out there in the ethers. We take all the precautions we can, but it's still our role in the world. I know it's hard, but it's a job that we must do because so few people are out there to do it."

"What about Riff?" she asked, looking back at the man currently collapsed on one of the big chairs in front of the fireplace.

"Riff's here," he called out. "I've been off doing my own stuff over the last couple months, but I'm still hoping you guys will come up with something to help me with my personal matter." He turned, glaring at Terkel.

"We may have a lead very soon," Terk replied in a clipped tone. "The gals are running it down, and, no, I'm not telling you until we know if it's a good one or not."

Riff straightened up in the chair slowly. "It needs to happen soon."

Just then Angela walked in, looked at Riff, and snorted. "Of course you would be here."

"Yeah, I'm right here," he snapped, with a negligent shrug. "The question is, why are you here?"

"I came to do my usual check on the babies."

"*Right,*" he muttered, getting to his feet. "I'll leave you to it then."

"You don't have to run away just because I'm here, you know?"

"Yes, I do," he declared, giving her a glare.

She shrugged. "Fine, if you're still running away, that's up to you. I thought maybe you'd grown up some."

He sucked in his breath, and everybody in the room sucked in theirs, waiting for an explosion. Riff slowly turned to face her, fire in his eyes. "What the hell does that mean?"

She stared at him, her hands going to her hips. "You know perfectly well what it means."

"No, I don't, and there's absolutely no point in talking to you until I have answers."

"The answers won't change the end result."

He stiffened, then nodded. "They won't change the end result, but they might change my attitude toward it."

"Ah, you better hurry it up then," she said, openly glaring now, "because I'm running out of patience." And, with that, she turned and walked out of the huge dining room. Riff exited via a doorway on the other side of the room.

Terkel glanced from Riff's back to Angela's back and then to Celia, who had a tiny smile tipping up the corners of her lips. Terk sighed. "We really do need to get answers for Riff."

"We do," she agreed, "but it'll be a while yet."

"I know, but hopefully not too long."

Just then Terk's phone rang. He checked the Caller ID and answered, "Hey, Bullard. How are you doing?"

"I'm okay, but I could use some help."

"You've got it. What do you need?"

"Somebody's hacking into my system."

"You don't need our help for that," Terk noted. "Your team is better on that IT sort of thing than we are."

"Yeah, except this is energy-related," he snapped. "I don't know what they're doing or how they're doing it, but they're attacking my system with energy."

"Energy?" Terk repeated.

"Yeah, somebody keeps shutting everything down."

"You might need to consider that it's not energy."

"I would, except for somebody named Tangerine—and who the hell names their kid after an orange? Anyway Tangerine, who calls herself Reeni, or whatever the hell she said," he muttered in disgust, "she came to my damn front door and announced that we needed help and that she was here to help us."

"You don't believe her?" Terk asked.

"Everything she's talking about makes life even more of a mockery," he admitted. "How do you listen to somebody named Tangerine in the first place?"

"Listen to her," Terkel ordered, "because she means it."

Bullard stopped, pausing before he spoke again. "Don't tell me that she's one of yours."

"She's not one of mine, and I don't know her. However, I can check her energy from right here, and she's got a lot of power," he shared. "More so, she's utilizing it to the benefit of others' good—to your good. So that's a very interesting combination."

"Great, but I don't trust her. I won't work with her if I don't have somebody from your team or at least somebody who's vetted Tangerine to say that she's on the up-and-up."

"Interesting, and you also need help solving who's after your system?"

"Of course I do," he snapped once more. "At least if you come and confirm what she's saying, then we'll have a better idea about what's going on—preferably before I lose all communications again. Pretty sure we've got hacking going on. I just don't know at what level and by whom, so send somebody and fast." With that, Bullard, as grumpy as ever, ended the call.

Terk looked around at everybody else seated at the big dining room table. "Do we have anybody? Most are off or at least committed to jobs here and there right now, aren't they?"

"We have a couple potentially available team members," Celia replied, "and we also have a bunch of applications for new hires. We just haven't had a chance to assess them."

"Yeah, well, they are hardly applications when they're sent in on the ethers," Terk pointed out, with a note of humor.

"Hey," Celia countered, rounding on him instantly, "you sent out a beacon saying that you had work, so don't be surprised when people respond in kind."

"I should never have done that," he muttered. "It brought in too many weirdos."

"They're all weirdos one way or another, and you know that."

"I know. I know. I know. I keep saying that it doesn't matter, but some of these people are very *unique*," he replied.

"And we need somebody unique right now," Celia stated, "somebody who can go into Bullard's place, handle all of it, and deal with whatever is going on in his world. We owe Bullard, and he's a friend, so we'll obviously help him."

"We'll definitely help him," Terk confirmed.

Just then everybody heard the front door opening. They all checked the energy, found friendlies approaching, and waited to see who had arrived. When Wade walked in, he smiled at everybody and pointed behind him. "Hey, guess who I found outside?"

Trevor stepped forward, a big grin on his face.

"Look who's here. It's the big man himself." Terkel hopped up, handed off the babies to Celia, and walked over to give this old friend a big hug. "Good God," he muttered, as he stared at Trevor. "I haven't heard from you in forever."

"Not until you sent out a damn beacon. What are you, nuts?"

"Yeah, I was discussing that just now with my wife."

At that term, Trevor's eyebrows popped up. "Wife?" He looked at the woman holding two babies and frowned. "Kids too?"

"Yeah," Terk stated proudly.

"So, you got soft in your old age or what?"

"I didn't think so, but that beacon idea wasn't my best,"

he admitted.

"On the other hand, it brought me in," Trevor said cheerfully. "So what kind of work have you got?"

"You ever been to Africa?" Gage asked from the sidelines, as he got up and walked over to shake hands.

"Yeah, but not for a few years though. That's where Bullard is."

"You know Bullard?" Gage asked.

"I do, although I'm not sure that he particularly likes my style. I'm a little too unrestrained for him."

"Oh, he's also mellowed quite a bit," Celia added, with a smile. "He's married with kids as well."

"Wow, the shocks just don't quit," Trevor murmured, still staring at the woman holding twins.

She got up, walked over, and introduced herself. "I'm Celia, and Terkel is my husband."

Her hands held two babies, so he didn't bother shaking her hand. "Pleased to meet you." He turned to Terkel and said, "Lucky guy, you. How did that happen?"

Terkel snorted. "Don't ask, but you're damn right, and I know it. I do have a job right now that needs somebody to turn around and head to Bullard's place."

"I'm on it," Trevor replied. "Do I get to find out what the job is now or later?"

Sophia came in and replied, "Later. Here's your file with all the information, but you need to get to the airport fast."

Trevor checked his watch, grabbed the file, then lifted a hand and waved. "We'll talk later, after this job." And, with that, Trevor was gone.

This concludes Book 11 of Terk's Guardians: Royce.
Read about Trevor: Terk's Guardians, Book 12

Terk's Guardians: Trevor (Book #12)

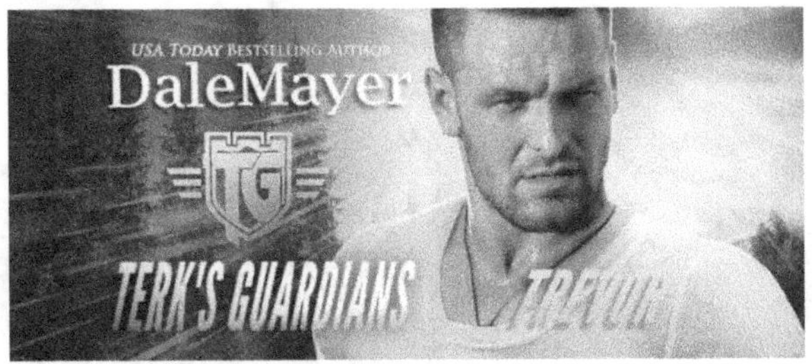

Answering Terk's beacon, Trevor walks into the castle, not quite prepared to turn around and leave instantly for a job in Africa, but that's exactly what happened. Finding Reenie pulling into Bullard's compound right behind him, he is delighted to be there. She is a curly carrottop with a free spirit, whose looks alone set most people back. Then, when she spouts on about alarms and warnings of an electrical kind, … well, no wonder no one is willing to listen.

Reenie hopes that people will take her seriously, but, so far, it hasn't worked out so well for her. However, finding Trevor at Bullard's just at the perfect time—to stand at her side and to validate her work—is both wonderful and awful that she needs that at all. Still, as the craziness unwinds around them, there's no one else she would rather with her.

Trevor and Reenie need to step up, as does each and every person in Bullard's compound. Everyone needs to be here 100 percent, as these attacks are, … let's say, … *very* personal.

Find Book 12 here!

To find out more visit Dale Mayer's website.

https://geni.us/DMSTrevor

Author's Note

Thank you for reading Royce: Terk's Guardians, Book 11! If you enjoyed the book, please take a moment and leave a short review.

Dear reader,

I love to hear from readers, and you can contact me at my website: www.dalemayer.com or at my Facebook author page. To be informed of new releases and special offers, sign up for my newsletter or follow me on BookBub. And if you are interested in joining Dale Mayer's Reader Group, here is the Facebook sign up page.
http://geni.us/DaleMayerFBGroup

Cheers,
Dale Mayer

About the Author

Dale Mayer is a *USA Today* best-selling author, best known for her SEALs military romances, her Psychic Visions series, and her Lovely Lethal Garden cozy series. Her contemporary romances are raw and full of passion and emotion (Broken But … Mending, Hathaway House series). Her thrillers will keep you guessing (Kate Morgan, By Death series), and her romantic comedies will keep you giggling (*It's a Dog's Life*, a stand-alone novella; and the Broken Protocols series, starring Charming Marvin, the cat).

Dale honors the stories that come to her—and some of them are crazy, break all the rules and cross multiple genres!

To go with her fiction, she also writes nonfiction in many different fields, with books available on résumé writing, companion gardening, and the US mortgage system. All her books are available in print and ebook format.

Connect with Dale Mayer Online

Dale's Website – www.dalemayer.com
Twitter – @DaleMayer
Facebook Page – geni.us/DaleMayerFBFanPage
Facebook Group – geni.us/DaleMayerFBGroup
BookBub – geni.us/DaleMayerBookbub
Instagram – geni.us/DaleMayerInstagram
Goodreads – geni.us/DaleMayerGoodreads
Newsletter – geni.us/DaleNews